P9-AQJ-718

The
Princess
of
Denmark

Also by Edward Marston

In the Nicholas Bracewell Series

The Queen's Head
The Merry Devils
The Trip to Jerusalem
The Nine Giants
The Mad Courtesan
The Silent Woman
The Roaring Boy
The Laughing Hangman
The Fair Maid of Bohemia
The Wanton Angel
The Devil's Apprentice
The Bawdy Basket
The Vagabond Clown
The Counterfeit Crank
The Malevolent Comedy

In the Domesday Book Series

The Wolves of Savernake
The Ravens of Blackwater
The Dragons of Archenfield
The Lions of the North
The Serpents of Harbledown
The Stallions of Woodstock
The Hawks of Delamere
The Wildcats of Exeter
The Foxes of Warwick
The Owls of Gloucester

The Princess of Denmark

Edward Marston

ST. MARTIN'S MINOTAUR
NEW YORK

www.minotaurbooks.com

Library of Congress Cataloging-in-Publication Data

Marston, Edward
    The Princess of Denmark : an Elizabethan theater mystery featuring Nicholas Bracewell / Edward Marston.—1st St. Martin's Minotaur ed.
        p. cm.
    ISBN-13: 978-0-312-35618-7
    ISBN-10: 0-312-35618-8
    1. Bracewell, Nicholas (Fictitious character)—Fiction.   2. Great Britain—History—Elizabeth, 1558–1603—Fiction.   3. Lord Westfield's Men (Fictitious characters)—Fiction.   4. Theatrical companies—Fiction.   5. Theater—Fiction.
    I. Title.

PR6063.I3175P75   2006
823'.914—dc22   2006041147

First Edition: August 2006

10 9 8 7 6 5 4 3 2 1

To Susan and John
with thanks for their warm hospitality
in Denmark

[DRAMATIS PERSONAE]

NICHOLAS BRACEWELL............book holder with Westfield's Men

LAWRENCE FIRETHORN............actor-manager

EDMUND HOODE....................playwright

BARNABY GILL.........................actor

JAMES INGRAM.......................actor

FRANK QUILTER.....................actor

RICHARD HONEYDEW..............boy apprentice

GEORGE DART.........................assistant stage-keeper

LORD WESTFIELD....................patron

ROLFE HARLING.....................his friend

ALEXANDER MARWOOD...........landlord of the Queen's Head

SYBIL MARWOOD.....................his wife

MARGERY FIRETHORN.............Lawrence Firethorn's wife

ANNE HENDRIK......................Nicholas's landlady and friend

ANTHONY ROOKER..................London merchant

ISAAC DUNMOW.....................York merchant

JOSIAS GREET.........................hired killer

BEN RYDEN............................hired killer

CAPTAIN SKRINE....................captain of the *Cormorant*

BROR LANGBERG.....................statesman

JOHANNA LANGBERG...............his wife

SIGBRIT OLSEN.......................Bror Langberg's niece

HANSI ASKGAARD....................her sister

KING CHRISTIAN IV.................king of Denmark

WILL DUNMOW.......................audience spectator

OWEN ELIAS...........................actor

PREBEN VAN LOEW..................Anne Hendrick's senior employee

The
Princess
of
Denmark

[CHAPTER ONE]

The fire was started by accident. Will Dunmow was a handsome young man, though nobody would have guessed it when they saw his blackened face and charred body resurrected from the ashes. Having come to the Queen's Head to watch Westfield's Men performing their latest play, he had enjoyed it so much that he insisted on adjourning to the taproom of the inn so that he could buy drinks for all members of the company. Wine and ale were consumed in glorious abundance, but the generous spectator made the mistake of trying to hold his own as a tippler against the actors. It was foolhardy. Only a veteran sailor could drink as hard and as relentlessly as a thirsty player, carousing at someone else's expense. Dunmow was soon so inebriated that he could barely speak a coherent sentence.

Yet he would not stop. As the taproom slowly began to empty, Dunmow remained, slumped at a table, imbibing merrily to the last. Still exhilarated by the play he had seen in the innyard that afternoon, he made a brave, if muddled, attempt at quoting lines from it when he could no longer even remember its title. Taking pity of their amiable benefactor, his last two drinking companions offered to convey him back to his lodging, but Will Dunmow refused to quit an establishment that had given him so much pleasure. Instead, he rented a room for the night and the two actors—Owen Elias and James Ingram—carried him up the rickety stairs. When they laid him on his bed, he fell instantly asleep.

"He'll not wake until doomsday," said Elias, looking down at the supine figure with a smile of gratitude. "Would that all our spectators were so free with their purses!"

"Yes," agreed Ingram, "he was a true philanthropist. And though he drunk himself into a stupor, there was good sport while he did so. He'll remember this day with fondness, I warrant."

"So will the rest of us, James."

"Let's leave the poor fellow to his well-earned slumber."

"Good night, good sir," they said in unison.

Elias snuffed out the candle that stood beside the bed, then he tiptoed out of the room after his friend. Lying in the darkness, Will Dunmow snored gently and dreamed of the performance of *The Italian Tragedy* that had set his blood racing that afternoon. Instead of being merely a spectator, however, he was now its hero, fighting to save his country from invasion, his own life from court intrigue, and his lover, the beauteous Emilia, from abduction by a foreign prince. Iambic pentameters poured from his lips like a golden waterfall. But his enemies closed furtively in on him. Stabbed by a dozen traitorous daggers, he came awake with a start and sat bolt upright in bed, relieved that he had evaded his assassins and desperate for a pipe of tobacco by way of celebration.

His hands would no longer obey him, flitting ineffectually here and there like giant butterflies with leaden wings. It was pure luck that one of them finally settled on the pocket in which he kept his pipe. It took him an age to find the tobacco and tamp it down in the bowl of the pipe. Inhaling its rich aroma seemed to revive him slightly, and after several attempts, he finally contrived to strike a spark that lit the tobacco. He drew deeply on its essence, letting the smoke curl around his mouth, down his windpipe, and deep into his lungs. The sense of contentment was overwhelming. A rare visitor to the capital, Will Dunmow believed that it had been the happiest day of his life.

Within seconds, he had dozed off again, lapsing into a sleep from which he would never awake. The pipe that had given him such fleeting joy now betrayed him. Falling from his hand, it spilled its glowing tobacco onto the bed. The fire began quietly, burning a hole in the sheet and sending up a column of smoke, imperceptible at first, then thickening and eddying until it filled the whole chamber. Meeting no resistance, the pungent fumes quickly overcame Will Dunmow. Having eaten its way through the bed linen, the fire tasted wood and its appetite proved insatiable. It gobbled everything within reach. By the time that the alarm was raised, the blaze was so loud, fierce, and triumphant that it defied arrest.

Panic seized the occupants of the inn. Guests and servants alike leapt from their beds and fled from their rooms in terror. Clad in his nightshirt, Alexander Marwood, the landlord, ran shrieking up and down passageways and staircases as if he himself had been set alight. The most deafening protests came from the horses locked in the stables, rearing and kicking in their stalls as the acrid smoke began to drift into their nostrils. Everyone rushed into the yard. The scene of so much sublime theater was now in the grip of a real drama. Flames danced madly along one whole side of the building as the inferno really took hold. From the windows of the houses opposite in Gracechurch Street, an audience watched apprehensively in case the blaze would spread to their properties.

Buckets of water were hurled onto the fire but they could only stifle its ominous crackle momentarily. After each dousing, it surged afresh and threw dazzling shadows across the yard. The horses were rescued just in time. No sooner had the last frantic animal been led out of the stables with a blanket over its head than the beam above one of the stalls collapsed, sending burning embers crashing into the straw. It ignited immediately and showers of sparks were flung high into the air.

One careless moment with a pipe of tobacco threatened to bring down the entire inn. At its height, the conflagration was so furious and uncontrollable that the whole of the parish appeared to be at risk. And then, suddenly and unaccountably, the miracle occurred. It began to rain. Nobody noticed it at first. Even those who stood aghast in their night attire did not feel the early drops. The fire had warmed them through so completely that they were impervious to any other touch. The storm then intensified, turning a fine drizzle into a gushing downpour and making people run for cover. Rain lashed down with competitive ferocity, matching itself against the blaze and determined to win the contest.

It was an extraordinary sight. Unchecked by human hand, the bonfire slowly gave ground to the deluge. Yellow flames were gradually extinguished. Billowing smoke was steadily beaten away. In place of the hideous roar there came a long, spiteful, exasperated sizzle as the fire reluctantly yielded to a superior force. It still burned on for another hour but its venom had been drawn. Though providential rain had saved much of the inn, a sizable amount had been destroyed beyond all recognition. Somewhere in the middle of the debris, quite unaware of the chaos he had caused, lay Will Dunmow.

We are done for, Nick," said Lawrence Firethorn sorrowfully. "Our occupation is gone."

"The Queen's Head can be rebuilt."

"But what of Westfield's Men in the meantime?"

"We do exactly what we did when we last had a fire," said Nicholas Bracewell. "We quit London and take our talents elsewhere."

"That was easy to do when the weather was fine and traveling was not too onerous. But the summer is past. Who will want to trudge around the provinces in cold, rain, and fog? Who will relish the idea of putting their shoulders to carts that are stuck ankle-deep in muddy roads? No, Nick," Firethorn added, stroking his beard ruefully, "we have been burned out of existence."

It was the following morning and they were standing in the yard, appraising the damage caused by the fire. Wisps of smoke still rose from some timbers, making it impossible for them to be moved by the servants who worked among the ruins. On the previous afternoon, Lawrence Firethorn, the company's actor-manager, had taken the leading role in *The Italian Tragedy* and convinced everyone there that they were watching treachery unfold in the Mediterranean sun. Not even his manifold talents could conceal the truth now. The innyard was a scene of utter devastation. Galleries where spectators had once sat no longer existed. Rooms where guests had stayed were empty shells, silhouetted against the gray sky. Nicholas Bracewell, a sturdy man in his thirties, was only the book holder with the troupe but he was always the first person that Firethorn turned to in a crisis.

"What are we to do, Nick?" he asked.

"The first thing we must do," replied the other practically, "is to help in every way to clear up this mess. We owe that to the landlord."

"We owe that scurvy knave *nothing!*"

"This disaster affects us all. We must honor our obligations."

"Had I been here when the fire started, I'd have been obliged to toss the landlord into the middle of the inferno. For that's where the wretch belongs. A pox on it!" Firethorn cried, seeing the very man approach. "Here comes the little excrescence. I'll wager he blames *us* for all this."

"Then leave me to do the talking," suggested Nicholas, only too aware of Firethorn's long-standing feud with Alexander Marwood. "This is not the moment to enrage him even further."

Marwood walked on. Sullen at the best of times, he was now thoroughly dejected, his eyes dull, his body slack, his movement sluggish. The nervous twitch that usually animated his ugly face was strangely quiescent. All the life had been sucked out of him, leaving only a hollow vestige.

"A word with you, sirs," he began with a note of deference.

"We are listening," said Nicholas. "There's much to discuss."

"I am on the brink of ruin."

"Surely not. The fire was bad but nowhere near as destructive as the one that burned down the whole inn. You learned from that dreadful setback, Master Marwood. You replaced the thatch with tiles and it slowed down the progress of the blaze."

"Yet it did not stop it from wreaking untold havoc, sir," said Marwood, indicating the shattered remains with a sweep of a skeletal arm. "My livelihood has been all but snatched away from me. I must talk to you of compensation."

Firethorn's ears pricked up. "I'm glad that you mention that," he said, entering the conversation for the first time. "Because we can no longer play here, Westfield's Men have sustained the most inordinate losses. How much compensation do you intend to pay us?"

"Pay *you?*"

"As soon as possible."

"But I am talking about the money that is due to *me,*" said Marwood, shaking off his torpor to adopt a combative pose. "It's you who should pay the compensation, Master Firethorn."

"Not a single penny, you rogue!"

"You were the cause of this catastrophe."

"I was nowhere near the Queen's Head last night!"

"Nevertheless, I lay the blame at your door."

"How can that be?" asked Nicholas, stepping between the two men before Firethorn could strike the landlord. "We are as much victims of this disaster as you, Master Marwood."

"Your actors set fire to my inn."

"That's a serious allegation."

"Yet one that I can uphold," said Marwood, wagging a finger under his nose. "Master Dunmow slept under my roof last night."

"I remember him well—a pleasant young fellow and the soul of generosity. He put a deal of money in your purse."

"Then took it straight out again."

Nicholas blinked in surprise. "He *stole* from you?"

"In a manner of speaking. The fire started in his room."

"How do you know?"

"Because we have the chamber directly above," said Marwood. "My wife is a light sleeper. It was she who first became aware of the danger. By the time we got to it, the room below was a furnace."

"Did your lodger escape?" said Nicholas with concern.

"He was too drunk to move. Yes—and that's another thing for which you must bear the responsibility."

Firethorn was scornful. "I told you that the rascal would blame us, Nick," he said. "Take him away before I lay hands on him."

"Let me hear all the facts," said Nicholas, gesturing for Firethorn to be patient. "Continue, Master Marwood. You claim that the fire began in the room below you. How?"

"How else?" retorted the landlord. "With the candle."

"What candle?"

"The one I left alight in his room when they carried him up to it. Two of *your* men, Master Firethorn," Marwood stressed. "They bore him up the steps between them. When they put him to bed, they must have forgotten to snuff out the candle. In the course of the night, Master Dunmow must have knocked it over and set my inn ablaze."

"That's pure supposition."

"The finger points at the Welshman and his friend."

"Owen Elias?"

"The very same. He drank till the very end."

"Yet remained sober enough to carry a man to bed," observed Nicholas. "I have more trust in Owen. He'd never leave a candle alight in such a situation."

"Then how did the blaze start?"

"Divine intervention," said Firethorn with a grim chuckle. "God finally tired of your miserable visage and lit a fire of retribution to send you off to hell where you belong."

"You were to blame," accused Marwood, voice rising to a pitch of hysteria. "If it had not been for your play, Master Dunmow would never have come near the Queen's Head."

"If it had not been for your heady wine," argued Nicholas, "he would never have taken a room here. You served him enough to make him drunk and incapable."

"Only because your actors urged him on."

"From what I remember, Master Dunmow did the urging."

"Yes," agreed Firethorn sadly. "Young Will was a most amenable host—and that's something we've never had at this inn before. If the fellow perished in the fire, I grieve for him."

"And so should you, Master Marwood," said Nicholas. "It must have been a gruesome death. As for the candle, let's suppose that it was indeed the villain. Who set it in the room?"

Firethorn pointed at Marwood. "He did, Nick."

"It all comes back to Westfield's Men," insisted the landlord. "You've been nothing but trouble from the start. This is not the first attack you unleashed on my property. When you performed *The Devil's Ride Through London,* you reduced the Queen's Head to ashes."

"An unfortunate mishap," said Nicholas. "Sparks flew up by accident into your thatch. We suffered as much as you while the inn was being rebuilt. We had to leave London."

"The shame of it is that you ever came back."

"Without us," said Firethorn, inflating his barrel chest, "this place would be deserted. Westfield's Men lend it true distinction."

Marwood curled a lip. "True distinction, eh? Is that what you call it?" he taunted. "I saw no true distinction when you played *A Trick to Catch a Chaste Lady*. You set off such an affray in my yard that the inn was almost pulled to pieces. I swore that you'd never perform here again after that."

"But wiser counsels prevailed," said Nicholas. "You allowed us back in time."

"And here is my reward." The landlord turned to survey the wreckage. "This how I am repaid for my folly. Never again, sirs! You are banished from my inn forever. As for the fire," he went on, rounding on them, "I'll seek compensation from you in the courts. I've been cruelly abused by Westfield's Men."

"Then add this to the list of charges," Firethorn told him.

Drawing his sword, he used the flat of it to hit Marwood's backside with a resounding thwack and sent him hopping across the yard with his buttocks in his hands. Firethorn laughed heartily but Nicholas was less amused.

"Nothing was served by attacking the landlord," he said.

"I had to do something to relieve my anger."

"He owns the Queen's Head—we do not. The day will come when we'll need to woo the testy fellow yet again. And we'll not do it with a sword in our hands."

"No," said Firethorn, sheathing his weapon. "As ever, you will be our ambassador, Nick. Soothing words from you will win that unsightly gargoyle over again." He heaved a long sigh. "Though it will be many months before your embassy can begin." He remembered something. "Our patron must hear of this. Lord Westfield will be mightily distressed at the tidings."

"I'll take on the office of telling him," volunteered Nicholas.

"Ask him if he can aid us in some way."

"Not with money, I suspect. His debts mount with each year."

"You are behind the times, Nick. Our esteemed patron has had good fortune at last. His elder brother died earlier this year."

"I knew that."

"What you did not know is that he left him half his estate. Lord Westfield is transfigured. He has finally paid off his creditors."

"Cheering news," said Nicholas, "yet I look for no munificence from him. Unlike poor Will Dunmow, he is not given to charity. And talking of our erstwhile friend," he added considerately, "we must send word to his family of his unfortunate end. Though we had only the briefest acquaintance with him, it behooves us to act on his behalf. The landlord will certainly not do so."

"He'll be too busy cooling his bum in a pail of water."

"Owen Elias spent the longest time with Master Dunmow. He'll know where the young man lodged in London and what friends he may have in the city."

"It's right to mourn for the dead but we must also have care for the living. Unless we can find somewhere else to play, the company will go into hibernation. A few of us will not fare too badly," said Firethorn, "because we have other irons in the fire, but most of the lads will suffer grievously. An actor without a stage is like a man without a woman, lacking in the one thing that allows him to prove his true worth." His gaze traveled around the yard. "Yesterday, we gave them *The Italian Tragedy*. This morning, we behold a real tragedy. Westfield's Men have gone up in smoke."

Nicholas was soulful. "That fate befell Will Dunmow," he noted. "We live to perform another day. For that, we owe a prayer of thanks."

"You are right, Nick." Firethorn doffed his hat and began to unbutton his doublet. "And I believe that we do have a duty to clear some of this rubbish away."

Nicholas slipped off his cap and his buff jerkin. "I've sent George Dart to fetch the others," he said. "This is work for many hands. When he sees us helping here, the landlord's heart may soften towards us." Firethorn gave a snort of derision. "And there will be compensation of a sort for you, Lawrence."

"Not from that death's-head."

"I was thinking of your wife. Margery will be delighted to see more of her husband in the next few months."

"That's a mixed blessing," said Firethorn, recalling his wife's violent temper. "But not in your case, Nick. Your domestic life is less troubled than mine. If the company goes to sleep throughout the autumn, you will see a great deal of Anne. That must content you."

"Unhappily, no."

"Why not?"

"Anne is planning another visit to Amsterdam."

L ocated in Broad Street, the Dutch Church had once been part of an Augustinian monastery. After the dissolution, it had been granted to royal favorites of Henry VIII, who had promptly shown their religious inclinations by using it as a stable. When his young son, Edward, succeeded to the throne, he gave the nave and aisles of the church to Protestant refugees, most of whom were Dutch or German, but they were not allowed to enjoy the gift for long. At the start of Queen Mary's reign, that devout Roman Catholic gave the foreign congregation less than a month to leave and she shunned them thereafter. The accession of Queen Elizabeth saw the immediate restitution of a building that resumed its title of the Dutch Church and acted as a central point for immigrant worshippers.

Anne Hendrik knew the place well and had attended many services there with her husband. A young Englishwoman with a quick brain, she had soon mastered Jacob Hendrik's native language and learned a deal of German from him as well. A happy marriage was then cut short by the untimely death of the Dutchman, and his wife inherited the hat-making business that he had set up in Bankside. Showing a flair and acumen that she did not know she possessed, she managed the enterprise with considerable success. The reputation it achieved was not all Anne's doing. Much of the credit had to go to Preben van Loew, her senior employee, a man whose talent and versatility brought in a stream of commissions.

It was the sober Dutchman who accompanied her on the long walk to church that morning. In a dangerous city, Anne was grateful for an escort, even one as taciturn as the emaciated old man.

"It's kind of you to come with me, Preben," she said.

"I like to pay my respects as well."

"You were a good friend to Jacob."

"We grew up together," he said.

"And fled to England together as well. It must have been a shock to you when he chose to marry someone like me."

"You were a good wife."

"I like to think so," said Anne with a nostalgic smile, "but you did not know that beforehand. You must have had serious doubts about me at first."

The Dutchman was tactful. "I cannot remember."

"A wise answer."

Side by side, they continued along the busy thoroughfare of Broad Street. They were making one of their regular journeys to the churchyard to visit the grave of Jacob Hendrik. It was always a sad occasion but there was some solace for Anne. Having paid her respects to her late husband, she would have an opportunity to call on the man who had replaced him in her life, Nicholas Bracewell, a dear friend who had begun as a lodger before finding himself her lover as well. Gracechurch Street was within easy walking distance of the Dutch Church. Ignorant of the tragedy that had befallen the Queen's Head, Anne proposed to stop there to watch a little of the day's rehearsal.

As she bore down on the church, however, her mind was filled with fond memories of Jacob Hendrik, a hardworking man who had been forced to settle south of the river because the trades guilds resolved to keep as many foreign rivals as they could out of the city. On arrival in England, her future husband had met with resentment and suspicion. When they reached their destination, Anne was suddenly reminded of what he had had to endure.

"Not another one!" said Preben van Loew with disgust.

"Tear it down," she urged.

"I wish to read it first."

"It's the work of a twisted mind, Preben."

"A man should always know his enemy."

The printed message was attached to the wall of the churchyard and had a stark clarity. Both of them read the opening lines.

You strangers that inhabit in this land,
Note this same writing, do it understand;
Conceive it well for safeguard of your lives,
Your goods, your children, and your dearest wives.

"They still hate us," said the old man, shaking his head. "I have been here all these years and I am still a despised stranger."

"Not in my eyes."

"You are the exception."

"No, Preben," she said stoutly. "London is full of good, decent, tolerant citizens who would be repelled by this libel. Unfortunately, the city also harbors cruel and vicious men who envy the success that foreign tradesmen have."

"They are many in number."

"I do not believe that."

"They are," he said, rolling his eyes in despair. "Have you forgotten how easily the apprentices were incited to riot against us? We are despised and always will be."

"When I see such vile accusations, it makes me ashamed to call myself English. At times like this," said Anne, glancing into the churchyard, "I feel proud that I have strong Dutch connections. I feel sympathy for all who sought refuge here. You and Jacob had so much to bear when you left your own country."

He shrugged. "It was no more than we expected."

Wanting to turn away, she felt impelled to read more of the angry verse and saw a scathing attack on the government for allowing strangers to enter the realm.

With Spanish gold you are all infected
And with that gold our nobles wink at feats.
Nobles, say I? Nay, men to be rejected,
Upstarts that enjoy the noblest seats,
That wound their country's breast for lucre's sake,
And wrong our gracious Queen and subjects good
By letting strangers make our hearts to ache.

"Take it down, Preben," she ordered. "Let us spare others the distress of having to read such hateful words."

"It is best to ignore it altogether."

"Remove it so that we may hand it over to a constable. It's a malicious libel and the law protects you from such things."

"They still keep coming," he said dolefully.

"Commissioners have been ordered to take the utmost pains to discover the author and publisher of these attacks. When they are caught, they will face a heavy punishment. Take it down," she repeated. "Nobody else can be insulted by it then."

"As you wish."

"And when you have done that, forget that you ever saw it."

The Dutchman smiled. "I've already done so."

Standing on tiptoe, he reached up to remove the verses from the wall. But they had a protector. No sooner did his hands touch the paper than a large stone was hurled from across the street. It struck his head with such force that his black skullcap was knocked off. Stunned by the blow, Preben van Loew fell to the ground with blood oozing from his head wound. Anne let out a gasp of alarm and bent down to help him. She did not see the figure that ran off quickly down a lane opposite. The libel on the wall of the Dutch churchyard was no idle jest. Someone was ready to enforce the warning against strangers.

[CHAPTER TWO]

They were all there. The entire cast of *The Italian Tragedy* had turned up at the Queen's Head, along with the stage-keepers and the tireman, to help in the mammoth task of clearing away the wreckage. In a sense, they were also dismantling their own home so the work was additionally painful. Rank disappeared. From the actor-manager down to the humblest hired man in the company, everyone did his share. The only actor who refused to dirty his hands, or to risk staining his exquisite attire by struggling among the filthy ruins, was Barnaby Gill, a brilliant clown onstage but a morose and egotistical man when he stepped off it. Since it was beneath his dignity to take part in physical labor, he simply watched sourly from the other side of the yard and deplored the fact that he would be unable to display his histrionic skills there again for a long time.

There was a crowning irony. Fire had robbed them of their playhouse yet they had to engage the self-same thief to dispose of the booty. Beams, floorboards, and furniture beyond recall were tossed on a bonfire in the middle of the yard. Bricks, plaster, and broken tiles were wheeled away in wooden barrows. Bed linen had been burned to extinction. Pewter tankards and utensils had melted in the heat of the furnace. Some things could be saved for reuse but most had perished during the night. There were consolations. The fire had not consumed the Queen's Head in its entirety, and because there had been no wind, sparks had not been carried to any of the adjacent properties.

It was Nicholas Bracewell who discovered the body. As he scooped up another armful of shattered tiles, he saw a foot protruding from the debris. It was bare and discolored. Since the fire had only claimed one victim, the foot simply had to belong to Will Dunmow. He was buried beneath some badly charred roof timbers.

"I've found him," said Nicholas, throwing the tiles aside. "Give me a hand, Owen."

"Gladly," offered Owen Elias, scampering across to him. "Are you sure that it's him?"

"Who else can it be?" Taking a firm grasp, between them they moved the first heavy oak beam. "The fire started in his bedchamber and that would have been directly above this spot."

"Poor Will! He had no chance."

"The landlord blames you for leaving a lighted candle there."

Elias was roused. "Then he needs to be told the truth," he said indignantly. "I made a point of snuffing out the candle before we left. You can ask James. He'll bear witness."

"I take your word for it, Owen," said Nicholas, "but that raises a question. If a candle did not cause the fire, then what did?"

"Who knows?"

Taking hold of the next beam, they heaved it aside to expose the upper half of the corpse. It was a grisly sight. Scorched and distorted, Will Dunmow's handsome face was a grotesque mask. His hair had burned down to the skull, his eyebrows had been singed, and both nose and jaw had been broken by the impact of the falling timber. Every shred of clothing had been burned off his body, leaving his flesh black and repellent. Nicholas felt a surge of compassion.

"His own mother would not be able to recognize him," he said. "I thank heaven that she did not see him in this condition." He turned to Elias, who was staring in horror at the corpse. The Welshman was visibly shaken. "What ails you, Owen?"

"It was true, Nick—hideously true."

"True?"

"What I said to James as we laid him on his bed last night. I said that Will would sleep until doomsday." Elias bit his lip. "I did not realize that doomsday would come so soon for him."

"How could you?"

"I feel so *guilty*."

"You were not to blame."

"It was almost as if I prophesied his death."

"That's a foolish thought. This was none of your doing." Nicholas became aware of the small crowd that had gathered to look at the body with morbid curiosity. Nicholas waved them away. "Back to your work, lads. Will Dunmow was kind to us. Do not stare so as if he were a species of monstrosity. Grant him some dignity." The others began to drift away. "I can manage here, Owen," he went on. "Fetch something to cover him from prying eyes."

"Yes, Nick."

The Welshman went off and left Nicholas to remove the rest of the debris that covered the dead man. He did so with great care, averting his eyes from the crushed legs that came into view. Pity welled up in him once more. In the course of his life, Nicholas had seen death in many guises but none so shocking and repulsive as the one that now confronted him. Will Dunmow had not merely been killed. He had been deformed and degraded. By the time the book holder had liberated the body completely, Elias had returned with a large white sheet that he had taken from the room where they kept their wardrobe. It was laid over the corpse with reverence, then the two of them lifted Will Dunmow up and carried him to a cart that stood nearby. They lowered him gently into it.

"There'll have to be an inquest," said Nicholas.

"I'll see the body delivered to the coroner."

"Thank you, Owen."

"Then I'll do what I can to track down the house where Will was staying while he was in London. He told me that it was in Silver Street," explained Elias, "and belonged to a friend. I'll find him if I have to knock on every door."

"Save yourself the trouble. I think this friend will come to us. He must have known that Will was at the play yesterday afternoon.

Since his lodger did not return last night, the friend will want to know why. In time, he'll turn up at the Queen's Head."

"Then he'll be met with dreadful news."

"Yes," said Nicholas. "And the worst part of it is that we cannot even tell him how the fire started."

"I could hazard a guess."

"Could you?"

"I've been thinking about what he said," remembered Elias. "When we carried him to his chamber, he kept calling for a bottle of sack. Will said that he'd like to drink some more and smoke a pipe of tobacco before he went to sleep."

"A pipe?"

"That might be the explanation, Nick."

"Indeed, it might."

"How he managed to light it, God knows, for he was as drunk as a lord. As soon as his head touched the pillow, he was asleep."

"He must have come awake again," decided Nicholas, "and tried to smoke a pipe. Will Dunmow would not be the first man to doze off and start a fire unwittingly with burning tobacco."

"An expensive mistake. He paid for it with his life."

"Take him to the coroner, Owen. Describe what happened here and tell him that we know precious little about Will Dunmow apart from his name and his generosity. I'll carry on here."

"Not for a while, Nick," said Elias as he saw two figures walking across the yard. "You have company."

Nicholas looked up to see Anne Hendrik and Preben van Loew heading toward him. They were looking around with dismay. Elias stayed long enough to exchange greetings with them before driving the body away in the cart. Anne was horrified by the amount of damage.

"What happened?" she asked.

"We are not certain," replied Nicholas, "and never will be, alas. But we think someone started the fire when he fell asleep with a pipe of tobacco still burning. He died in the blaze. Owen is just taking him to the coroner."

"We expected to find you rehearsing today's play."

"Out of the question, Anne."

"So I see."

"It will be next spring at least before we return to the Queen's Head. The landlord would rather that we never came back." Nicholas glanced at the bandaging around the old Dutchman's head. "But enough of our troubles. Preben seems to have encountered some of his own. I thought you both went to the churchyard this morning."

"We did, Nicholas," Preben said solemnly. "There was another vicious libel on strangers, I fear."

"It was on the wall," said Anne. "When Preben took it down, he was hit on the head by a stone. We did not see who threw it. It was a bad wound. We had to find a surgeon to dress it."

Nicholas was sympathetic. "I'm sorry to hear that. Another libel, you say? That's bad. Let's stand aside," he said, moving them away from the noise of the clearance work behind him. "Now—tell me all."

Lord Westfield gazed in wonder at the miniature then let out a cry of delight. Holding the portrait to his lips, he placed a gentle kiss on it.

"I love her already!" he announced. "What is her name?"

"Sigbrit, my lord," said his companion. "Sigbrit Olsen."

"A beautiful name for a beautiful lady."

"That miniature was painted only last year."

"And is she as comely in the flesh?"

"I've every reason to think so," said Rolfe Harling. "I've not had the pleasure of meeting her yet, but when I spoke with her uncle in Copenhagen, he could not praise her enough. He described his niece as a jewel among women."

"I can see that, Rolfe. The creature *dazzles*."

Lord Westfield was so enraptured by the portrait that he could not take his eyes off it. Framed by silken blond hair, Sigbrit Olsen's face combined beauty, dignity, and youthfulness. Her skin seemed to glow. Lord Westfield pressed for details.

"How old is she?"

"Twenty-two."

"Less than half my age."

"Such a wife would take years off you, my lord."

"That's my hope. Has she been married?"

"Only once," stressed Harling, "and her husband died in an accident soon after the wedding. There was no issue. At first, she was overcome with grief. After a decent interval of mourning, however, she is now ready to start her life afresh and she prefers to do it abroad. Denmark has too many unhappy memories for her."

"Then I must take her away from them."

"That would be viewed as a blessing, my lord."

"By me as well as by her."

He kissed the portrait again. Lord Westfield was a short, plump man of middle years with a reddish complexion lighting up a round, pleasant face. Thanks to a skillful tailor, his slashed doublet of blue and red gave him a podgy elegance and his breeches cunningly concealed his paunch. He had been married twice before but had outlived both of his wives. Though he led a sybaritic existence that involved the pursuit of a number of gorgeous young ladies, he had now decided that it might be time to wed for the third time.

"How do you think that Sigbrit would look on my arm, Rolfe?"

"You will make a handsome couple, my lord," flattered Harling.

"She would be the envy of all my friends."

"That thought was in my mind when I chose her."

"You have done well, Rolfe."

"Thank you," said Harling with an obsequious smile. "It has taken time, I know, but a decision like that could not be rushed. I did not wish to commit you until I was absolutely convinced."

"I would have preferred it if you had actually *seen* Sigbrit."

"So would I, my lord, but she was visiting relatives in Sweden when I was there. Her uncle is eminently reliable, I assure you, and I've had good reports of the lady from others. Until her marriage, she was a lady-in-waiting at court."

"That, in itself, is recommendation enough."

"The dowager queen likes to surround herself with beauty."

Lord Westfield beamed. "And so do I, Rolfe."

They were in the house that Lord Westfield used when he was staying in the city. His estates were in Hertfordshire, north of St. Albans, close enough to London to allow easy access to and fro yet far enough away to escape the stench and the frequent outbreaks of plague that afflicted the capital. He had been waiting for weeks for the return of Rolfe Harling. Since his reputation for promiscuity was too well-known in England, Lord Westfield had chosen to look elsewhere for a wife, and Harling had been dispatched to find a suitable partner for him, searching, as he did, through three other countries before settling on the woman whose portrait he had brought back.

Rolfe Harling was a tall, thin individual in his thirties with long, dark hair and a neat beard. He wore smart but sober apparel, and with his scholarly hunch and prominent brow, he conveyed an impression of intelligence. That he spoke four languages had made him an ideal person for the task in hand.

"Do you ever regret leaving academic life?" asked Lord Westfield.

"Not at all, my lord. Oxford has its appeal but it can seem very parochial at times. Travel has taught me far more than I could learn from the contents of any library."

"That depends on where you travel."

"Quite so," said Harling. "As an Englishman, there are some countries that I have no desire to visit—Spain, for instance. I would never have dared to foist a wife from that accursed nation upon you. Spain is our enemy, Denmark our friend."

"And likely to remain so."

"That, too, was taken into consideration."

"You have been diligent on my behalf," said Lord Westfield, "and I thank you for it. My brother's death was a bitter blow but it brought a welcome change of fortune to me. Hitherto, I balked at the idea of asking a woman to share my poverty with me. Now that I can afford to marry again, I will do so in style."

"Sigbrit Olsen will not disappoint you. Through her uncle, she makes only one request, and that is for the wedding to be on Danish soil. I was certain that you would abide by that condition."

"Gladly. Let her nominate the place."

"She has already done so."

"Copenhagen?"

"No, my lord," said Harling. "The lady prefers her hometown. In her native tongue, it is called Helsingor."

"And what do we call it in English?"

"Elsinore."

Preben van Loew was a very private man who had remained single by choice because of his excessive shyness and because of a lurking fear of the opposite sex. He liked and respected Anne Hendrik, but even she was not allowed to get too close to him. When they returned to her house in Bankside, therefore, he refused her offer to examine the wound and dress it with fresh bandaging. Still in pain, he wanted to get back to his work in the premises adjoining her house to put the incident at the Dutch churchyard out of his mind.

"You are not well enough to go back to work," Anne said.

"I am fully recovered now," he told her.

"Your face belies it, Preben. That stone was thrown hard."

He gave a pale smile. "You do not need to remind me."

"If you feel the slightest discomfort, you have my permission to leave at once. Do not tax yourself. Every commission we have has been finished ahead of time. You are under no compulsion."

"Thank you."

"And when you do want the dressing changed, come to me."

"I will," he said.

But she knew that he was unlikely to do so. He had such a strong sense of independence that he hated to rely on anyone else, especially a woman. Preben van Loew was an odd character. When he had been struck on the head, he was less concerned with the searing agony than with the embarrassment he felt at having been attacked in Anne's presence. Having set out that morning as her protector, it was he who now needed protection. It was an affront to his pride.

"Do not tell them about this in Amsterdam," he requested.

"But they will all ask after you, Preben."

"Tell them that I am well."

"But you are not," she said.

"I want them to hear only good news about me. If they know about the attack, my family and friends will only worry about me."

"And so they should."

"Spare them the anguish," he said. "Tell them the truth—that I live a happy life among people I admire, and do a job that I have always loved. I want no fuss to be made of me, Anne."

Anne became reflective. "You sound like Jacob," she recalled. "During his last illness, when he lacked the strength even to get out of bed on his own, he kept telling me not to cosset him. He hated to put me to the slightest trouble. I was his wife yet he would still not let me pamper him. Can you understand why?"

"Very easily."

"Then you and he are two of a kind." She thought about the narrow, dedicated, industrious, almost secret existence that Preben led and she changed her mind. "Well, perhaps not. As for your injury . . ."

"These things happen. We just have to accept that."

"Well, I'll not accept it," she said with spirit, "and neither will Nick. You saw how angry he was when we told him about it."

"But there was no need to do so, Anne. It's far better to remain silent. All that I had was a bang on the head. Think of the problems that Nicholas is facing after that fire. You should not have bothered him with this scratch that I picked up."

"It was much more than a scratch, Preben."

"It will heal in time."

"Someone deserves to be punished."

"We do not know who he was."

"Nick will find out."

"How can he?" asked the old man. "He was not even there."

"Perhaps not, but he cares for you, Preben. That's why he took such an interest in the case."

"I'd rather he forget it altogether."

"Then you do not know Nick Bracewell," she said proudly. "If his friends are hurt, he's not one to stand idly by. You may choose to forget the outrage but he will not. Sooner or later, Nick will make someone pay for it. You will be avenged."

* * *

After toiling away for most of the morning with the others, Nicholas Bracewell left the Queen's Head to call on their patron. Lord Westfield liked to be kept informed about his troupe and this latest news would brook no delay. Having cleaned himself up as best he could, therefore, Nicholas made his way to the grand house he had often visited in the past. In times of crisis for Westfield's Men—and they seemed to come around with increasing regularity—the book holder always acted as an intercessory between the company and its epicurean patron. He had far more tact than Lawrence Firethorn and none of the actor's booming self-importance. As a result of Nicholas's long association with the company, Lord Westfield appreciated the book holder's true worth. It made him the ideal messenger.

The servant who admitted him to the house was not impressed with his appearance, but as soon as he gave the name of the visitor to his master, he was told to bring him into the parlor at once. Nicholas was accordingly ushered into the room and found Lord Westfield, sitting in a chair, scrutinizing a miniature that he held in his palm. It was moments before the patron looked up at him.

"Nicholas," he said with unfeigned cordiality. "It is good to see you again, my friend."

"Thank you, my lord."

"What brings you to my house this time?"

"Sad tidings."

"Oh?"

"There has been a fire at the Queen's Head."

"A serious one?"

"Serious enough," said Nicholas.

He gave Lord Westfield a detailed account of what had happened, speculating on the probable cause of the blaze and emphasizing the dire consequences for the company. To Nicholas's consternation, their patron was only half-listening and he appeared to be less interested in the fate of the troupe that bore his name than he was in the portrait at which he kept glancing. When he had finished his tale, the visitor had to wait a full minute before Lord Westfield even deigned to glance up at him.

"Is that all, Nicholas?" he asked.

"Yes, my lord."

"Sad tidings, indeed."

"We have been wiped completely from the stage."

"And you believe this man started the fire?"

"It is only a conjecture," admitted Nicholas.

"Then it could just as easily have been arson."

"Oh, no, my lord."

"But we have jealous rivals," Lord Westfield reminded him. "They have often tried to bring us down before. Someone employed by Banbury's Men could have burned us out of our home."

"There is no suggestion of that."

"But it is a possibility."

"No, my lord."

"Why not?"

"Because they would not have lit the fire in that part of the inn," reasoned Nicholas. "Had someone wanted to inflict real damage on us, they would have started the blaze on the other side of the building so that the rooms where we keep our wardrobe, our scenery, and our properties would have been destroyed. Without all that, we would be unable to stage a play anywhere."

"A fair point," conceded the other.

"The seat of the fire was in Will Dunmow's bedchamber. That much is certain. It was started by accident."

"Accident or design, Banbury's Men will applaud the result."

"There is nothing we can do to stop them," said Nicholas. "They and our other rivals will gloat over our misfortune. That is why I came to you, Lord Westfield."

"Go on."

"We are hoping that you may lighten our burden."

"In what way?"

"It may be possible for us to play at the Rose on rare occasions but that will hardly keep our name before the public. You have many friends, my lord. In the past, you have been kind enough to commend us to them and we have been invited to play in their homes."

"True."

"May we prevail upon you to do so again, please?"

Lord Westfield gazed down at the miniature again and went off into a trance. Nicholas tried to catch his attention by clearing his throat noisily but the other man did not even hear him. He was far too preoccupied. The book holder grew steadily more annoyed. He had just brought terrible news about Westfield's Men yet all that their patron could do was to ignore him. At length, Lord Westfield did raise his eyes, blinking when he realized that he had company.

"Did you want something, Nicholas?" he said.

"Yes, my lord. I begged a favor of you."

"Ah, yes. You wanted to be recommended to my friends."

"We would be most obliged," said Nicholas politely. "Actors like Lawrence Firethorn and Barnaby Gill will always be in demand for private performances, and Owen Elias can sing sweetly enough to make a living at it. But for most of the company, that fire is the road to penury and suffering. If you could find us work from those in your circle, you would lessen that suffering. May we count on you to do that, my lord?"

"No," said the other flatly.

Nicholas was taken aback. *"No?"*

"I would not even consider it, Nicholas."

"As you wish, my lord—though I find your decision surprising."

"It was made for me," said Lord Westfield, getting up from his chair and coming across to him. He held out the miniature. "Look at this, please." Nicholas hesitated. "Go on—take it."

The book holder did as he was told. He studied the portrait and wondered why it held such fascination for the other. Lord Westfield watched him carefully.

"Well?" he prompted.

"It is well painted, my lord. The limner knows his trade."

"Forget the artist. Consider only his subject."

"The lady is very beautiful," observed Nicholas.

"Is that all you have to say about her?"

"What else is there to say except that she is young, well-favored, and of high birth? She has great poise and charm, my lord. Who the lady is, I do not know, but I think that she might well hail from a Scandinavian court."

Lord Westfield was pleased. "Why do you believe that?"

"This is not an English face," said Nicholas, "and I'll wager that you will not find any of the ladies at court with their hair worn like this. The limner has painted a foreigner."

"You are very perceptive."

"I do have an advantage, my lord."

"Advantage?"

"Yes," confessed Nicholas. "There have been occasions when I've worshipped at the Dutch Church in Broad Street. It does not only serve the needs of those from the Low Countries. Other nations are also represented–Germans, Swedes, Norwegians–and you learn to pick out the differences between them."

"And what does this tell you?" said the other, taking the portrait back so that he could feast his eyes on it once more. "This dear lady is the reason that I will not let my company spend their talents in the drafty halls of my friends. Where does she come from, Nicholas?"

"Why do you ask?"

"Answer the question–it's important to me."

"Then I return to my first guess," said Nicholas, still mystified. "What you hold in your hand is a Scandinavian aristocrat. If you force me to name a country, I will do so."

"Then name it."

"Denmark."

Lord Westfield shook with laughter. Slapping his visitor on the back by way of congratulation, he thrust the portrait in front of Nicholas's gaze once more.

"You have hit the mark," he said jubilantly. "This is no English beauty. She transcends anything that we could produce here. You are looking at a veritable saint. Her name is Sigbrit Olsen–a princess of Denmark!"

[CHAPTER THREE]

Though they worked extremely hard to clear the debris from the innyard, they neither expected nor received any thanks from Alexander Marwood. Westfield's Men knew the landlord too well to look for any sign of gratitude from him, still less for any reward. Pessimistic by nature, Marwood was plunged into despair, seeing the end of the world foreshadowed in the destruction wrought by the fire. Instead of planning to rebuild his inn, he was mentally composing his will. The taproom of the Queen's Head was virtually unscathed but the troupe did not even consider retiring there at the end of their exhausting labors. Marwood still blamed the troupe for the disaster and neither he, nor his flint-hearted wife, Sybil, would serve them. The actors therefore walked up Gracechurch Street to the Black Horse, a smaller and less comfortable tavern but one where they were at least guaranteed a warm welcome.

Seated at a table, three of the leading members of the company picked away desultorily at their food and discussed their prospects. They looked bleak. Lawrence Firethorn, Barnaby Gill, and Edmund Hoode were not the only sharers, but they customarily made all the major decisions affecting Westfield's Men. Hoode, playwright and actor, felt that, in this case, the decision had been made for them.

"We must disband until next year," he said gloomily.

"That would be fatal, Edmund," said Firethorn. "We must stick together at all costs or the company will lose heart. Who knows? There may be room for us at the Rose from time to time, and we may even have the opportunity to perform at court in due course."

"Neither outcome is likely," said Gill with a dismissive flick of his hand. "The Rose already has its resident company and we will hardly be invited to play at court if we disappear from sight. We have to be seen onstage in order to catch the eye."

"Barnaby is right," agreed Hoode. "To all intents and purposes, Westfield's Men have ceased to exist."

"No," said Firethorn, banging the table.

"We have nowhere to perform, Lawrence."

"There may be another inn ready to help us out."

"We've never managed to find one before. The Queen's Head is our home. When people hear the name, they think of us."

"And so they should," said Firethorn, thrusting out his jaw. "I've given some of my finest performances on the boards there. And you have helped me to do so, Edmund. Your plays have inspired me to reach the very peak of my art."

"What about me?" asked Gill peevishly.

"You frolic down in the foothills."

"I surpass you in everything I do, Lawrence."

"You surpass me in pulling faces, dancing jigs, and singing bawdy songs, that much I grant you. As a tragedian, however, I cannot be matched in the whole of Christendom."

"Your modesty becomes you," said Gill waspishly.

"Where would the company be without me?"

"Better off in every way."

"It could certainly spare *your* meager talents, Barnaby."

"Stop this argument," said Hoode, taking his usual role as the peacemaker. "You two never meet but you fall to quarreling. The truth is that all of us—whatever our talents—have been put out of work by this fire." He chewed the last of his meal meditatively. "What does Nick say?"

"What does it matter?" countered Gill sharply. "You seem to forget that Nicholas is merely a hired man with no real standing in the company. It is *we* who decide policy, not the book holder."

"Nevertheless, his advice is always sound."

"Not in this case," said Firethorn with a sigh. "Nick thought that we should take to the road and hawk our plays around England."

"I'll not turn peddler for anyone," said Gill defiantly.

"You've done so before."

"Only under duress—and only in spring or summer."

"Strolling players are on tour throughout the year," noted Hoode. "They take no account of bad weather."

Gill was insulted. "We are not strolling players, Edmund," he said huffily. "We are members of a licensed company. We have a patron and wear his livery. That sets us worlds apart from the ragamuffins who call themselves strolling players."

"For once, I agree with Barnaby," said Firethorn. "We have high standards and we must never fall below them. As for touring, it's the wrong time of the year to walk at the cart's arse."

"I dispute that," said Hoode. "If we have no audience in London, we must go in search of one. We can brave a little rain for the sake of keeping our art in good repair."

"I refuse to stir an inch from London," declared Gill with finality.

"Then we'll have to go without you."

"I'll not allow it."

"I side with Barnaby on this," said Firethorn. "In another month, it will not only be rain that will harass us. Frost, fog, and freezing cold will hold us up. Roads will be like swamps. Rivers will be swollen. Icy winds will get into our very bones."

"Stop it, Lawrence," ordered Gill. "My teeth chatter already."

Gill pushed away the remnants of his dinner and reached for his wine. His companions fell silent. The despondent atmosphere that hung over the table pervaded the whole taproom. Actors sagged in their seats or conversed in muted voices. There was none of the happy banter that normally invigorated them. For the sharers—those with a financial stake in the company and who therefore enjoyed a share of its profits—the future was cheerless. For the hired men—jobbing actors employed for individual plays—it was far worse. Being out of work was a form of death sentence for them. With no wages to sustain them, and with a harsh winter ahead, many would fall by the wayside.

The sense of dejection was almost tangible. Nicholas Bracewell noticed it as soon as he entered the inn. He collected a few nods and words of greeting but none of the raillery for which the actors were famed. When he stopped beside Firethorn's table, he was met with blank stares from all three men seated around it.

"I've been to see Lord Westfield," he announced.

"Did you tell him that his company is posthumous?" asked Gill. "For that is what we are now—mere ghosts that no longer have any corporeal shape or function."

"Speak for yourself, Barnaby," chided Firethorn. "I am no ghost but a flesh-and-blood titan. All that I lack is a stage on which to unleash my power." He looked at the newcomer. "Find a seat, Nick, and tell us the worst. Was our patron shocked by the news?"

"No," replied Nicholas, bringing an empty stool to the table and lowering himself onto it. "Lord Westfield was not shocked."

"Horror-struck, then?"

"No, Lawrence."

"Alarmed?"

"Not even that."

Hoode was puzzled. "Lord Westfield is not insensible," he said. "When you told him about the fire at the Queen's Head, he must have expressed *some* emotion."

"He did, Edmund."

"Anguish—fear—disappointment?"

"None of those things."

"I do not believe it," said Gill irritably. "You'll be telling us next that he was glad his company were driven out of their home by the blaze. Let's have no more of this jest, Nicholas. It's in poor taste."

"It's no jest, I assure," Nicholas promised. "Our patron was sad that we had been evicted from the Queen's Head but he was far from crestfallen. He saw it as an act of God."

"Except that God, in this instance, went by the name of Will Dunmow for it was *he* who started the fire that ruined us. Act of God, indeed!" said Gill, clicking his lips. "I've never heard such nonsense."

"Lord Westfield thinks otherwise."

"Was he not even upset at our loss?" said Firethorn.

"To some degree."

"Does he *want* us swept from the boards?"

"Of course not," replied Nicholas, "but, given the situation, he is quick to take advantage of it."

"Advantage!" howled Firethorn. "What advantage?"

"I see none," said Gill. "You are teasing us, Nicholas."

"I would never do that," said the book holder.

"Then stop speaking in riddles," urged Hoode. "The troupe is a credit to our patron. We bear his name and proclaim his status. Since we are the best company in London, we add luster to Lord Westfield. Can he sit calmly by and watch all that cast away?"

"No, Edmund," said Nicholas. "He would never do that. He has our best interests at heart."

"Then why is he not as downcast as the rest of us?"

"For two reasons." Nicholas took a deep breath before imparting the news. "First, Lord Westfield is to marry."

Firethorn was astounded. "Marry?" he exclaimed. "That old goat? Why does he need to take another wife when he can enjoy all the pleasures of marriage without one?"

"I did not know that there *were* any pleasures in marriage," said Gill, a man who looked upon any relations between the two sexes with a jaundiced eye. "The love of man for man is the only source of true happiness."

"How would you know, Barnaby? The only man you ever loved is yourself. You've spent a whole lifetime courting mirrors. But no more of that," Firethorn went on, turning back to Nicholas. "Are you in earnest?"

"Never more so," said the other.

"Who is the lady?"

"Her name is Sigbrit Olsen."

"A foreigner?"

"She lives in Denmark and comes of good family."

"Whatever possessed him to marry a Dane?"

"She is a lady of exceptional beauty. I saw her portrait."

"How old is she?"

"Still young, Lawrence."

"I can understand Lord Westfield pursuing *her*," said Hoode, "but what does he have to offer a Danish beauty? Nobody could call him handsome and he relishes every vice in the city."

"Not all of them," murmured Gill to himself.

"He means to mend his ways," said Nicholas. "As to what must have attracted her, I would have thought it was obvious—he is wealthy, since his brother's death, he has a title, and he has us."

"Westfield's Men?"

"Our reputation goes before us, Edmund. It seems that her uncle—and it is he who has brokered this match—saw us perform when we played at Frankfurt once as we traveled across the Continent. He had never forgotten the event and has filled his niece's ears ever since with tales of our excellence."

"That's gratifying to hear," said Firethorn, "but the lady is not being asked to wed *us*. She will be sharing a marriage bed with our patron, an aging voluptuary."

"Just like you, Lawrence," remarked Gill nastily.

"I resent that gibe."

"Truth is always painful."

"Nothing could be more painful than the sight of your repulsive face, Barnaby. It's a monument to sheer ugliness."

"Many people account me well-featured."

"Blindness is a terrible handicap."

"You are at it again," scolded Hoode, pushing them apart with his hands. "Forbear, both of you. Listen to Nick. I think he has something very important to tell us."

"I do," confirmed Nicholas.

"You said that there were two reasons why Lord Westfield was not as worried as he might have been. What's the second?"

"Our loss is his gain, Edmund."

"Could you speak more plainly?"

"You are all very slow to pick up my meaning," said Nicholas, amused by their bafflement. "In short, the position is this. Since our patron means to marry—and since his future wife is fond of the theater—he intends to take us with him."

Firethorn gaped. "Take us where, Nick?"

"To Denmark."

"Is that where the wedding will be held?"

"Yes, Lawrence. At Kronborg Castle in Elsinore."

"That's hundreds and hundreds of miles away," complained Gill.

"It matters not. We are offered work."

"But only after an interminable journey."

"Why must you always see only the hazards of an enterprise?" said Hoode, grinning broadly. "This is splendid news. We are to perform at the Danish court."

"And we will doubtless be invited to show our skills elsewhere," said Nicholas. "Remember what we discovered on our other visit to Europe. We have no rivals there. English companies excel all else. If we go to Elsinore, we will be feted."

"Then we'll go, Nick."

"Nothing would stop me," said Firethorn, elated. "Westfield's Men will be the toast of Denmark. We'll tell you of our many triumphs when we return, Barnaby."

Gill was disconcerted. "What do you mean?"

"You will be discarded from the company."

"But I've every right to go."

"Earlier on, you said that you refused to stir from London."

"True," admitted Gill, "and I still have qualms about this new venture. But, then, it has its undeniable attractions. A court is my natural home. I flourish before royalty."

"We will all flourish," said Firethorn, leaping to his feet to address the whole room. "Do you hear that, lads?" he yelled. "Cast off your misery. Order more drink. Lord Westfield is to marry and we will perform a play to celebrate the occasion. Kiss your wives and mistresses good-bye, dear friends. We are going to Denmark!"

Owen Elias was so pleased at the turn of events that he sang to himself in Welsh as he strolled down Gracechurch Street. Chance had contrived their salvation and turned unhappiness into sheer joy. He was still exercising his rich baritone voice when he turned into the yard of the Queen's Head. When he confronted the scene of destruction once more, however, the ditty died on his lips. Because of the concerted efforts of the company, much of the debris had been burned or taken away but enough still remained to bring him to a halt. Instead of looking at one side of the inn, he was staring over piles of rubble at the houses beyond. It was dispiriting.

Out of the corner of his eye, he detected movement and swung round to see the landlord shuffling toward him with a stranger. The other man was in his forties, tall, stooping, and in need of a walking stick. From his appearance, Elias could tell that he was a man of substance. He wore a smart brown suit, a fine hat, and he had an air of prosperity about him.

"You come upon your hour, Master Elias," said Marwood. "This gentleman has come in search of a friend who stayed here last night."

"Will Dunmow?" asked Elias.

"The very same. I'll leave him in your hands. I am so weighed down by what has happened that I can barely speak." Marwood shot them both a baleful glance. "Excuse me, sirs."

"The landlord was not very helpful," said the stranger as Marwood walked off. "I had difficulty prising a word out of him."

"Then you are fortunate, my friend. This morning, a whole torrent of abuse surged out of his mouth and it was aimed at us." Elias offered his hand. "My name is Owen Elias and I belong to Westfield's Men." They shook hands. "What have you learned about Will?"

"Nothing beyond the fact that he spent the night here and died in the fire. I am Anthony Rooker, by the way," said the other, face lined with anxiety. "I'm a friend of Will's father and offered the son bed and board while he was visiting London."

"He was very grateful, sir, and spoke well of you."

"That's good to hear."

"Will told us that he was here to do business on his father's behalf but that he intended to enjoy himself while he did so. He was cheerful company and generous to a fault."

"The lad has always been openhanded."

"His father is a merchant in York, I believe."

"Isaac Dunmow and I were partners in the city until I moved to London, but we still transact business together if the occasion serves. However," said Rooke, lips pursing in trepidation, "I am not sure that our friendship will survive this. I was meant to look after Will. I was *in loco parentis.*"

"He was too old to be fathered and too young to drink with actors. That was Will's undoing, alas."

"Tell me what happened."

Elias gave him an honest, straightforward account of Will Dunmow's fateful visit to the Queen's Head, ashamed of the way that he had helped to get him helplessly drunk, thereby making him so vulnerable. Anthony Rooker listened with a mingled sadness and unease, stunned by the details of the death and wondering how he could break the news to the father when he wrote to him. He was not surprised to hear of Will Dunmow's readiness to carouse.

"His father is inclined to severity," he explained, "and frowns upon most of the pleasures of life. It is only when he journeys south that Will can enjoy drink, lively company, and entertainment."

"What about women?" asked Elias.

"He has not neglected them while he was here."

"I ask that because he was so enamored of Emilia."

"Emilia?"

"A character in *The Italian Tragedy,* the play that moved him so much. When he acted as our benefactor, the person he most wished to meet was Emilia. Thinking her to be the gorgeous young lady he had seen onstage, Will blushed deep crimson when he realized that the part had been taken by Dick Honeydew, one of our boy apprentices."

"He is not well-versed in your conventions."

"It shocked him that he was entranced by a young lad."

"It would have shocked Isaac even more."

"One thing you may tell the father," said Elias, "not that it will soften his grief. But his son died happy. While he was with us, Will was in ecstasy and said so in round terms."

"Then I will certainly mention it in my letter."

"I'll gladly write to his father myself, if that would help."

"No, so," said Rooker quickly. "This is wholly my obligation. I mean no disrespect to you, Master Elias. The truth is that Isaac does not hold players in high regard. This tragedy will only serve to confirm his prejudices."

"What of the body?"

"I'll see it taken to York for burial."

"You will have to wait until the coroner releases it," said Elias. "I would add this warning. Will was badly burned. It would pain you to look on him and you must advise his father not to open the coffin. His son should be remembered as he was in life."

"That's good counsel. I'll follow it."

"If there is anything we can do, Master Rooker, do call on us."

"You've told me all I need to know."

"The truth was harsh but it had to be spoken."

"I bid you farewell, sir."

"One moment," said Elias as he remembered something. "You told me earlier that you and Will's father were partners at one time."

"For several years."

"Why did you go your separate ways?"

A shadow fell across the face of Anthony Rooker. "We parted by mutual consent," he said evasively. "Isaac Dunmow has many virtues and every attribute that a merchant must have. But he was not the easiest person with whom to get along."

"You and he had an argument, then?"

"In asking that, you presume far too much."

"Then I apologize," said Elias, holding up two penitent hands. "It is just that wine tends to loosen the tongue and it certainly set Will's free. When he talked of his father, it was not with affection. Will said that he sometimes resorted to violence."

Rooker's eyes flashed. "Good day to you, sir," he snapped.

Turning abruptly, he hobbled away on his walking stick.

It is an accident that heaven provides," said Anne Hendrik, taking his hands. "By all, this is wonderful, Nick!"

"It has certainly rallied Westfield's Men."

"No wonder. Instead of being deprived of work, they will be able to win new friends in a foreign country. My only regret is that you will not be able to perform in Amsterdam while I am there."

"Denmark will keep us fully occupied."

"Your patron, too, by the sound of it. Having outlived two wives, I never thought that he'd take a third."

"When he was deep in debt," said Nicholas Bracewell, "he was in no position to do so. An inheritance has transformed his outlook. The lady in question would enchant any man."

"I hope that you were an exception."

"Of course—I am already spoken for."

Anne laughed and brushed his lips with a kiss. It was late evening and they were in her house in Bankside. At the end of a long and eventful day, Nicholas was grateful for some peace and some warm companionship. Anne, too, was able to relax for the first time as they sat side by side in the parlor.

"Describe her to me," she requested.

"Who?"

"This paragon whose portrait you saw in miniature. Is she really a princess of Denmark?"

"Only in Lord Westfield's mind."

"Is she dark or fair?"

"Fair."

"What of her eye, her lip, her cheek?"

"She has the requisite number of each," said Nicholas, "but she still does not compare with you, Anne. You have one crucial advantage over Sigbrit Olsen."

"And what is that?"

"I can see you as you really are—a lovely woman in the prime of life with virtues too numerous to name. All that I know of Lord Westfield's bride is what I gleaned from her portrait. Limners can be deceptive," he pointed out. "And they are there to please their clients."

"You mean that they will hide any blemishes?"

"And enhance any finer points of a countenance."

"This lady still has considerable charm," said Anne. "The most artful hand cannot turn an ugly face into a beauteous one. What does she know of the man she has agreed to marry?"

"Only what her uncle has told her. The match has been arranged by him and by a man whom our patron engaged to find a suitable bride."

"So she had not seen a portrait of Lord Westfield?"

"No, Anne. She is taking him on trust."

"Then she is in for an unpleasant surprise," she said. "Of the two of them, Sigbrit Olsen is getting by far the worst of the bargain."

"We shall see," said Nicholas tolerantly. "All that concerns me is that we have been rescued from idleness by this marriage. More to the point, it enables me to spend more time with you."

"How so?"

"I thought that you would sail for Amsterdam alone."

"I still intend to do so. I've promised to visit Jacob's family and I will not let them down. My plan is to leave next week."

"Stay your hand and we may sail together. A ship that sails for Denmark is likely to visit the Low Countries as well. Indeed, I'll make sure that it does before I commit us as passengers." He smiled fondly. "Would you rather go with or without me?"

"You know the answer to that," she said, touching his arm. "There's nobody I would rather have beside me. You are a good sailor, Nick. I am not. You have voyaged around the whole world. All that I managed to do was to sail across the North Sea."

"That, too, can have its perils."

"Then I'll gladly share them with you."

He put an arm around her and she nestled into his shoulder. Dappled by the shadows thrown by the candles, they sat there in restful silence for a long time. Nicholas's memory was then jogged.

"How is Preben?" he asked.

"Still pretending that there is nothing wrong with him."

"He looked as pale as death when I saw him."

"That stone all but knocked him senseless," said Anne, "and he lost a lot of blood. He was so upset that I should see him like that."

"Did you report what happened?"

"Yes, Nick. We gave that document to a constable and charged him to pass it on to the authorities. They will be as angry as we were by that message of hatred. Steps will be taken to find the culprits."

"There have been no arrests so far."

"The villains have been too cunning."

"Then a trap needs to be set for them."

"It's not your place to get involved, Nick."

"I gave Preben my word," he said.

"And it caused him great disquiet," said Anne. "To have anyone acting on his behalf only distresses him. Preben would prefer that the whole matter was forgotten."

"His head was cracked open. Retribution is due."

"Humor him, please. For his sake, do not pursue the matter. We had a shock this morning and we are over it now. With so much to do before you leave for Denmark, you will not have time to go to the Dutch churchyard."

"I'll find the time somehow."

"What is the point?" she said. "Your chances of success are very slim. It may well be that what we saw was the last of these libels against strangers. Those who put them there know the dire penalties that they face. I think that they will be frightened away."

The watchmen plodded along side by side in the dark like two old cart horses pulling a heavy load. Broad Street was no less noisome by night than by day. A compound of unpleasant smells hung in the air to assault their nostrils, and their feet squelched through all kinds of filthy refuse. But they knew their duty. When they reached the Dutch churchyard, they paused to look inside, using their lanterns to illumine even its darkest corners. All that they found was a dog, curled up beside one of the gravestones. Dispatched with a kick, it yelped aloud and scurried away. The watchmen were content. Leaving the churchyard, they checked every inch of the wall to see if anything had been hung there again.

"Nothing," said one.

"We are good scarecrows," said the other.

"Yes, Tom. We frightened them away at last."

Chuckling quietly, they went on their way, patrolling the streets of the parish at the same slow, tireless, unvarying pace. They were soon swallowed up by darkness. When the distant echo of their footsteps finally died away, someone came out of a doorway opposite the churchyard and trotted across to it. Seconds later, another vile attack on foreigners was attached to the wall.

The villains had struck again.

[CHAPTER FOUR]

Margery Firethorn was a gregarious woman who loved to have people around her. Her house in Shoreditch was not merely home to her husband and children, it also contained two servants and the four boy apprentices who belonged to Westfield's Men. In addition, it was the regular meeting place for certain members of the company, so visitors were coming and going all the time. Margery greeted them all with maternal warmth and made sure that refreshment was always on hand. That morning, however, her pleasure at seeing her friends was tempered by the thought that she might not lay eyes on them again for a long time. When the troupe sailed off to Denmark, five people who slept under her roof would disappear along with all of her most cherished callers. The house in Old Street would seem very empty.

Nicholas Bracewell was the first to arrive and she always reserved her most cordial welcome for the book holder. When she embraced him this time, however, there was sadness in her face and a hint of desperation in the way that she clung to him. He understood why. Margery stepped back to appraise him.

"I shall miss you, Nick," she said.

"Not as much as I'll miss you," he said gallantly. "There's nobody in the whole of Denmark who will look after us as well as you."

"Thank you."

"The pity of it is that we cannot take you with us."

"The same must be true of Anne, surely?"

"No, Margery—she will be joining us."

"Oh?"

"Anne is going to Amsterdam to visit relatives and friends of her late husband. She'll sail with us part of the way."

"Would that I could do so as well!"

"We'd be honored to have you."

She kissed him on the lips, gave him an impulsive squeeze, then took him into the parlor, where Lawrence Firethorn was poring over a manuscript. He looked up.

"Nick, dear heart," he said, rising from his chair. "As ever, you are the first here even though you have to travel farther than anyone."

"I enjoy a long walk," said Nicholas.

"It must have taken you past the Queen's Head."

"It did. The place looks forlorn. By now, I fancy, the landlord will have pulled out the last remaining tufts of hair in vexation. It will be months before the inn returns to anything like its former glory."

"It can only do that when Westfield's Men play there again," said Margery loyally. "The sooner that happens, the better." The door-bell clanged. "That will be Edmund."

She left the room and let the newcomer in, enfolding him in her arms for a moment before ushering him into the parlor. Margery then vanished into the kitchen. After an exchange of greetings, the three men sat down. Firethorn picked up the manuscript on the table.

"I've been reading your latest play again, Edmund," he said. "I know that it did not find favor with the Master of the Revels but it might have a kinder reception in Denmark."

"I doubt it," said Hoode. "*Sir Thomas More* will be a poor play if I take out all the lines that offended the censor. He hacked it to pieces."

"His writ does not run in Elsinore."

Hoode sat up. "We perform the piece exactly as it is written?"

"That's my suggestion," said Firethorn, leafing through the pages. "Sir Thomas is a part I yearn to play. He towers over the drama like a colossus and his execution will move the hardest of hearts. *Sir Thomas More* would grace any stage."

"Thank you, Lawrence," Hoode said, touched. "I have never had a play savaged by the Master of the Revels before and I was deeply wounded. To have it performed in Denmark would be a balm to my injuries." He turned to the book holder. "What's your opinion, Nick?"

"I think it's a fine play," said Nicholas. "One of your best."

"It's settled then," declared Firethorn, tossing the manuscript onto the table. "That's one problem solved."

"I disagree, Lawrence."

"I thought you liked the play."

"I admire it greatly," said Nicholas, "but it is hardly a suitable choice for a wedding. Lord Westfield will expect laughter and gaiety. We cannot celebrate the occasion with a tragedy."

Hoode nodded. "Nick makes a telling point."

"Then we play *Sir Thomas More* elsewhere," said Firethorn, determined not to be deprived of the chance to create a superb new role. "They'll have a comedy for the wedding and a tragedy at some other venue in Denmark."

"I'm sorry to challenge you again, Lawrence," said Nicholas, "but I have to question the wisdom of that decision."

"Why?"

"Because the name of Sir Thomas will mean little to a Danish audience. He may live fresh in our memory but they have their own heroes and men of integrity. But there is an even stronger argument against the play," Nicholas went on. "It was rejected in its present form and there was a good reason for that."

"Yes," said Firethorn with a scowl. "Sir Edmund Tilney does not appreciate the talent of Edmund Hoode. Our celebrated Master of the Revels sliced the play wide open."

"Only because he thought it politic to do so. And you malign him unjustly. He's an admirer of Edmund's work and has never turned one of his plays away before. What alarmed him was the coincidence."

"What coincidence, Nick?"

"I can tell you that," interjected Hoode. "At the time when Sir

Thomas was undersheriff of London, there was great unrest over the number of foreigners in the capital. It's dealt with in three separate scenes. Unhappily," he said with a grimace, "the same hatred of strangers has been whipped into a frenzy again."

"Look what happened to Anne and Preben yesterday," resumed Nicholas. "They learned just how much resentment is felt against foreigners. Without intending to do so, certain scenes in Edmund's play might excite that resentment even more."

"Perish the thought!" said Hoode.

"Such objections could not be raised in Denmark," argued Firethorn. "We would hardly arouse enmity against strangers there."

"No," conceded Nicholas, "but we would show England in a very poor light. Remember this—whenever we perform, our patron and his bride will be in the audience. No play will endear itself to the new Lady Westfield if it portrays this city as a cauldron of hatred and intolerance."

"*Sir Thomas More* is a history play."

"History has a nasty habit of repeating itself, Lawrence, as in the case of our present troubles. Denmark will not be unaware of those. Among the strangers here," Nicholas pointed out, "we have Danes as well. Their letters home are bound to talk of the outrages against foreigners."

"Nick has persuaded me," said Hoode. "My play is withdrawn."

Firethorn raised a palm. "Not so fast, Edmund. I'll not yield up a wonderful role so easily. To make it more acceptable, all that we have to do is to remove the scenes that deal with strangers."

"In other words, we ape what Sir Edmund Tilney did."

"He tore the play apart. We will merely amend it."

"It amounts to the same thing. If the play is not performed in its entirety, then it will not take the stage at all. No more argument," said Hoode as Firethorn tried to speak. "I'll not be party to anything that might cause embarrassment to Lord Westfield and his bride." The doorbell was rung hard. "That will be Barnaby. I'm glad that we discussed *Sir Thomas More* before he arrived. He disliked the play."

"Only because he had such a minor role," said Nicholas.

"Yes," said Firethorn, "the only scenes he bothered to read were those in which the clown appeared. It was ever thus. He judges the quality of a play by the number of lines he has and the number of comic jigs he's allowed to dance."

Moments later, Margery showed the latest arrival into the room before disappearing again. There was a flurry of greetings, then Gill took a seat. He distributed a warning glance among the others.

"I hope that you've not been rash enough to make any decisions without me," he said, "because I shall countermand them all."

"Three votes will always count against your one," said Firethorn.

"I only see two sharers in the room."

"Nick's opinion has more weight than anyone else's."

"Even when he is nothing more than a hired man?"

"Stop harping on that, Barnaby," said Hoode wearily. "Nick has already stopped us from taking one unsuitable offering to Denmark and he'll do so again. Nobody knows our stock of plays better than he, and what costumes, scenery, and properties are needed for each one. Since we can only carry a limited amount of baggage, such details need to be taken into account." Margery entered with a bottle of wine and four glasses on a tray. "We'll put it to the test."

"You come on cue, my love," said Firethorn, massaging her buttock as she put the tray on the table. "Of the four of us, who is the best judge of a play?"

"Nick Bracewell," she replied promptly.

"And the finest actor?"

"Do not fish for compliments, Lawrence," she said, pouring the wine out and handing the glasses around. "When you are in the same company, you do not compete. You act with each other."

Hoode smiled his approval. "Well said, Margery."

"Every team needs a leader," Firethorn commented.

"He leads best who does not have to impose his will upon others," she said, handing a drink to her husband before moving away. "Bear that in mind, Lawrence."

"Heed your wife," Gill advised. "Margery spies your weakness."

"She spied yours at a glance," riposted Firethorn.

"I did not come here to be abused."

"Then refrain from inviting abuse."

"I'm here to make important decisions."

"And so is Nick—let that be understood."

"It's not only the choice of plays that must exercise us," said Nicholas. "There is the far trickier problem of selecting those who act in them. Lord Westfield has kindly volunteered to pay for our passage to Denmark but his bounty ends there. To defray expenses, we must travel with a smaller company and that will mean shedding several of our hired men."

"We must take musicians," insisted Firethorn. "They will expect songs and dances from us."

Gill preened himself. "And especially from me," he boasted.

"There's not room for everyone," said Hoode somberly.

"Alas, no," agreed Nicholas. "Instead of musicians, we must have actors who can play an instrument. Their other skills should also be taken into account before we come to a decision."

"Other skills?" said Firethorn.

"Oswald Megson once worked as a carpenter. He will be sorely needed to make new scenery or repair anything that gets damaged. Harold Stoddard was apprenticed to a tailor. He must be both actor and tireman. As for David Knell—"

"Oh, no!" protested Gill. "I draw the line at him—anyone but David Knell. His face is so mournful that it makes me feel unwell. When he smiles, it is like a grave opening up. Forget him, Nicholas. Whoever else comes with us, we do not take Death Knell."

"No," said Firethorn, disheartened at the prospect before him, "we simply sound it for those we have to set aside. Very well—let us be fair but firm. As well as the sharers, who else comes to Denmark?"

How do things stand, my lord?" asked Rolfe Harling.

"Preparations are almost complete."

"In so short a time?"

"There's no point in delay," said Lord Westfield. "Once I made the decision to take my company with me, it was simply a case of leaving the arrangements to Nicholas Bracewell."

"And who might he be?"

"An estimable fellow in every way. Though he is only the book holder with Westfield's Men, he virtually carries them on his broad shoulders. He is our talisman. What he has done in the course of one week is extraordinary."

"A remarkable man, clearly," said Harling.

"And he has one outstanding quality."

"What is that?"

"He is a born sailor," said Lord Westfield, "and we need someone like him to comfort us on the voyage. Nicholas is the son of a Devon merchant. He went to sea with his father many times."

"Only across the English Channel, I daresay. I can tell you from experience that the North Sea is far more perilous."

"Do not talk of peril to Nicholas Bracewell."

"Why not?"

"In younger days, he sailed around the word with Drake. He survived storms and tempests, the like of which we can only imagine. The North Sea holds no fears for such a man."

"I look forward to meeting him, my lord."

"I reserve my anticipation for my dearest Sigbrit."

Although he knew every detail of her countenance from incessant study of the miniature, Lord Westfield took it from his pocket yet again and looked in wonderment at her. They were dining together in his favorite tavern and he was anxious for events to move as swiftly as they could.

"You've written to her uncle?"

"My letter will have arrived by now."

Lord Westfield was worried. "We may have set sail before his reply comes. Oh!" he cried, slapping his leg with a petulant hand. "Is there anything more vexing than the tyranny of distance?"

"Have no fears," Harling told him.

"But I need to know that I am expected and wanted."

"You are, my lord, I assure you."

"Supposing that she has changed her mind? Or fallen ill and is unable to go through with the marriage? Supposing that I do not *please* her enough?"

"You are all that she could wish for," said Harling, sampling the Madeira wine in his glass. "Her uncle and I took every aspect of the marriage into account. We do not leave for another ten days. There is no chance that his reply will fail to reach me."

"What if the ship should miscarry before it reached our shore?"

"Even then, we would have no reason for alarm."

"I need to see her acceptance in the form of a letter."

"And so you shall, my lord—when we reach Flushing."

"Flushing?"

"Yes, my lord," explained Harling. "Our vessel first calls there. I took the precaution of having any letters for you from Denmark sent to the governor's home in Flushing. They will not even have traveled by sea but been carried overland by couriers."

"What a clever fellow you are, Rolfe!"

"I did not want any correspondence to go astray. All that we have to do is to call on Sir Robert Sidney and retrieve any letters."

"You have put my mind at rest." After glancing at the portrait once more, he slipped it back into his pocket. "All things proceed to a successful outcome."

"I think you will find that every detail has been considered."

"And we will be housed in the castle?"

"Kronborg Slot awaits you."

Lord Westfield blinked. "Where?"

"It's what they call the castle in Elsinore."

"I could want a more mellifluous name for a place where I will marry the most beautiful creature in the world. However, if it contents Sigbrit, I'll raise no complaints. Will the king be in residence?"

"He'll be sure to attend the ceremony," said Harling, "and he will certainly not miss any performances given by your troupe. English players have visited Denmark before with distinction."

"Lawrence Firethorn will outshine all of them."

"Even he will taken second place to Sigbrit Olsen."

"I'll be fast married to her before I let him near her," said Lord Westfield with a grin. "Lawrence has an eye for the ladies. When absent from his wife, he has been known to seek pleasure elsewhere. But not from my Sigbrit—she is one woman he will never ensnare."

"How many performances will your company give?"

"As many as they can."

"They will be in demand at Kronborg Slot and in the town of Elsinore itself, I daresay. And if King Christian admires them—as he is certain to do—he may well invite them to play in Copenhagen."

"What do you know of this new king?"

Harling pondered. "He is well-educated, ambitious, and far-sighted," he said at length. "His mother was Sophie of Mecklenburg so he speaks perfect German. His father, King Frederick II, was a man of strong convictions and had an interest in the arts. His son shares that interest. Until his coronation earlier this year, the country was under a regent. King Christian IV has succeeded to the throne with the fire of youth in his veins."

"You seem unduly well-informed, Rolfe."

"I have traveled widely in Europe. One picks up all the gossip."

"This is more than gossip."

"When I was in Copenhagen," explained Harling, "I found out all I could. You must remember that I am a scholar at heart. I've been trained to gather all the evidence before reaching a judgment."

"I have been the beneficiary of your thoroughness."

"You paid me well."

"No man can set a price on happiness."

"I like to render good service."

"And so you did," said Lord Westfield, raising his glass. "I toast my future wife—the divine Sigbrit Olsen!"

"Sigbrit Olsen," echoed Harling as they clinked glasses.

"She will be so thrilled with my wedding present."

"Which one, my lord?"

"My theater company, of course."

"Ah, yes."

"What other bridegroom could turn up at the altar with the finest troupe in Europe at his side? And there'll be another surprise for her, Rolfe."

"Will there?"

"Westfield's Men are to perform a play in her honor."

"What is it called?"

"What else, man—*The Princess of Denmark?*"

But there is no such play in our stock," said Owen Elias, "and even someone with as fluent a pen as Edmund's could not write one in the short time before we leave."

"Nevertheless, we will perform *The Princess of Denmark.*"

"How can we, Nick, when she does not even exist?"

"But she does," said Nicholas, "hidden beneath another name."

"Well, I do not know what it is."

"Think hard, Owen."

The two of them were in Elias's lodging and the Welshman was eager for any information relating to their imminent trip abroad. As a sharer and as one of the company's most versatile actors, he was among the first to be listed among those making the voyage. Others had been less fortunate and it had fallen to Nicholas Bracewell to pass on the bad tidings to many of the hired men who served the troupe. It had been an ordeal for him. Bitter tears had been shed and heartbreaking entreaties made but he had no authority to alter the decisions that had been made. Having at last finished his thankless task, he had called in on his friend.

"Do you remember our visit to Prague?" asked Nicholas.

Elias was rueful. "I am hardly likely to forget it, and neither is Anne. She was abducted in the city."

"What was the title of the play we performed at the wedding?"

"*The Fair Maid of Bohemia.*"

"No, Owen."

"It was—I swear it."

"What the audience *thought* they saw was a play of that name," said Nicholas. "In fact, what they were watching was *The Chaste Maid of Wapping,* an old comedy new-minted by Edmund to give it the sheen of novelty. He will use the same trick again."

"Turn a chaste maid into a princess?"

"Find a play from the past that will fit an event in the future. With my help, Edmund has done so. We chose *The Prince of Aragon.*"

"But that is a dark tragedy."

"Not in its new incarnation," said Nicholas. "The prince becomes a princess, Aragon is translated into Denmark, and the death of the hero is changed into the wedding of the heroine. All demands are satisfied. Lord Westfield and his bride will think the piece was conceived with them in mind."

"You are a magician, Nick!"

"I merely provided the play. Edmund will fashion it anew."

"Oh, I am so looking forward to this adventure!"

"I, too," said Nicholas, "but we have unfinished business first."

"Do we?"

"I still worry that we've heard no more about Will Dunmow."

"There's nothing else to hear. I told you about that man with whom Will was staying."

"Yes—Anthony Rooker."

"When the body was released by the coroner, he was going to have it transported back home for burial. He must have done that by now. A letter was sent to York in advance."

"That's what perplexes me, Owen."

"Why?"

"Put yourself in the father's position," suggested Nicholas. "Your son sets out for London on business. The next thing you hear is that he's been killed in a fire. What would you do?"

"Mourn his death."

"Nothing else?"

"Await the return of his body."

"Then we would make very different fathers."

"What do you mean?"

"If a son of mine died in those circumstances, I'd be in the saddle the moment I heard about it. I'd come to London to find out every last detail of the tragedy. Nobody else would be allowed to send Will's body north. I'd ride with it myself."

"Yes," said Elias, thinking it through, "I suppose that I would as well. I'd seek out those who last saw Will alive."

"Owen Elias and James Ingram."

Elias shuddered. "We have that grim distinction."

"Has the father been anywhere near either of you?"

"No, Nick. As far as I know, he is still in York."

"I find that odd."

"So do I. On the other hand," said Elias, "Will did tell us how glad he was to get away from him. There was no love lost between them. Will was bent on living life to the full while he was in London because he was not allowed to do that in York. His father was a martinet—Anthony Rooker confirmed that."

"I wish that I'd met him myself."

"He was not the most pleasant of men, Nick."

"That's irrelevant," said Nicholas. "I still feel that this whole business is not yet over somehow. We were *involved*—you, especially. To a man, we liked Will Dunmow."

"He was a true friend."

"I would like to know what happened to him. When was the body dispatched and what sort of funeral will it have? What manner of man is the father? Why has he not been in touch with you?"

"I think that he probably despises me, Nick."

"Why?"

"I helped to get his son into that state," admitted Elias. "James and I carried him to his bed that night. I snuffed out the candle but I forgot that he had a pipe with him."

"We are not even sure that that is what started the fire."

"I'm sure, Nick—and I still feel culpable."

"No blame attaches to you or to James. You could not foresee what might happen. However," Nicholas continued, "let's leave Will Dunmow and turn to the other unfinished business."

"And what is that?"

Nicholas leaned in closer to him. "I need to ask a favor of you."

The Dutch churchyard lay wrapped in the thick blanket of night. Dutch, German, and other languages were etched on the gravestones but they were unreadable in the darkness. All that could be seen were the blurred outlines of monument and tombstone. An owl perched on a stone cross. Moles were busy underneath the soft earth. Rats came sniffing through the grass. Locked against intruders, the church itself loomed over the dead that were buried in its massive shadow. A homeless beggar slept on the cold stone in its porch.

The old watchmen approached on their nightly patrol. When they got close to the churchyard, their lanterns threw a flickering light on an ancient cart abandoned near the entrance. All that they could see in it was a large pile of sacks and a broken wheelbarrow. They moved on to the churchyard to conduct their usual search and disturbed the owl. Leaving its perch, it flew high up into a tree before settling on a branch and keeping them under wide-eyed surveillance. As they meandered between the gravestones, they looked for signs of desecration. They found none. They sauntered back toward the gate.

"Look to the wall, Tom," said one.

"Aye," replied his companion.

"That's where they publish their damnable lies."

"Except that they're not all lies."

"What's that you say?"

Tom did not reply. They left the churchyard and examined the wall that ran alongside it. Nothing had been left there. The first man repeated his question.

"What's that you say?"

"There are too many of them, Silas," grunted the other.

"Too many?"

"Strangers—they are everywhere. I heard tell that they counted their numbers. Do you know how many we have in London?"

"No, Tom. Hundreds, I expect."

"Over four thousand."

"Never!"

"That's the figure I heard and I believe it. They are never satisfied, Silas, that's their trouble. They always want more."

"The foreigners I know all work very hard."

"Yes," said Tom grumpily, "but they do not work for us. They sneer at what we have in our shops and warehouses. They open their own instead. It's not right. It's not fair."

"That's not for us to say."

"Strangers are strangers. They'll never belong."

"Anyone would think that *you* wrote those libels, Tom Hubble."

"Not me, Silas. I despise most of what they say." Tom spat onto the ground. "But I do agree with bits of them."

"Shame on you!"

"England must look first to the English."

"Let's move on."

"Over four thousand of them, Silas—and the numbers grow."

"They are exiles, Tom," said the other with compassion, "driven out of their own countries."

Tom Hubble sniffed. "There are too many of them."

They trudged off down Broad Street until their lanterns were slowly extinguished in the gloom. There was a long pause. Someone then emerged warily from a doorway on the opposite side of the road and trotted across to the churchyard. Confident that he was alone, he unfurled a poster and started to fix it to the wall. He was soon interrupted. A figure suddenly rose up in the back of the abandoned cart and shook off the sacking under which he had been concealed. The man at the wall was so terrified that he dropped his scroll and ran for his life. He did not get far.

Nicholas Bracewell darted into the street from his hiding place and grabbed him by the shoulders, hurling him against a wall to knock some of the breath out of him. But the man was young and strong. Recovering quickly, he pulled out a dagger and slashed at Nicholas. The book holder eluded the weapon with ease. He had been involved in many brawls and knew how to stay light on his feet. When his assailant thrust the dagger at his heart, therefore, Nicholas turned quickly sideways and grabbed the man's wrist as it flashed past him. There was a brief tussle but Nicholas's superior strength soon brought the fight to an end. Forcing this adversary to drop the knife, he flung him against the wall again, then struck him with a relay of punches that left him cowering on his knees against the brick. Whimpering piteously, the man begged for mercy.

Owen Elias had been hidden in the cart. When he joined his friend, he was not happy about his accommodation.

"I swear that those sacks were filled with horse manure at some point," he said, curling his nose. "I must stink to high heaven."

"Our efforts were rewarded, Owen. We caught him." Nicholas hauled the young man to his feet and held him by the throat. "This is one piece of business that is now finished."

[CHAPTER FIVE]

George Dart was the smallest and most timid member of the company. As an assistant stage-keeper, he performed a whole array of menial tasks with a willingness that never flagged. On occasion, much to his discomfort, he was also compelled to take part in a play, albeit in a minor capacity. For the most part, however, he loved his work and looked upon Westfield's Men as his true family, even though the apprentices sometimes teased him and the actors frequently used him as their whipping boy. Expecting to be discarded for the visit to Denmark, he was overwhelmed to be one of those selected to go. Dart was bursting with gratitude.

"A thousand thanks, Nicholas," he said.

"It was not my decision, George."

"But you spoke up for me. I know that. If it had been left to Master Firethorn and the others, they would not have given me a second thought—except to laugh at me."

"I know your true worth," said Nicholas fondly. "You do the work of three men and are always ready to learn. Dear old Thomas Skillen is our stage-keeper but you do most of the tasks that should rightly be his. Since his ancient bones would never survive a voyage across the North Sea, he urged that you should go in his place."

Dart was amazed. "But all that he ever does is to box my ears."

"That is his means of instruction."

The two of them had come to the Queen's Head to take away

the scenery and properties that would be needed on tour. There was a limit to how much they could carry. Weight and bulkiness were thus crucial factors. Guided by their book holder, Lawrence Firethorn and the others had chosen to perform plays on tour that could share many of the same items as well as most of the same costumes. Duplication would simplify matters. Nicholas took out the key. When he unlocked the room where everything was stored, there was barely enough space among the clutter for them to stand side by side.

"Read out the list, George," said the book holder, handing him a scroll. "I'll try to find the things we need."

Dart unrolled the paper. "*Item,* one pope's miter, one imperial crown, one throne."

"The throne is far too heavy. If we play in a castle, I'm sure that we can borrow a high-backed chair that will serve our purposes."

"They may also furnish us with a crown."

"That would be too much to ask," said Nicholas, taking two objects specified down from a shelf. "It would be impertinent of us to ask King Christian to abdicate for a couple of hours so that we could make use of his crown." He put the items aside. "Here we are—one miter, one crown. What's next?"

"*Item,* one rock, one tomb, one cauldron."

"The tomb must come—it's used in three separate plays—but we will have to find a rock in Denmark—a real one, probably. It is so with the cauldron. The castle kitchens will furnish that."

"What about the steeple and maypole for *Love and Fortune?*" asked Dart. "I doubt that we will find those so easily. Big as they are, we'll have to take them with us."

"No," said Nicholas, putting the wooden tomb outside the door so that it would not impede them, "they will stay here. When we reach the castle, Oswald Megson will make us a new steeple and maypole. He's been told to bring his tools."

"I forgot that he was trained as a carpenter."

"It's the reason that Oswald was picked to go."

Before they could continue, they heard footsteps in the corridor outside, then the face of Alexander Marwood appeared in the doorway.

"I want all this taken away," said the landlord peremptorily.

"It will be," replied Nicholas.

"Every trace of Westfield's Men must leave my inn."

"The costumes have already been removed by Hugh Wegges, our tireman. George and I will clear this room today as well. When we have picked out the items that we need to take to Denmark with us, we'll return with a larger cart and carry everything else away."

"Not before time!" snarled Marwood. "Since we lost almost half of the Queen's Head in the fire, we need to use every room we have."

Dart was curious. "This will become a bedchamber?"

"It will have to. Eight rooms were lost in the blaze."

"But what happens when we come back?"

"You will not be allowed on my premises."

"We do have a contract with you, Master Marwood," Nicholas reminded him, "and it was signed in good faith. You have no legal right to put us out on a whim."

"That contract—accepted against my better judgment, I may tell you—stipulates that Westfield's Men may play in my yard for the next year. But I no longer *have* a yard," asserted Marwood, jerking a thumb over his shoulder, "and so the contract is null and void."

"Only until you rebuild the inn."

"That will never happen."

"But it must," pleaded Dart. "This is our home."

"It was *our* home until it was burned down, young sir. It was the place that gave us our livelihood. You and the others may sail off across the sea to earn a living. We do not have that luxury. My wife and I are stuck here in the ruins of our inn."

"Have you spoken to a builder yet?" asked Nicholas.

"What is the point?"

"The Queen's Head can arise anew."

"Only at a high price, Master Bracewell. Where am I to get the money to pay it? I do not have a wealthy patron like you."

"Come now," said Nicholas, "you can hardly plead poverty. The weather has been kind to us all year. Throughout spring and summer, we filled your yard with paying customers. They bought your refreshments during the performances and thronged your taproom after it. Six days a week, you made healthy profits."

"Yes," Dart put in, "and it would have been seven days had we not been banned from staging a play within the city limits on the Sabbath."

"We bring in most of your custom, Master Marwood."

The landlord sneered. "You also bring cunning pickpockets and greasy prostitutes to my inn. I watch them mingle with the crowd as they go about their nefarious business. I will be well rid of such vile creatures."

"You will also lose the gallants and their ladies who inhabit your galleries," said Nicholas persuasively, "not to mention those members of the court who spend their money so freely here. Great men of state have sat on cushions at the Queen's Head in order to watch us. Would you spurn them as well?"

"I will spurn anyone in order to keep Westfield's Men at bay."

"But we need each other," wailed Dart.

"My mind is made up—you are expelled forever."

"Rebuild," advised Nicholas, pointing through the open door at the yard beyond. "Rebuild your inn and rebuild your faith in us."

Marwood was adamant. "The only thing that I will build is a high wall to keep out you and that infernal company of yours. I am sorry, Master Bracewell," he went on, "you are a decent man and have always dealt honestly with me, but Lawrence Firethorn and his crew have tortured me enough." He indicated the wooden tomb at his feet. "This is your monument—Westfield's Men are dead and buried. Away with the whole pack of you!"

With a derisive gesture, he turned on his heel and stalked off.

Dart was distraught. "Did you hear that, Nicholas?"

"I've heard it all too often."

"He means to evict us. We have nowhere to perform."

"Yes, we do," said Nicholas, "we have the castle in Elsinore and other places in Denmark. That is all that concerns me at the moment, George. Pay no heed to the landlord. When we are gone, he will rue his harsh words. Now," he went on briskly, "let us carry on. Read out the next items on the list."

* * *

Turning it gently in her hands, Anne Hendrik examined the hat with an expert eye. Light green in color, it was round with a soft crown and a narrow brim. Twisted gold cord surrounded the crown. An ostrich feather sprouted out of the top of the hat.

"This is good," she said with admiration.

"It will pass," said Preben van Loew. "It will pass."

"It will do for more than that. Are you sure that Jan made this?"

"Quite sure."

"He has improved so much in the last year, Preben."

"Apprentices must work hard if they are to master their trade."

"Jan has certainly done so. You must be proud of him."

"I am teaching him all I know," said the Dutchman. "I showed you this latest example of his craft to prove that you need have no fears while you are away. The business will continue. Jan is now able to make hats that are worthy of sale. The lad is no longer a burden on you. He is helping to earn his keep."

"And maintaining the tradition that Jacob established."

"That is very important."

Anne had invited Preben into her house so that they could discuss how the business would be run in her absence. There were enough commissions to keep them busy for months and there was always the possibility that more might come in. She had no worries about the making of the hats because Preben van Loew would oversee that. Where he needed advice was in the areas that she usually reserved for herself—the buying of the materials and the pricing of the finished article. What the Dutchman and the others made, she then sold. Her side of the operation was one in which the old man did not excel.

"We will get by somehow," he assured her.

"I know, Preben."

"How long will you be away?"

"I'll not stay much more than a week in Amsterdam."

"I still have many friends there. Will you carry letters for me?"

"I'll insist upon it."

"Thank you, Anne."

It was early evening and they were seated in the parlor where candles had already been lit to dispel the shadows. Anne had no regrets about marrying into a Dutch family. She had not only acquired some charming relatives, she had also made many friends from the Low Countries and been impressed by the diligence and simplicity of their lives. She did not merely keep in touch with her relatives by marriage out of a sense of obligation. It was a pleasure to make rare visits to see them. Unwilling to return to his homeland himself, Preben van Loew valued her excursions there because she always brought back news and letters for him.

"I feel that I can leave with a clear conscience now," she said.

"Conscience?"

"Nick did what he vowed to do."

"Ah," Preben said, realizing. "The Dutch churchyard."

"He and Owen kept vigil there for three nights in a row before they caught that young man."

"I know, Anne. I'm very grateful."

"He was the same person who threw the stone at you that day we were there. He admitted as much to Nick."

"But he did not write those cruel verses about strangers."

"No," she agreed, "but he endorsed every word of them. He'll be punished severely for his part in the outrage. He'll not be able to hang any more libels on the wall of the churchyard."

"Somebody else will do that."

"I doubt it."

"They will, Anne," Preben said with an air of fatalism. "He can easily be replaced. The only way to stop these attacks is to arrest the men who write and publish them. Nicholas would never catch them. They are far too clever to put themselves at risk. They stay hidden while someone else spreads the poison on their behalf. The young man who was captured last night was suborned by others."

"Their names will soon be known, Preben."

"He'll not yield them up willingly."

"Nick says that he's been taken to Bridewell to be examined," she told him. "We both know what that means."

Preben van Loew swallowed hard. A sensitive man, he recoiled from the idea of pain, even when it was inflicted on others. The young man in custody had broken open the Dutchman's head with a sharp stone yet he could still feel pity for him. Examination in Bridewell condemned the prisoner to torture. Instruments that could inflict the most unbearable agony were kept there. The very notion made Preben van Loew squirm. He tried to change the subject.

"Do you wish me to see you off, Anne?"

"We're not sailing for another couple of days."

"Will you want me at the quayside?"

"No, Preben. You are much better off here, carrying on with your work and helping Jan to improve even more. If he or any of the others have letters or gifts they wish me to take to Amsterdam, they only have to ask."

"I'll pass that message on to them."

"Good."

"It's a pity that you cannot go on to Denmark as well."

"Oh, I do not have time enough for that."

"But you would like to be with Nicholas, would you not?" he said with a quizzical smile. "And you have always enjoyed watching Westfield's Men—do not deny it."

"I would never dare to do that. I've spent many happy afternoons at the Queen's Head and hope to spend many more in the future. And, yes," she added, warming to the thought, "I would love to go with them to Denmark. But, then—if truth be told—I'd gladly go anywhere with Nick Bracewell."

On the eve of their departure, Nicholas Bracewell called at the house in Shoreditch to confirm arrangements with Lawrence Firethorn. Once again, he was clasped to Margery's surging bosom, hugged for a long time, then kissed repeatedly.

"Let him go, my love," said Firethorn with a chuckle, "or you'll squeeze the life out of him. Above all else, we need Nick on this voyage. He's the one true sailor among us."

"Then I charge you to bring him back safely to me," she told her husband, releasing the book holder. "For I have my needs as well."

"It's always a delight to satisfy them, Margery." She let out a merry cackle and gave her husband a playful push. "Well, Nick," he continued, "is everything in order?"

"I believe so."

"Where are our costumes, scenery, and properties?"

"Awaiting us at the quayside. I rented space in a warehouse."

"What of the items we leave behind?"

"Hugh Wegges has stored the costumes in his own home. All else has been stowed with our carpenter in Bankside. It hurt me to tell Nathan Curtis that he would not be sailing with us, but there is no room in the company for someone who does not act."

"Then why are we taking Barnaby?"

Margery laughed. "Do not be so wicked, Lawrence!"

"Have you spoken to our patron again, Nick?"

"Yes," replied Nicholas, "I've just come from Lord Westfield's house, as it happens. He and his servants will sail with us tomorrow on the *Cormorant*—and so will his adviser."

"Adviser?"

"A man named Rolfe Harling. I met him earlier on. It seems that he was responsible for helping to arrange this match. He has been combing Europe for a suitable bride."

"I found mine right here in England," said Firethorn, slipping an affectionate arm around his wife's plump waist, "and she has been the light of my life. But more of that later," he whispered into her ear. "I have never heard of Rolfe Harling," he admitted, turning back to the book holder. "Is he part of Lord Westfield's circle?"

"Far from it," said Nicholas.

"Why so?"

"Because he would look out of place among the other hangers-on. Our patron likes the company of flamboyant young men and powdered young ladies. Rolfe Harling is too sober and diffident a man in every way," said Nicholas. "He's quiet, watchful, intelligent. I take him to be a scholar of some sort."

"Perchance he is tutoring Lord Westfield in Danish."

"Our patron relies heavily on him, I know that."

"And we rely heavily on you, Nick."

"I would never trust myself to pick out a bride for another man."

"When are you going to marry the one you have picked out for yourself?" asked Margery bluntly. "Anne clearly adores you."

"And I, her," confessed Nicholas. "But she prefers to remain a widow for the time being and I respect her wish. A lady should not be rushed into marriage."

"I was—and happy to be so."

"And what about this Sigbrit Olsen?" said Firethorn. "It seems that she is being taken to the altar at a mad gallop. Lord Westfield has not even met the lady yet he wants to move posthaste to the marriage bed."

"It would appear that she is agreeable to the plan."

"Then we must abide by it ourselves and perform *The Princess of Denmark* by way of celebration. How does Edmund fare?"

"Four acts are completed. Even now, he works on the last one."

"Changing an old play is swifter work than writing a new one."

"Trust him—the piece will be ready in time."

"I hope that the same is true of everyone else," said Firethorn sternly, "for the *Cormorant* will not tarry. It leaves on the morning tide. I know that the others will want to take a fond farewell from their wives and lovers tonight, but we do not want them still sleeping between the thighs of a woman while we sail down the Thames. Did you make that clear to them, Nick?"

"Crystal clear. The whole company will be there tomorrow."

"What of you, Nick? Will you roister with them tonight?"

"No, I'll spend a quiet evening in Bankside with Anne. We will have to be up early to get to the quayside."

"So will we," said Margery. "I have a husband, two children, and four apprentices to roust out of bed. I'll manage it somehow."

Firethorn chortled. "You'll have us up, washed, dressed, and fed long before dawn, my love. Would that everyone had some like you to haul them from their slumbers." His brow furrowed. "Owen Elias is my real concern."

"He's as eager as any of us to go to Denmark," said Nicholas.

"I do not question his eagerness, Nick. What troubles me is the way that he'll spend the night. Owen is a Welsh mountain goat. The rest of us—except Barnaby, that is—are content to lie in the arms of one woman. Owen will seek out three or four and swear undying love to each. Do you see why I worry? What state will he be in, in the morning?"

Owen Elias was determined to enjoy his last night in London. In the company of James Ingram and Frank Quilter, two other actors who would be going to Denmark, he spent a couple of riotous hours in the Black Horse, drinking his fill. Aware of the passage of time, he then peeled off from his friends and strutted off toward the first house he intended to visit that night. A buxom young woman was awaiting him, her appetite whetted by the fact that she might not see him again for some time. Elias planned to spend an hour or so with her before rolling on to his second port of call. He was so elated at the thought of what lay ahead that he did not hear the footsteps behind him or sense any danger.

The attack came when he turned down an alleyway. Seizing their moment, the two men who had been trailing him ran forward and started to belabor him with cudgels. Taken unawares, Elias was beaten hard around the head and shoulders. He put up his arms to protect himself and spun round to face his attackers. Two brawny men were flailing away with their cudgels, trying to knock him senseless. One blow opened a gash above his eye, another sent blood cascading down from his nose.

Elias surged with anger. He was a powerful man and he fought back with fury. Ducking and weaving, he managed to catch one of the cudgels in his hand and wrested it from the grasp of the man who had been holding it. With a weapon of his own, he was not such an easy target. The second man continued to strike at him but Elias was able to parry the blows with his own cudgel, punching at his attacker with the other fist. Swerving out of the way of another murderous blow, he kicked the man in the groin and made him double up in pain. Elias increased his victim's agony by rapping him hard on the skull with his cudgel and making blood spurt out.

The first man was not finished. Deprived of his cudgel, he drew a sword and tried to run the Welshman through. Elias reacted swiftly. He parried the blade, grabbed the man's jerkin, and lifted him a foot into the air before hurling him to the ground. Elias stamped on his hand to make him let go of the sword, then landed a series of stinging blows with the cudgel. His attackers had had enough. Dragging himself to his feet, the man limped away as fast as he could. His companion was close behind him, still clutching his groin and moaning with pain. Bruised, dazed, panting for breath, and covered in blood, Owen Elias forgot all about the women on whom he had promised to call.

He tossed the cudgel aside and staggered off into the night.

The *Cormorant* was a small galleon, used, for the most part, as a cargo vessel but ready to take a certain number of passengers as well. Built in the Netherlands, it had recently been bought and renamed by an English merchant. It was a three-masted ship, square-rigged on the fore and main, and with a lateen sail on the mizzenmast. It had good carrying capacity and its shallow draft allowed it to sail along inshore waters with comparative safety.

Nicholas Bracewell was pleased with what he saw. Having sailed on many vessels during his youthful apprenticeship to his father, he could assess the finer points of a ship at a glance. Anne Hendrik stood beside him on the quay and appraised the *Cormorant*.

"Why are there so many cannon?" she asked.

"Piracy is still a hazard in the North Sea," he replied. "That's why she is so well armed. There are gunports along the main deck and the quarterdeck. At a guess, I say that she had at least thirty cannon aboard."

"Well, I hope they are not needed."

"They will frighten off smaller vessels, Anne. A show of strength is sometimes all the defense that you need." He indicated the gangway. "You may as well go aboard."

"What about you?"

"I'll wait here to check off all the names."

There was a flurry of activity at the quayside. The last of the cargo was being loaded and the passengers were starting to embark. When he saw Edmund Hoode, the book holder beckoned him over.

"Good morrow, Edmund."

"Good morrow to you both," returned the other.

"Have you brought *The Princess of Denmark* with you?"

Hoode patted the leather satchel slung from his shoulder. "She is right here, Nick." He smiled at Anne. "But I see that you have your own princess."

"Thank you, Edmund," she said, beaming at the compliment.

"Be so good as to take Anne aboard," said Nicholas. "I must stay here until the last." He consulted the list that he held. "We are still missing four people."

"What about Lord Westfield?" asked Hoode.

"He and his servants are already aboard. Take the trouble to introduce yourself to Rolfe Harling, who travels with our patron. It was Master Harling who found this young bride and who therefore made possible our voyage to Denmark."

"Then he deserves all our thanks." Hoode turned to Anne. "Are you ready to come aboard?"

"Yes." She tossed a worried glance at the cannon. "I think so."

Hoode led her to the gangplank and let her walk up it first. Nicholas, meanwhile, was able to cross another name off his list as Barnaby Gill came into view, marching along the quay in a peach-colored suit and an elaborate wide-brimmed hat. In his wake was a porter, groaning under the weight of the luggage he carried. Of all the actors, Gill was easily the most vain and he was taking by far the largest wardrobe with him. Since nobody had come to see him off, he went aboard immediately.

Some members of the company preferred to stay on land until the very last moment to be with the families and friends who had come to see them off. Oswald Megson was entwined with his young wife. Frank Quilter was caressing the cheek of his new mistress. Unable to go to Denmark himself, Thomas Skillen, the wrinkled old stage-keeper, was giving copious advice to George Dart. Lawrence Firethorn was part of a tearful huddle that comprised his wife, children, and the boy apprentices.

What touched Nicholas was the number of hired men who had come to wave the company off even though—like Skillen—they would not be part of the adventure. Hugh Wegges, the tireman, and Nathan Curtis, the stage carpenter, were both there along with several actors whose main source of income was Westfield's Men.

They put on brave faces as they wished their fellows well. Two more of the travelers arrived with their bags and Nicholas was able to cross off the names of Harold Stoddard and James Ingram. As the latter strolled along the quay, Nicholas went to greet him.

"Well met, James," he said.

"I'm sorry if I am late, Nick," Ingram apologized, a hand to his brow. "I drank far too much last night and I am paying for it now."

"Where is Owen?"

"I thought that he would be here by now."

"He's the one person who is missing."

"Owen will be here anon," said Ingram confidently. "He talked of nothing else when we were in the Black Horse with him last night."

"Your lodging is close to his," said Nicholas. "I expected that the two of you would come together."

"No, Nick. He told me that he had calls to make first thing this morning. Owen Elias spreads his love far and wide. He did not want three or four ladies turning up here together, each thinking that she alone would get a farewell kiss." Ingram smirked. "Owen is probably visiting them in turn."

"Then he needs to visit the *Cormorant* as well—and be quick about it." Nicholas looked back at the ship. "The cargo is loaded and everyone else is starting to go aboard. You go and join them, James."

"I will."

"And pray that Owen gets here in time. We'll not wait."

Ingram hurried on down the quay to be greeted by the other actors. They moved excitedly across to the gangway. Nicholas saw that Lawrence Firethorn was simultaneously holding his children in his arms and kissing his wife. It was an affecting scene. Other farewells were being taken yet there was still no sign of Owen Elias. The book holder was alarmed. It was far too late to go to the Welshman's lodging, and he might, in any case, not even be there. It was worrying.

Nicholas remembered the fear that Firethorn had expressed the day before, that an excess of pleasure might hinder Elias. If that was the case, Westfield's Men would be deprived of one of their finest actors as well as of someone whose sunny disposition helped to keep spirits high in the company. He would be a grave loss and Firethorn would never forgive him for letting them down. Nicholas was hurt. Elias was a particular friend of his. He felt betrayed by his absence.

The last of the passengers were clambering aboard and the crew would soon be preparing to cast off. Nicholas could delay no longer. He walked sadly down the quay toward the *Cormorant*.

"Nick!" cried a familiar voice. "Wait!"

The book holder turned to see Owen Elias, moving gingerly toward him with a large bag slung from his shoulder. Nicholas was shocked. Not only was the Welshman walking with difficulty, he was patently injured. There was thick bandaging beneath his hat, around one knee, and on both hands. His face was covered in bruises and one eye was virtually closed. Nicholas ran toward him.

"What happened to you?"

"Bullies set upon me in an alleyway," replied Elias, his swollen lips making speech painful. "But I fought them off in the end."

"Give me the bag," said Nicholas, taking it from him, then helping his friend along with the other hand. "We thought we would have to leave without you."

"No hope of that. I'd have crawled all the way here, if need be."

"You obviously took some punishment."

"The two of them had cudgels."

"Were they after your purse?"

"No," said Elias. "They wanted something else—revenge."

"For what?"

"The way I helped to catch that villain at the Dutch churchyard. He has desperate friends. You are lucky that they did not come after you as well."

Nicholas was puzzled. "Are you sure that this has something to do with those libels against strangers?"

"Of course, Nick. I'm a foreigner myself, remember—I'm Welsh."

"Why should they pick on you and not on me?"

"I had no chance to ask them that," said Elias, wincing as he struggled along. "I was too busy fighting for my life."

"I am still not convinced."

"I am—those cudgels were very persuasive."

"They might have simply been trying to rob you."

"No," said Elias firmly. "They were hired ruffians, ordered to break my bones. I've had the whole of the night to think about it, Nick, for I could get no sleep in this condition. The assault *must* be linked to what we did at the Dutch churchyard that night." He hunched his shoulders. "Who else could possibly want to have me beaten like that?"

Dressed in black, the man was tall, thin, angular, and beetle-browed. His features were unprepossessing enough in repose. When he was roused, as now, his face turned into a mask of ugliness, eyes staring, teeth bared, and veins standing out on the forehead.

"You let him get away!" he yelled, glaring at them. "There were two of you against one of him—and he *escaped*?"

"Only after we gave him a sound beating," said the man with the black eye. "We thrashed him hard."

"I ought to do the same to the pair of you."

"We're here for our money, sir," said the second man, nursing a badly bruised arm. "You told us to come to the tavern this morning."

"Only if you'd done what you were told to do."

"We deserve something, sir."

"He helped to kill my son," snarled Isaac Dunmow, clenching a fist. "A beating is not enough. I wanted him dead."

"We did our best," said the first man, "but he fought like a demon. You can see what he did to us." He smiled ingratiatingly. "Give us another chance, sir. We'll track him down, I swear it, wherever he's gone to. We'll murder him next time."

"Yes," added his companion. "I'll shoot him, sir. Then we'll cut off his head and bring it to you."

Isaac Dunmow studied them through narrowed lids. Since he was a rich man, money was no problem to him. He could afford to pay handsomely for vengeance. He remembered the moment when his son had arrived back in York in a wooden box. He had forced open the lid and seen something that he would never forget. Will Dunmow had been turned into a black, shrunken monster. Someone had to atone for that. Extracting some coins from his purse, he tossed them onto the table in front of him and the men snatched them up.

"No," he said vindictively. "I don't want you shoot Owen Elias. That would be too kind a death. I want him burned alive."

[CHAPTER SIX]

The *Cormorant* made good speed. With a strong wind filling her sails, she glided down the busy Thames estuary and out into the sea beyond, creaking all over as she dipped and rose over the waves. Since it was a dry day, with the sun occasionally peeping out from behind the clouds, most of the company stayed on deck to watch the coastline of England receding slowly behind them. Nicholas Bracewell stood at the bulwark with Anne Hendrik, hoping that the rest of the voyage would be as smooth as its beginning but knowing that many hazards could well lie ahead. George Dart joined them on the crowded deck.

"Are you reminded of your days as a sailor, Nicholas?" he said.

"Yes, George," replied the other.

"This ship must be much smaller than the *Golden Hind*."

"Oh, no. The *Cormorant* is bigger in every way."

Dart was disappointed. "But the *Golden Hind* is famous."

"Not for its size," said Anne. "I've seen her."

"I lived in her for almost three years," recalled Nicholas, "so I know her dimensions by heart. She was seventy feet in length whereas the *Cormorant* must be at least twenty feet longer. The *Golden Hind*'s beam was nineteen feet, narrower than the one we have here. While we carried eighteen cannon, they have almost double that number on board today. Our reputation made the ship seem much larger than she really was, George."

"If you were to sail around the world again," asked Dart, "which of the two vessels would you choose?"

"Neither of them," said Nicholas with a smile, "because I never wish to undergo such trials and tribulations again. When we left London, we had five ships. Only one returned to Plymouth—that tells its own story. I lost a lot of good friends on the voyage," he went on wistfully. "The sea can be a cruel tyrant."

"I hope you lose none of us on this ship."

"So do I, George."

"Nothing could be worse than drowning."

Dart looked anxiously down at the sea, smacking the bows of the ship as it plunged into another wave. Spray was thrown up into his face and there was a salty taste on his lips. He was soon diverted. When he saw Owen Elias come up on deck, he moved across to the Welshman to stare at his injuries with ghoulish interest. Anne noticed the battered face for the first time.

"Whatever happened to Owen?" she asked.

"He was set on by two ruffians last night."

"Why?"

"Drink had probably been taken," said Nicholas, not wishing to divulge what he had been told. "It's all that some need men in order to pick a fight."

"There must have been more to it than that, Nick."

"I think not. Owen is a strong man—he beat them away. His injuries will heal in time. They will have to, because he could not act on a stage like that. The sea air will be good for him."

She eyed him shrewdly. "You are hiding something."

"Why should I do that?"

"You must tell me."

"There's nothing to tell, Anne."

"I know you too well," she said, looking him straight in the eye. "When you conceal things, it's usually because you want to protect me. What is it that you are keeping from me this time?"

Nicholas shrugged. "It is only a silly idea of Owen's."

"Tell me about it." He hesitated. "I'll not be balked, Nick. I have a feeling that this might concern me."

"It does," he conceded, electing to tell her the truth. "Owen believes that he was attacked because of the way he helped to catch that man at the Dutch churchyard."

She blanched. "Then I *am* involved here."

"No, Anne."

"Had I not told you about that incident there, you and Owen would not have mounted a vigil at the churchyard. In other words," she said guiltily, "I must take some of the blame for his injuries."

"That's foolish talk."

"Preben told you not to bother on his account."

"I thought only of you, Anne," he said, taking her hand. "The stone that hit Preben could just as easily have been hurled at you. Imagine that. You might have been disfigured or even blinded."

She tensed slightly. "That did occur to me at the time."

"I wanted to catch the man responsible and put an end to the foul messages he was leaving at the churchyard. Owen agreed to help me. But what happened to him last night," he added rapidly, "has no connection to the arrest we made. If someone really sought revenge, *I* would have been the person they attacked, not Owen. He did not even touch the fellow. It was I who fought with him."

"Then you are in danger as well."

"There *is* no danger, Anne. Put the whole thing out of your mind. Owen was set on by some thieves, that is all."

"Is it?"

"Yes. That's the end of the story."

Anne was not so certain but she did not press the matter. She glanced across at Elias again, who was making light of his injuries in front of the others but evidently in pain. When she turned back to Nicholas, he was gazing contemplatively out across the sea. Rolling waves seemed to stretch to infinity.

"I wonder if they have an *English* churchyard there," he said.

"Where?"

"In Elsinore."

"Why do you ask?"

"When we get to Denmark," he pointed out, "we will know how it feels to be the outsiders—*we* will be the strangers."

* * *

Lord Westfield occupied a small cabin belowdecks in the stern of the ship. It was tidy, compact, and equipped with solid oak furniture. Ensconced in a chair, he sipped a cup of wine and discussed plans with Lawrence Firethorn and Rolfe Harling.

"Life is full of surprises," he observed genially. "A month ago, I would never have dreamed that I would one day be sailing to Denmark to meet my young bride."

"We, too, have been swept away by the tide of events, my lord," said the actor. "But for that fire, we would still be entertaining our audiences at the Queen's Head."

"Instead of which, you will play before royalty."

"We intend to conquer the whole of Denmark."

"Your journey may not end there, Master Firethorn," said Harling knowledgeably. "When an English company visited the court ten years or more ago, they were sent on to Dresden to earn even more plaudits. King Frederick II also recommended them to the elector of Saxony and word of their excellence spread."

"That's encouraging to hear, Master Harling."

"Expecting to stay weeks, they remained abroad for months."

"Oh, I do not think that my wife would approve of that," said Firethorn with a chuckle. "If I stay away too long, Margery is likely to swim the North Sea in order to drag me back home."

"I will stay in Denmark for as long as Sigbrit wishes," said Lord Westfield, taking the miniature from his pocket to pass to him. "Here, Lawrence. This is the reason we are all sailing on the *Cormorant*. Is she not divine?"

"Words could not describe her, my lord," said the actor, almost drooling over the portrait. "She is the perfection of womanhood."

"You are looking at the next Lady Westfield."

"However did you find her, Master Harling?"

"It took time," said Harling, "for there are so many things to be weighed in the balance. Beauty is only one attribute required. In Sigbrit Olsen, I found someone who answered every demand."

Firethorn studied him. Try as he might, he could not warm to the man. Harling was too cold and reserved. There was no doubting his intellectual brilliance but such a quality rated little with Firethorn. He preferred wit and conviviality in his friends.

After another glance at the miniature, he gave it back to its owner.

"You did well, Master Harling," he said appreciatively. "Was this lady your sole reason for going to Europe?"

"By no means. Government business took me there in the first instance but it allowed me a deal of leisure. I was therefore able to make inquiry on behalf of Lord Westfield and my search eventually led me to Denmark."

"The most important thing is that she *wants* me," said Lord Westfield. "Age does not matter to her. Quality is all. She accepted me as soon as she realized who I was."

"It involved a lot of negotiation, my lord."

"I leave all that to you, Rolfe."

"Fortunately, her uncle was very amenable."

"What about her parents?" asked Firethorn.

"Both dead, alas," said Harling. "She lives with her uncle Bror. His full name is Bror Langberg and you will see a lot of him. He's a man of great influence."

"Does he know that an entire theater company is on its way?"

"You were mentioned in all my letters."

"How are we likely to be received?"

"With open arms," said Lord Westfield. "According to Rolfe— and he has been to Denmark—they will not stint us. The king is very wealthy, is he not?"

"Yes, my lord," replied Harling, "and he has Kronborg Slot to thank for that. It's the name of the castle in Elsinore," he explained to Firethorn. "That's the source of his fortune for it controls the way in and out of the Baltic Sea. Every ship has to sail through a sound less than a mile wide. For centuries now, Denmark has imposed sound dues on the vessels. They are not only paid in money. Sometimes, part of a cargo is taken as well."

"What if a ship refuses to pay the dues?" said Firethorn.

"Nobody would dare to do that."

"Why not?"

"Because they would be blown out of the water by the cannon mounted on the ramparts. It all began well over a hundred and fifty years ago when Erik of Pomerania was on the throne. Not that that was his real name," he said pedantically, "but that's beside the point."

"Rolfe is steeped in Danish history," noted Lord Westfield.

"King Erik declared that every ship wishing to sail past Elsinore should dip its flag, strike its topsails, and cast anchor so that its captain might go ashore to pay a toll to the customs officers in the town. Well over a thousand vessels a year were involved," continued Harling, "so the amount of money collected was enormous."

"What did the ships get in return?" wondered Firethorn.

"Free passage to or from the Baltic Sea and protection from the pirates who used to haunt it."

"Pirates?"

"They are still there but in far smaller numbers. The Danish navy has hunted them for generations. In the days of King Erik, any pirates captured were first broken on the wheel and then executed. Their heads were stuck up on poles as a warning."

"The same fate should meet those who pirate our plays," said Firethorn vengefully. "We've had more than one stolen from us. There was a comedy printed last year that bore a close resemblance to one that Edmund Hoode had written for us long ago."

"What was the name of the author?"

"None was given. He skulked behind anonymity. But I'll swear that he filched Edmund's work and sold it as his own. That man's head should be stuck on a pole outside the Queen's Head." Firethorn laughed harshly. "I'd suggest that the landlord's head stood beside it but that would only frighten our audiences away."

"Nothing will frighten them away in Denmark," said Harling.

"As long as we can keep the company together."

"You will have no difficulty doing that," said Lord Westfield.

"We might, my lord. Were we not told that each vessel that sails into Elsinore harbor had to yield up a portion of its cargo?"

"True," confirmed Harling. "Customs officers have the right to come aboard to see what a ship is carrying. At first, the toll was levied on the vessel itself, then, about thirty years ago, a man called Peder Oxe, treasurer to King Frederick II, pointed out that they could increase their revenue substantially if the weight of the cargo was the deciding factor. Within twelve months, they had trebled their income from sound dues. Most ships carry large and valuable cargoes. The Danes are entitled to a fixed proportion of it."

"That's what disturbs me," joked Firethorn. "*We* are part of the cargo. I do not want any of my actors confiscated by way of a toll."

"They are quite safe, sir—unlike your patron."

Lord Westfield blinked in astonishment. "Me?"

"Yes," said Harling, his thin smile warning them that he was about to make a rare jest. "When Erik of Pomerania first imposed harbor dues, the toll was paid in gold. It was one English noble." He gave a brittle laugh. "The only English noble aboard is Lord Westfield."

Their good fortune soon deserted them. After a couple of hours of relative calm, the *Cormorant* ran into choppier water. The wind gusted, the skies darkened, and the ship began to heave much more. Most of actors began to feel queasy and only a gallant few had the courage to stay on deck. The others went below and huddled together, their gaze fixed immovably on a wooden bucket in case they should have need of it. Informed that a woman was traveling with the company, Lord Westfield kindly invited Anne Hendrik to share his cabin for a while, and with a storm brewing, Nicholas Bracewell insisted that she take advantage of the offer. The book holder was interested to hear her opinion of Rolfe Harling.

Nicholas remained steadfastly on deck and so, improbably, did Owen Elias. Clutching the bulwark to steady himself, the Welshman was talking to James Ingram. Nicholas adjusted his feet to the roll of the ship and went over to them.

"I would have thought you'd be sleeping below by now, Owen," he said. "You need rest."

"I cannot settle, if I lie down," complained Elias. "Strange as it may seem, I find it easier to stand up."

"You'll not find it easier for much longer."

"Why not?"

"There's a squall coming. Stay on deck and you'll be soaked."

"Yes," said Ingram, looking up at the sky. "Those clouds are ominous. When the rain comes, I'll join the others."

"How do you feel now?" asked Nicholas, taking an inventory of Elias's injuries. "Are you still in pain?"

"Every part about me throbs or aches, Nick, but it's my pride that hurts the most. I was so careless."

"Careless?" repeated Ingram.

"I should have heard those two villains coming up behind me."

"Your mind was elsewhere."

"It was, James, and that's another thing that rankles. I'd made assignations. Three lovely women were expecting me to call. When I think of what I missed last night, I shudder at my loss. If only I had not gone to the Dutch churchyard with you, Nick."

"That was a separate venture," said Nicholas.

"No," said Elias. "I was punished for my part in the capture."

"Then why was I left unharmed? For it was I who laid rough hands on the man we caught. If his friends wanted recompense, they would have come after me."

"I side with Nick," said Ingram. "His argument is sound."

"Then who gave me these injuries?" demanded Elias, indicating his face. "Tell me that, James. Who attacked me?"

"Enemies."

"I have no enemies."

"I can think of some."

"Who?"

"A certain husband, for a start," said Ingram. "When you left us at the Black Horse last night, you told us that you first intended to visit a married woman whose husband was away from London."

"He was—he had business in Norwich."

"Perhaps he had qualms about leaving his wife behind."

Elias cackled heartily. "With good cause!"

"What better way to ensure his wife's fidelity than to have her lover cudgeled by ruffians? You were found out, Owen."

"Never—I've had too much practice at the game."

"Well, *someone* took offense at you."

"It was those rogues who penned verses against strangers."

"They would not even know your name," contended Nicholas, "still less where to find you. There is another explanation here, and seeing the pair of you together, I began to spy it. Cast your minds back to the night of the fire at the Queen's Head."

"I try not to think about that," said Ingram.

"This is important, James. You and Owen were left alone with Will Dunmow, were you not?"

"Yes. He took a room at the inn. We put him to bed. After we left him there, I went straight back to my lodging."

"I did not," said Elias with a grin. "Beth's husband was away from the city that night as well."

"The fact is," said Nicholas, "that you were the last people to see him alive. Owen confessed as much to Anthony Rooker."

"Why should I deny it? We did nothing wrong."

"You did in the landlord's eyes."

"Ignore that scurvy knave."

"He believes that you left the candle burning there."

"Owen snuffed it out," said Ingram. "I saw him."

"I'm sure that you did but the landlord does not believe you. It's possible that Will Dunmow's father might not believe you either."

"What does he have to do with this?"

"Everything," said Nicholas. "His only son is sent to London on his behalf and he dies in a fire. Any father would want to know how."

"He would have listened to Master Rooker's report."

"Yes," said Elias. "The father did not even come anywhere near us. Anthony Rooker traveled to York and delivered Will's body. He must have been buried some time ago."

"Grief plays strange tricks on a man's mind."

"What do you mean, Nick?"

"Only this—the father might have been moved to rage. Think how he must have felt when he looked inside the coffin."

"I warned him against doing that through Master Rooker."

"What father would heed such advice?" asked Nicholas. "I know that I would not. It was a terrible sight to behold. It must have filled him with blind anger. Will told you that his father could be violent."

"He had no reason to use violence against Owen," said Ingram. "We *helped* his son. We looked after him."

"You both know that, James—he does not. All that the father has been told is that his son got drunk in the company of actors, and that you were the two people who caroused with him to the very end. My suspicion is that the father will be deeply hurt, bereaved, and desperate for someone to blame."

"Will was the true culprit," said Elias sadly. "There's no other explanation. He must have started the fire with that pipe of his."

"His father may not accept that. He will blame you."

"Even though we took such care of his son?"

"What he knows is that a group of people got his son so completely drunk that Will had to be put to bed. The only details he will have came from Master Rooker—and where did *he* get them from?"

"Me," said Elias.

"So yours is the name he will recognize," said Nicholas. "From everything I've heard about the father, he does not sound as if he would let such a serious matter pass lightly. According to Will, he was strict, unloving, and possessed of a temper." As the sky darkened even more above him, Nicholas reached his conclusion. "I begin to wonder if you were not the victim of that temper, Owen."

Denmark!" exclaimed Isaac Dunmow.

"That's what I've been told. They sailed this very morning."

"And did Owen Elias go with them?"

"I should think so."

"Death and damnation!"

When he called at the inn, Dunmow found the landlord in the yard, staring in consternation at the huge gap where part of his premises had once stood. Alexander Marwood was still exercised by the thought that he was on the brink of ruin. With the loss of his stables, he could no longer keep horses at livery for travelers who came to the city. Since eight rooms had been destroyed, the number of guests who could stay at the Queen's Head had been almost halved. With no plays being performed in the yard, a major part of his custom had vanished. As a result, the steady flow of income had turned into a mere trickle. It made him quiver with apprehension and a nervous twitch attacked three distinct areas of his face so that his eyelid, his cheek, and his lip trembled uncontrollably in unison.

"Which part of Denmark?" asked Dunmow.

"How should I know?" replied Marwood brusquely.

"They played here, man. They ate and they certainly drank at your inn. Since you are so close to Westfield's Men, you must know where and why they went across the sea."

"I was just glad to be rid of them, sir."

"Why is that?"

"Because they burned down my inn."

"Yes," said Dunmow, eyes glinting beneath the beetle brows. "My son was inside it at the time. It's important that I should find out everything I can about the actors who got him drunk that night. Now, tell me why they sailed away this morning."

"Their patron is to be married in Denmark," said Marwood, discomfited by the man's intense glare. "Westfield's Men are to perform plays to celebrate the event. Nicholas Bracewell, their book holder, did tell me the name of the place where the wedding would be held but it has gone quite out of my mind."

"Was it Copenhagen?"

"No, sir."

"Roskilde, the old capital?"

"It was not that either."

"Elsinore, perhaps?"

"Yes," said Marwood, scratching his mottled pate, "that sounds more like it. You impress me, Master Dunmow. I could not even tell you where Denmark is yet you actually know the names of its towns."

"I'm a merchant," said the other, "and I've traded with a number of Baltic towns in the past. As it happens, Elsinore is one of them. In my younger days, I went there. It's an agreeable place."

"Then I hope Westfield's Men stay there forever."

"Do you detest them so much?"

"They've made my life a misery, sir," said the landlord. "They bring the riffraff of London into my yard, the very sweepings of the city. The actors show me no respect and they hound every wench I employ here. They are lewd and ungovernable."

"Tell me about the night of the fire."

"It pains me to recall it."

"Please," said Dunmow. "I must know the truth."

"Then you shall have it. Your son watched *The Italian Tragedy* here and was so moved by the performance that he came into my taproom and opened his purse to the company. They drank deep, as actors always will. There was merriment into the night. When your son began to fade, only two of them remained."

"Owen Elias was one of them."

"The worst offender, Master Dunmow. It was he who kept urging you son to drink and drink. And it was he, I believe, who left a lighted candle in the room. It was knocked over in the night and set the bedsheets on fire."

"And poor Will was unable to escape."

"I doubt if he even woke up."

"Why did you not bring charges against Elias?"

"Because nothing could ever be proved."

Isaac Dunmow had heard enough. The rage that had been simmering inside him flared up again. In his febrile mind, one of the actors was chiefly responsible for the death of his son and would be held to account for it, but the whole company was at fault as well. The merchant wanted to punish Westfield's Men in some way.

"What will happen to them when they return?" he asked.

"They'll not play here again, I know that."

"Where will they go?"

"Nowhere, sir," said Marwood, "for the theaters already have their companies and no other inn would take Westfield's Men. They will be homeless."

"So they will try to get into your good graces again."

"Most assuredly. They will set Nicholas Bracewell onto me, the only honorable man among them."

"And what will he do?"

"He has a most persuasive tongue and has charmed me into letting them stay here before. I'll not make that error again," said the landlord rancorously. "I'd sooner starve than have them here again."

Dunmow raised an inquiring eyebrow. "There's no danger of starvation, surely?"

"There is. Our custom has shrunk almost to nothing. While we flounder, our rivals take over our trade."

"When your inn is rebuilt, that will soon change."

"How can I rebuild it when I lack the funds to do so?"

"Borrow the money."

"But I'll then have to pay it back," said Marwood, his voice filled with pathos. "That's the dilemma I face, sir. With all their faults—and they are far too many to name—Westfield's Men do bring in most of our custom. If I borrow heavily, the only way I can repay the loan is by letting the company return and I'll not do that."

"Supposing that the money came from elsewhere?" said Dunmow thoughtfully. "Suppose, for instance, a benefactor helped you to rebuild the Queen's Head."

"Such people do not exist."

"You might be talking to one such."

The landlord was startled. "*You*, Master Dunmow?"

"Possibly. I'm a rich man."

"But what interest would you have in helping us out?"

"I'd make that clear in the terms of the contract."

"I do not follow."

"It's quite simple," said Dunmow levelly. "I will consider helping you on strict conditions. First, that the bedchamber in which my son died is to be rebuilt and named the Will Dunmow Room."

"I accede to that request at once."

"Secondly—and I'll have this in writing so that there can be no equivocation—that Westfield's Men will never again be allowed to perform in your yard. It was their play that lured my son here and their actors who contrived to get him drunk afterwards. Those crimes must be answered," Dunmow went on, pounding a fist into his other palm. "I want the whole devilish company forced out of London forever."

The squall was not especially severe but it seemed so to those who were not sailors. Crowded together belowdecks, the actors sat in disconsolate groups, clutching their stomachs and wondering whose turn it would be to use the wooden bucket next. As the *Cormorant* bucked and tilted, they began to have second thoughts about the wisdom of the whole enterprise. Barnaby Gill acted as a self-appointed spokesman for the suffering passengers.

"This is naught but a floating coffin," he protested. "Each and every one of us is doomed."

"It's not a violent storm," said Nicholas Bracewell soothingly. "I think we'll come through it without any mishap."

"But we are all sick to our stomachs."

"That's because you have no sea legs as yet."

"I do not *want* any sea legs," said Gill, shifting his position to gain a modicum of relief. "What I want is dry land on which I can walk in perfect safety. I don't wish to be tossed around like this." There was a collective moan of agreement. "We should never have accepted the invitation to go to Denmark in the first place."

"You were all in favor of it at first, Barnaby."

"Yes," agreed Owen Elias, slumped opposite him. "You heard about those pretty Danish boys in Elsinore. And you never miss a chance to disport yourself in front of royalty."

Gill was livid. "I do not disport myself, Owen," he said with withering contempt. "I leave that to underlings like you. I dance, I sing, and I act without compare."

"Then give us one of your jigs to cheer us up."

"I could not stand, let alone dance. The floor would keep moving under my feet." Gill pointed at Nicholas. "I hold you responsible for this," he said accusingly. "You arranged our passages. Why on earth did you put us aboard this disgusting cargo vessel?"

"Because it was the first ship sailing for Denmark," replied Nicholas, "and that's what Lord Westfield requested. Unlike you, he is willing to endure a little discomfort in order to reach our destination."

"But he's doing so in the privacy of a cabin. That's a form of luxury compared to this. Lawrence is in there with him and so is Master Harling." Gill sat up indignantly. "I should be in there as well."

"There was no room, Barnaby."

"Only because your friend took my place."

"Lord Westfield invited Anne to share his cabin."

"Quite rightly," affirmed Elias. "Woman have precedence in situations like this. It will be uncomfortable enough in the cabin. I'd hate it if Anne had to put up with our misery."

The ship suddenly pitched and rolled, hurling them about and making them groan even more. Cargo occupied most of the space belowdecks. They inhabited the small, dank, drafty, fetid area that was left, sitting on wet floorboards and listening to the waves that pounded the side of the ship so mercilessly. Rain lashed the deck above their heads and the wind howled with ever-increasing stridency. Blown to and fro, the ship's bell clanged ceaselessly. The loud yells of the crew added to the cacophony. Diving forward, George Dart made use of the bucket for the third time.

Gill looked away in disgust. "I deserve better than this!"

"Then swim back to England," advised Elias.

"I demand a cabin of my own."

"Then you'll have to find another ship," said Nicholas, "for the *Cormorant* cannot satisfy you. Hold fast, Barnaby—and the rest of you. The squall will soon blow over."

"It sounds as if it's getting worse, Nick," said Elias.

"Oh, no. Trust me. The rain is starting to ease off."

As if to contradict his prediction, the ship veered over sharply to starboard and sent a couple of them tumbling across the deck in a heap. One of the victims, Edmund Hoode, rubbed his bruised elbow.

"Will we ever get out of this alive, Nick?" he asked.

"Yes, Edmund. It's only a question of time."

Nobody believed him. They resented that Nicholas was completely untroubled by the squall or by the cramped conditions in which they sailed. He was patently at ease. Though it was years since he had been on a voyage, he felt at home aboard a ship. The only other person not struck down by seasickness was James Ingram.

"Will this storm have blown us off course, Nick?" he said.

"I fear so, James."

"Are we likely to meet more bad weather?"

"Very likely," said Nicholas. "The North Sea can be like a cauldron at this time of year. It's all a matter of luck."

"Well, *we've* had none!" complained Gill.

"I disagree. We've been let off lightly."

"Are you mad?"

"This is a nightmare," said Hoode.

"But it's almost over," Nicholas told him. "Listen, Edmund."

"To what?"

"Just listen."

They all pricked up their ears and soon realized something. The rain had stopped. The wind was less punitive, too, and the ship no longer rocked quite so wildly. She was still rearing and diving through the waves but with less discomfort for the passengers. The worst was definitely over. Within a quarter of an hour, there had been a marked improvement in the stability of the *Cormorant*. Some of them actually began to relax. Nicholas got to his feet and moved to the stairs.

"I'll see what's happening up there," he said.

"Be careful," warned Elias.

"Yes," said Hoode. "We don't want to lose you, Nick."

Lifting the hatch, Nicholas let in a blast of cold air. He went swiftly up on deck and lowered the hatch again. The first thing he noticed was how much lighter the sky was. Dark clouds had given way to patches of blue. Since the deck was so slippery, he moved slowly to the bulwark, taking a firm grip on the timber rim. Two men were at the wheel and Nicholas could see that they were no longer struggling to steer the vessel. Working his way toward the quarterdeck, he went up the steps and approached the captain, a solid man in his forties, wearing a cape and hat that were glistening from the downpour.

"Stay below, sir," he cautioned. "It's safer there."

"I'm a seasoned mariner," said Nicholas cheerily. "I've been through many squalls. If you ever have need of me, Captain, look upon me as another member of the crew."

"I'll remember that, my friend."

"We came through it well."

"The *Cormorant* is a fine vessel. She'll survive almost anything. The Dutch have good shipwrights."

The captain broke off to bark some orders to the crew and Nicholas went to the stern of the ship. Somewhere below him, Anne was sharing a cabin with Lord Westfield and the others. He hoped that she had not been too jangled by the storm. There was no sign of land in any direction but his sharp eyes did descry a sail in the middle distance. Another vessel had ridden out the storm and was slowly gaining on them. Nicholas watched it for a long time until he was certain. They were being followed.

He drew the captain's attention to the other ship. Putting his telescope to his eye, the captain studied the vessel for several minutes before coming to a grim conclusion.

"Pirates," he said.

[CHAPTER SEVEN]

After failing at the first attempt, the two men were eager to make amends by satisfying the demands of their paymaster. A personal interest was involved. They still bore the marks of the beatings they had received at the hands of Owen Elias and they wanted immediate revenge. Offered a handsome reward for their murderous work, they were determined not to falter again. When they were given their orders, however, they blenched.

"They've sailed to *Denmark?*" cried Josias Greet, the elder of the men. "However can we reach him there?"

"By going after him," said Isaac Dunmow.

"Across the sea?"

"I know of no other means of travel."

"Why not wait until they return to England, sir?"

"Because that might be several weeks away and I'll not tarry that long. My anger needs to be appeased now." Dunmow looked from one to the other. "I can see that you are not the men for me," he said curtly. "I'll find someone with more mettle. Good day to you."

"Wait," said Greet quickly. "Let us think about this."

"Then do so quickly."

They were in the taproom of the inn where Dunmow was staying. While the merchant sipped a cup of wine, the two men had tankards of ale on the table in front of them. They exchanged a glance. Greet was clearly perturbed but Ben Ryden, his confederate, was not so easily put off an assignment that could bring in a large amount of money. Shorter and stockier than his companion, Ryden had a flat face spreading out from a snub nose, with thick, black hair and beard. Because he had been a sailor in his younger days, the sea held no fears for him. He had other worries.

"Denmark is a country of islands," he said. "I've been there. How would we know where to find Westfield's Men?"

"They'll go first to Elsinore," explained Dunmow, "and are like to stay a week or more as guests at the castle. The company is there to celebrate the wedding of their patron." He drained his cup in one gulp. "I want them to attend the funeral of Owen Elias as well."

"How will we be paid?" asked Greet.

"You'll have some of the money now but most of it when the deed is done. That will encourage you to dispatch him quickly. It will also prevent you," Dunmow added pointedly, "from simply taking your payment and vanishing before you have earned it. I'll not allow that."

"What about the cost of travel, sir?"

"I'll arrange passports for both of you," said Dunmow, "and put money in your purses to pay any charges you may incur along the way. You have a score to settle with this man. Remember that."

"We do," murmured Greet, rubbing his sore chin.

"We'll burn him to a cinder," said Ryden with a smirk. "My only worry is that we may never catch up with him. By the time we reach Elsinore, he and the others may have left."

Dunmow shook his head. "I doubt that. They sailed on the *Cormorant* and she is due to call in at Flushing and Amsterdam on the way. That will delay them. In a few days, the *Speedwell* sets out for Elsinore, her first port of call. You'll be on board. It may well be that you overtake them and reach the town first."

"If they stay at the castle, they'll be out of reach."

"You bide your time." Dunmow's face darkened. "I loathe plays myself," he said with scorn, "and I've even more cause now to loathe the actors who put them on. But the theater is ever popular with many people. Westfield's Men are certain to be invited to perform in the town. Make sure that you are there when they do so. All that you have to do is to wait, watch, and choose your moment."

"We'll know where to find them afterwards," said Ryden.

"And where's that, Ben?" asked Greet.

"The nearest inn. The breweries of Denmark are famous for the strength of their beer. I've tasted it, Josias."

"Then I'll test its power as well."

"Make sure you do not drink any of it before you strike," warned Dunmow. "Keep your heads clear. Bring me back certain word of his death. Only then can my son be truly laid to rest."

"Owen Elias is a good actor," said Ryden grudgingly. "We've seen the Welshman onstage at the Queen's Head more than once. When they lose him, Westfield's Men will suffer badly."

"That's only the start of their suffering."

"How so, Master Dunmow?"

"There's more to come. Whatever it takes, I mean to bring the whole company down for what they did to my son." Dunmow gritted his teeth. "They do not know what misery lies in store for them."

The main deck of the *Cormorant* was a scene of frantic activity. The crew had clapped on full sail and the vessel was surging on through the North Sea with an urgency she had never possessed before. Her canvas flapped noisily and the eerie creaking of her timbers was louder than ever. Being at the mercy of a storm was a regular occurrence and the sailors had learned to cope with the situation. Finding themselves pursued by pirates, however, induced a real fear. If captured, they would not merely sacrifice their ship and her cargo. Their lives would be at risk as well.

Nicholas Bracewell remained on the quarterdeck and watched the chasing vessel getting inexorably closer. Up in the crow's nest, the lookout was trying to pick out as much detail from the other ship as he could. When he had counted her guns, he called the number down.

"Twenty or more, Captain!"

Even though the pirates had fewer cannon aboard, Nicholas was disturbed. Evidently, their vessel was smaller than the *Cormorant* but she was also faster and easier to maneuver. Since they made their living by preying on other ships, the pirates would be expert gunners.

Nicholas did not think that his own crew would be so experienced and well trained. If the *Cormorant* was boarded, the pirates were bound to have the advantage in hand-to-hand fighting.

The captain stood beside him and used his telescope again.

"I think she's Spanish," he decided.

Nicholas was positive. "She is, Captain."

"How do you know?"

"Because she's like other Spanish galleons, built high so that she can grapple with more effect. I've seen dozens like her and had the pleasure of helping to sink one or two of them."

"When was that?"

"When I sailed on the *Golden Hind*," said Nicholas, seeing a look of admiration in the captain's eyes. "If it comes to a fight, I know how to fire a cannon, so I'm at your disposal. I've counted only thirty-four in your crew. That's well short of the number you'd need to sail the *Cormorant* and man all the guns."

"We are glad to have you aboard, sir."

The book holder flashed a smile. "I'm not sure that I'm glad to be here at this very moment."

"Your name, sir?"

"Nicholas Bracewell."

"I am Captain Skrine," said the other. "I sailed on the *Victory* with Sir John Hawkins so I am well accustomed to action. My hope is that we can outrun them but our heavy cargo is slowing us down. If she attacks us, we'll need every man we can get. Is there anyone else who might help?"

"None who've been sailors, Captain, but I can think of three at least who could man a cannon if they were taught how. And most of them can handle a weapon if we are boarded."

"Instruct your three friends now, Master Bracewell," said the captain, "but do not tell the others of our danger. We may yet escape. There's no point in spreading alarm too early."

"Time is against you."

"In what way?"

"If she maintains her speed," said Nicholas, "she'll overhaul us before long. Then everyone aboard will know that we have a fight on our hands. I think it best to warn them now."

"You heard my orders," asserted Skrine.

"I'll obey them to the letter."

"You're on the *Cormorant* now—she's mine to command."

Nicholas took no offense at the crackle of authority in Captain Skrine's voice. He was confident and decisive. Those qualities would be needed in the engagement that lay ahead. Excusing himself, Nicholas went below to seek out some of the actors.

When the storm abated, Lawrence Firethorn thanked their patron for his hospitality and left the cabin to join the others. Anne Hendrik felt that it was her turn to go as well.

"I'm very grateful to you, my lord," she said, about to rise, "but I think that you're entitled to have the cabin to yourself now."

"Stay as long as you wish, dear lady," Lord Westfield told her, gesturing for her to remain. "You are delightful company and it's far more comfortable in here than anywhere else."

"I'll not deny that."

"Though not without its hazards," noted Rolfe Harling wryly.

During the inclement weather, he had fared badly. The others had been queasy but Harling came off worst of all and he had been obliged to rush out of the cabin at one point. Firethorn was amused by his sudden departure. It somehow relieved the discomfort he was feeling himself. When he returned to the cabin, Harling had been deeply embarrassed. He was still uneasy.

"I've sailed across the North Sea a number of times," he said, "but I can never get used to its vagaries. I'm a land creature."

"So am I," confessed Anne.

"That makes three of us," said Lord Westfield.

"Crossing the Thames by boat is the only voyage that I enjoy."

"I hope that you stop your ears against the blasphemy of the watermen. It's not fit for a lady to hear. I sometimes think that sailors and boatmen were put on this earth to mangle the English language. Unlike Rolfe here," he continued, indicating Harling with a gloved hand, "who can talk politely in several foreign tongues."

"I've devoted my life to their study," said Harling.

"Do you speak Dutch?" asked Anne.

"Very well."

"It took me some time to master it."

"I once spent three months in the Low Countries. By the end of that time, I was fluent."

"You'll have to teach me a few words in Danish," said Lord Westfield. "I would like to show consideration to my bride."

"You do that by marrying her, my lord," observed Anne.

He beamed. "Yes, I suppose that I do. But I would still like to greet her in her own language and to have a telling phrase or two at my command. Will you be my tutor, Rolfe?"

Harling nodded, clearly still troubled by seasickness. "I begin to wish that I had found your new wife in England, my lord," he said. "Then I'd have been spared this voyage."

"I endure it willingly as proof of my love to Sigbrit."

"Is the lady ready to leave Denmark?" said Anne.

"She will go anywhere with her husband."

"I felt the same when I was married."

"Yet you stayed in England."

"Jacob—my husband—set up his business there."

"From the way you talked about him earlier, it sounds to have been a happy marriage."

"Very happy, my lord."

"That reassures me," said Lord Westfield. "I know that our kings have married foreign brides—Henry VIII did so more than once—but only for political reasons. I am prompted by the heart."

"And so is your bride," said Harling.

"My princess of Denmark."

"You'll not be disappointed, my lord. In every way, Sigbrit Olsen will be a good wife." Harling noticed the sudden concern in Anne's eyes. "Is something amiss?"

"I hope not," she said.

The two men were sitting with their backs to the window. Occupying a chair opposite, Anne could look over their shoulders and see the water being churned into a bubbling whiteness in the wake of the vessel. She could also see the ship that was following them. Lord Westfield and Harling glanced over their shoulders.

Anne was fretful. "Are we being chased?"

"That's no English ship," said Harling. "I dare swear that."

"She's probably another merchant vessel," said Lord Westfield airily, "trying to overtake us. There's no call for anxiety."

"I'm not so sure, my lord."

Anne shared Harling's apprehension. She sensed trouble.

Nicholas Bracewell worked quickly. Having taken the three men up on deck, he told them about the likelihood of an attack, then instructed them in how to load and fire a cannon. Lawrence Firethorn, James Ingram, and Frank Quilter had been selected because they were the most able-bodied members of the company. Owen Elias would also have been a natural choice but he was handicapped by his injuries. Shocked at the news that they were being pursued, the actors were keen to do anything within their power to repel an attack.

"What of the others, Nick?" said Ingram.

"They'll all be needed," replied Nicholas, "even the apprentices. If they hit us with a broadside, there are bound to be fires. The lads can help to throw buckets of water over it."

He ran quickly through the names of the company, allotting tasks to them in the event of combat. If they were boarded, every one of them—including their patron—would need to defend himself with a weapon. Nor would Anne Hendrik be content to stay hidden belowdecks while the battle raged above her. Nicholas knew that she would insist on being involved. She was not squeamish. Anne would readily tend the wounded. In a crisis, nobody could be excused.

The other ship was getting closer all the time, its sails billowing, its prow carving an undulating path through the waves. Firethorn waved a fist at it and emitted a roar of defiance.

"Spanish curs!" he yelled. "We defeated your Armada and we'll send you to the bottom of the sea to join them!"

"Brave words," said Nicholas, "but you speak too hastily. There may be no Spaniards at all aboard."

"You told us that it was a Spanish galleon."

"No question of it. However, that proves little. The *Cormorant* is a Dutch ship yet Anne is the only person here with links to the Low Countries. No," Nicholas continued, "piracy attracts men of all nations and they'll commandeer the finest ship they can find. The crew could be French, Portuguese, Dutch—even English."

"English!" shouted Firethorn. "They would kill their own kind?"

"They are not interested in our country of origin. All that they see is a rich prize, there for the taking. It's only a question of time before they try to take it."

"We'll be ready for the rogues!"

"Yes," said Quilter, slapping the cannon. "Let them come on. We three will prove doughty gunners. We'll blow the blackhearted devils to smithereens."

"Keeping them at bay is all that we need to do," said Nicholas. "If the action is too hot for them, they'll withdraw. We just have to pray that they do not get too close."

"Why, Nick?"

"Because they will rely on light guns and superior manpower. Their aim is to grapple and board."

"I'll kill the knaves with my bare hands," said Firethorn.

"They'll have swords and daggers, Lawrence—guns, too, in some cases. I'll make sure that we all have weapons. Without them, Westfield's Men will become extinct."

Captain Skrine had done all he could to shake off the pursuit but his efforts were in vain. Though the *Cormorant* changed course repeatedly and zigzagged through the open sea, she could neither elude nor outrun the pirate vessel. With a series of sharp commands, he deployed his crew at the gunports on both decks and on both sides of the ship. The helmsmen were ordered to bring the *Cormorant* around in a wide arc. The Spanish galleon was now less than two hundred yards behind them. Beckoned by the captain, Nicholas climbed swiftly up to the quarterdeck.

"Alert the others, Master Bracewell," ordered the captain.

"Aye, aye, sir."

"We'll need every man jack of them."

"You shall have them."

Nicholas went off at speed. Lord Westfield was the patron and Lawrence Firethorn the actor-manager of the troupe, but it was the book holder who was in charge now. Given his greater naval experience, nobody would dare to challenge his authority. He went first belowdecks to warn his colleagues that the ship was in danger of attack and that they would all be required to defend it. Nicholas gave them no opportunity to fly into a panic. Pointing to each in turn, he assigned specific tasks to them before sending them up on deck. Necessity was a ready cure for seasickness. Even those most severely afflicted somehow managed to rally. To his credit, Barnaby Gill was the first to mount the steps, shedding his habitual selfishness and making common cause with the others.

Weapons were essential. Taking both George Dart and the limping Owen Elias with him, Nicholas went to the storeroom that was being unlocked by the master-at-arms. They grabbed swords, pikes, and daggers to give to the others. While his friends rushed up on deck, Nicholas knocked on the door of Lord Westfield's cabin before opening it. When they saw the weapons that he was carrying, all three occupants leapt to their feet at once.

"What's happened, Nick?" asked Anne.

"We have pirates on our tail."

"Pirates!" cried Lord Westfield with disgust. "How dare they! I'll not be kept from my bride by *anybody*. Give me a sword, Nicholas," he said, taking one from him. "I'm yours to command."

"Here's a weapon for you as well, Master Harling," said Nicholas, handing him a cutlass. "Do you know how to use it, sir?"

"No," confessed the other, quailing.

"You'll soon learn."

"What about me?" said Anne.

"If they engage us, there'll be serious injuries."

"I'll look to the wounded. I'm not afraid of the sight of blood." She glanced through the window at the other ship. "I had a feeling that they were getting very close."

"Too close," said Nicholas. "Let's see if we scare them away."

He led the way up the stairs to the main deck. Everyone was at his station. After telling the newcomers where to stand, and what to do if the ship was fired upon, Nicholas went off to join Captain Skrine on the quarterdeck. From his elevated position, he had an excellent view of the pirate ship, sitting high in the water. Her gunports were open and her cannon at the ready. When the vessel got within a hundred yards of them, Nicholas turned to the captain.

"They have no long-range guns," he said, "or they'd have fired on us well before now."

"That's what we did in the *Victory,*" said Skrine. "We fired heavy shot low down from three hundred yards. We crippled some ships and took much of the boldness out of others."

"They are after our cargo so they'll try not to damage it too much. They mean to board us. Their intent is to disable us first. With your permission, Captain, we'll make use of Martin Yeo."

"Martin Yeo?"

"One of our boy apprentices," said Nicholas, pointing to the lad on the main deck. "Martin is also a fine musician. I told him to bring his trumpet with him. When we fire, he'll blow hard in triumph. When their cannon sound, he will respond with a mocking fanfare."

"I like the notion," said Skrine, grinning. "Permission granted."

"Thank you, Captain." Nicholas signaled to Martin Yeo, who gave a nervous smile of acknowledgment. "The others all have instructions. I'll make sure that they abide by them."

Carrying a sword, Nicholas went down to the main deck so that he would be in the thick of the action. The *Cormorant* had, meanwhile, come round in a wide arc so that she was heading toward the other ship at an acute angle. At the command of Captain Skrine, a single shot was fired across the bows of the pirate vessel, passing within twenty yards of her bowsprit before plopping harmlessly into the sea. The response was immediate. Instead of being warned off, the ship altered its course sharply so that it could come alongside the *Cormorant*. A broadside was inevitable but Skrine was determined to fire his first. As they drew level with the three-masted pirate galleon, he gave the signal and the guns thundered. Martin Yeo played a shrill fanfare on his trumpet.

His celebration was premature. Before the echoes of the first broadside had died away, and before they could see what damage they had inflicted, a second one boomed out and the *Cormorant* was hit so hard that she rocked in the water. Some cannonballs flew over the heads of the crew but others struck the bulwark, holing it instantly and sending showers of splinters into the air like so many wooden bullets. One man was instantly blinded, another's face was horribly disfigured by a hail of splinters. There were other casualties. Two men were crushed to death beneath the weight of their cannon when it suffered a direct hit and jumped into the air before pinning them to the deck. A third member of the crew had his leg fractured by flying debris.

Anne Hendrik could hear their screams but she had to wait until the smoke had cleared before she was able to find the injured men. Clearing his throat, Yeo did his best to play a derisive fanfare. Still on the main deck, Nicholas was pleased that none of the company had been wounded. He was also impressed with the way that his three friends had fired their cannon and were trying to reload. James Ingram was lifting a heavy iron cannonball while Frank Quilter held the wooden ram to pack the charge home. Lawrence Firethorn had put more gunpowder in the touchhole and stood by to apply a spark to the linstock.

"Wait there, James," said Nicholas, stepping forward to pick up a different cannonball. "Use stone instead of iron. It will shatter on impact and cause more damage. Let me show you."

He supervised the reloading then waved his friends back. The other ship had passed them and they were now looping around her stern. Nicholas saw his opportunity. Without waiting for an order, he picked his moment, then lit the slow match, moving smartly aside so that he would not be caught by the vicious recoil of the gun and its solid wooden carriage. The lint burned down and the gunpowder ignited with an earsplitting bang. The stone shot was lethal. Smashing its way through the windows of a cabin below the quarterdeck, it went straight through a door then sped along the main deck until it hit the mainmast with juddering force.

Stone flew everywhere, killing two men and wounding several others. Razor-edged shards also sliced through the rigging and cut dozens of holes in the canvas sails. One well-aimed shot had caused pandemonium on the pirate ship. Aboard the *Cormorant,* they could hear the screams of pain and confusion. Martin Yeo found much more breath to blow his trumpet. But the action was not over yet. As soon as the ships came alongside each other again, the pirates retaliated with another broadside. It was more destructive this time, holing the *Cormorant* in a number of places just above the waterline and raking the main deck. The broadside also caused a barrel of gunpowder to explode, hurling men in every direction by the force of the blast.

Three of the crew were killed outright and some of the actors were injured. A fire started. Nicholas was everywhere, helping the apprentices to douse the flames with water, calling Anne's attention to wounded men in need of bandaging, then replacing a gunner whose arm had been shot away. On a signal from Captain Skrine, they discharged their own broadside with deafening volume. A mixture of stone and iron shot had been used, the former splitting on impact to spread its terror far and wide, the latter punching large holes in the bulwark and knocking two cannon out of commission.

Though they did not know it, the stone ball fired by the three actors had the most dramatic effect. Striking the mainmast, which had already been badly weakened by the earlier impact, the heavy stone opened up a split that widened within seconds. The mast's own massive weight told against it, pressing down on the fissure until it burst asunder. There was a loud crack, then the mainmast came crashing down like a tall tree in a forest, demolishing everything in its way and bringing the battle to a sudden end. Everyone aboard the *Cormorant* gave a rousing cheer.

Over the distant howls of agony came the loudest fanfare yet.

W hen will they arrive, Uncle?" asked Sigbrit Olsen.

"Not for some time yet."

"But they are on their way?"

"Oh, yes," said Bror Langberg. "They will have set sail by now. When they reach Vlissingen—the English call it Flushing—there will be letters from me awaiting them. I've explained how delighted you are with the match."

Sigbrit was hesitant. "Yes, Uncle."

She was a slender young woman of middle height with the white skin of a true Scandinavian. She had a cambric ruff above her stiffened bodice and a hooped skirt whose hem brushed the ground and concealed her slippers. Worn high on the forehead and away from the sides of her face, her fair hair had a natural sheen. Bror

Langberg, her uncle, was a tall man in his fifties with broad shoulders and a substantial paunch. Wearing a long gown over his doublet and hose, he had a ruff of yellow, starched linen. Langberg had a pleasant, round, open face and a warm smile. He was visiting his niece at an apartment in Kronborg, the castle at Elsinore. The closer the visit of Lord Westfield became, the more reassurance she would need.

"Will he like me?" she wondered.

"He already loves you, Sigbrit."

"But he has not even met me."

"Yes, he has," said Langberg, "albeit through intercessories. He has two portraits of you—one in miniature and the other in life-size, painted with my own words. Rolfe Harling described you in detail and his master was enchanted."

"Will I find Lord Westfield agreeable?"

"Of that, there is no doubt."

"What will he expect of me?" she said anxiously.

"That you are a good wife to him. Love and loyalty are all that he asks for, Sigbrit. Pledge yourself to him." Still worried, she turned away. He took her by the shoulders. "Away with these silly fears," he whispered in her ear. "His only wish is to make you happy. Do you not want to live in England as Lady Westfield?"

"I do not know, Uncle." She faced him once more. "I would like to visit England because there are too many sad memories to vex me here, but I am not sure if I could live there. And I do not believe that I could ever love as I did once before."

"You will in time, Sigbrit."

"I do not believe it."

"You will and you must," he said softly. "It is right that you should mourn your husband but he would not have wanted you to pine forever. Consider Lord Westfield—he has grieved over the death of two wives yet he has enough spirit and hope to seek a third. He wants to pluck joy out of sorrow. You must do the same."

"I know."

Her nod of obedience concealed her misgivings. Sigbrit Olsen loved, respected, and trusted her uncle. She treated him as a father and, as a rule, accepted his advice unquestioningly. In this instance, however, she was assailed by doubts. While the prospect of marrying a member of the English nobility was tempting, it was also daunting. She wished that she could feel more enthusiastic about it.

"Take heart," said Langberg, reading her thoughts. "It is all for the best, I promise you. Do you think that I would have entered upon these negotiations unless they were to the advantage of my niece? You will gain so much, Sigbrit—wealth, position, and fine houses both in London and in the country. You will have real importance."

"Yes, yes, I understand all that."

"Then there is another aspect, of course."

"You have already talked to me about the king."

"He approves of this match. Denmark has enemies so we must be sure to strengthen bonds with our friends. King Christian wishes us to be closer to England and this marriage will be one small way of achieving that end." He lowered his voice. "We do not want to disappoint the king, do we?"

"No, Uncle Bror."

"Look to the future."

"The future?"

"Yes," he explained. "King Christian's sister is herself married to a king, James VI of Scotland—a most happy union. Queen Elizabeth is old and tired. She will not rule England much longer. Just imagine if the person to succeed her was King James. What would that mean?"

"England would have a Danish queen," she said.

"Someone you know and love."

"Anne was good to me."

"Your friendship will blossom again, Sigbrit—but not if you stay here in Elsinore, your mind forever entombed with your late husband. You must break away from Ingmar," he insisted. "Honor his memory but build your life anew with another man."

"Yes, Uncle."

"I ask it for your own sake and for that of your country." After a moment, Sigbrit nodded. Langberg kissed her on the cheek. "That is better," he continued. "Lord Westfield has a wedding gift for you that even King James could not match."

"When he got married in Oslo," she recalled, "he brought four

Negroes with him to dance in the snow at the wedding. I was there and saw them dance so prettily. But the cold was too much for them," she added with a wan smile. "All four died of pneumonia."

"No more talk of death," said her uncle, showing his irritation. "Think only of life, Sigbrit. Lord Westfield does not come with four dancers but with a whole company of actors."

"Yes," she said, brightening at last. "I long to see them."

"They are the finest troupe in England and they will be yours."

Her doubts returned. "Will they?"

Celebrations aboard the *Cormorant* were short-lived. Having crippled the pirate ship and sailed out of range of her cannon, they took stock of their casualties. They were heavy. Five members of the crew had been killed and even more had been wounded. Only one member of Westfield Men had died—Harold Stoddard, crushed to death—but several had suffered injuries. Barnaby Gill had been knocked unconscious by a glancing blow from a falling spar and Edmund Hoode's hands had been badly lacerated by flying splinters when he brought them up to protect his face. None of them had escaped without at least some cuts and grazes. Two of the apprentices had slight burns from the fires on board. To his annoyance, Owen Elias added a facial gash and a head wound to his other injuries.

Nicholas was proud of them all, especially of Anne Hendrik. Working tirelessly throughout, she had torn her clothing into pieces to bandage wounds, saving more than one man from bleeding to death. When she had finished with the more serious cases, she washed and dressed the minor wounds of crew and actors alike with great tenderness. It was she who poured the brandy into Gill's mouth. It made him open his eyes again.

"Well," said Elias with a cackle, "that's a sight I never thought to see in a hundred years—Barnaby in the arms of a woman."

The other actors laughed. Gill started. When he realized that Anne was cradling him, he sat quickly up and pushed her hands away, rubbing his sore head where he had been struck.

Burial of the dead was one of the first tasks. Captain Skrine did not want the gruesome, blood-covered corpses left on board to upset his crew so he officiated at a simple ceremony. Along with the others, Harold Stoddard was sewn into a piece of canvas and consigned to the deep. Damage had been extensive and many repairs were necessary. Nicholas volunteered the services of Oswald Megson, actor and carpenter, and undertook the most onerous duty himself. Lowered over the side of the ship on ropes, he mended the holes that had been opened during the action by cannonballs.

It was slow, laborious, tedious work and the constant movement of the vessel made it highly dangerous. Nicholas was soaked to the skin by the waves but he ignored the discomfort and stuck at it, knowing how crucial the repairs were. When he was finally hauled back on deck again, he was dripping wet.

"Well done," said Captain Skrine. "We owe you our thanks."

Nicholas grinned. "It's the pirates who get *my* thanks. They holed us just above the waterline. Had they hit us lower, we would be in real difficulty. I know what it is to make repairs on the hull below the sea. It's not an experience I'd care to repeat."

"Get below and change into dry clothing, Master Bracewell."

"I will, sir. Do you know where we are?"

"Yes," said Skrine, "I've taken bearings. We were blown right off course by the storm and chased further north by the pirates. I'm minded to change our plans."

"Why?"

"Most of the cargo is destined for Elsinore and we've to take some on board there. If we make for Denmark first, we can call at Amsterdam and Flushing on the voyage home."

"That will please Lord Westfield," said Nicholas, shaking out his wet hair, "for it will get him to his new bride sooner than he expected. But it will not suit everyone."

Nearby, Anne Hendrik was bandaging Lawrence Firethorn's wounded arm. Constant effort had taken its toll. Her hair was disheveled, her face streaked with perspiration, and the remnants of her skirt splashed with the blood of a dozen patients. Nicholas crooked a finger to call her over.

"Do you hear that, Anne?" he said.

"What?"

"The *Cormorant* is to make for Denmark first."

"I see," she said, crossing over to them.

"She'll call at Amsterdam on the return voyage."

"It will add a long time to your journey, I fear," apologized Skrine, "but it suits our purpose. The *Cormorant* is, after all, a merchant ship and the fate of her cargo is paramount. You were the only person bound for the Low Countries."

"Do not worry, Anne," said Nicholas. "When we reach Elsinore, you may well find a ship that will get you to Amsterdam much sooner than this one."

"But I prefer the *Cormorant*," she announced.

"Oh?"

"I feel like part of the crew, Nick. And since you made me ship's surgeon, I would like to keep an eye on my patients. Besides, I'll not complain about a few days spent in Denmark. It will give me a chance to see Westfield's Men perform again."

"Then you are welcome to join us."

"I would also like to meet the lady."

"What lady?" he asked.

"Sigbrit Olsen. Lord Westfield talked about her so much when we were in his cabin during the storm. He's deeply in love with her."

"I know, Anne. That's why he braved this voyage."

"I look forward to seeing this princess of Denmark."

"So do we," he said seriously, "for much hangs on this marriage. We must please his new wife and win her blessing because we must, above all else, keep our patron. Everything depends on Lady Westfield. Should she take against us, we may discover that we have made a long journey to the graveyard."

"In what way?"

"Our patron is truly infatuated. He could refuse his bride nothing. We must pray for her approval. If he were forced to choose between Sigbrit Olsen and his theater company, there is no question of the outcome." Nicholas gave a philosophical shrug. "Westfield's Men would disappear into oblivion."

[CHAPTER EIGHT]

Margery Firethorn was not a woman to grieve over the absence of her husband and to sit brooding alone until his return. Because he was such a commanding presence, she missed him dreadfully and she missed the whole company as well. But she still had children to bring up, a house to run, and a life to lead, and she did all three with the bustling energy that defined her. Margery also had another important function. She had been appointed as an emissary on behalf of Westfield's Men. Knowing that they were in serious danger of losing their innyard playhouse, Lawrence Firethorn had asked his wife to pay an occasional visit to the Queen's Head to use her powers of persuasion on its egregious landlord.

It was a role that Margery had taken on once before and she had learned a valuable lesson in the process. There was one sure way to influence Alexander Marwood and that was to win over the person who really made all the decisions. When she next visited Gracechurch Street market, therefore, Margery went out of her way to call in on Sybil Marwood.

"Good day to you," she said cheerily.

"What is good about it?" asked Sybil, looking around a taproom that was virtually empty. "Our custom is pestilence dead."

"I am sorry to hear that."

"Your husband must take some of the blame."

"Lawrence did not start the fire."

"Someone involved with Westfield's Men did."

Margery remained cool. There was no point in arguing with Sybil Marwood, a fierce, resolute, dogmatic woman with a forbidding countenance and a hostile glare that could turn weaker vessels to stone. Podgy and unlovely, she had devoted her middle years to a period of sustained regret over the follies of her younger days, chief among which was the disastrous marriage into which she believed she had been inveigled. Seeds of bitterness had been planted in her soul and they had produced a flourishing crop that grew inside her like a field of large ulcers. Closing one hooded eye, she peered at her visitor through the other.

"Marriage is truly a veil of tears for women," she declared.

"I have never found it so, Sybil," said Margery, hoping, by the familiar use of her Christian name, to move the conversation onto a more friendly level. "Never a day goes by but I realize how blessed I am in Lawrence. Being the wife of a famous actor brings with it certain disadvantages—I'm very much aware of them at this time—but they pale beside the many benefits of marital life."

"Benefits—ha!"

"I see that our experience differs."

"Being married has turned me against all men."

"But it's only through a man that we achieve full womanhood."

"Then I wish I'd remained a spinster."

"But think what you would have missed, Sybil."

"Nothing that I would not gladly spare."

"It was love that brought you and your husband together in the first place." Sybil curled a contemptuous lip. "Never forget that. And together, you produced a beautiful daughter. Do you not look at Rose and recall those first magical years of conjugal bliss?"

"No, Mistress Firethorn," retorted the other woman. "I simply hope that Rose does not have to endure the misery, boredom, and toil that comes with the title of wife. Men are little better than beasts."

"Some men, perhaps."

"All of the breed. A cruelty in nature shaped them for pleasure and us for pain. We are born to slavery."

It was strange comment from someone who dominated her husband so completely that she kept him in gibbering servility, but

Margery did not point this out. She found it easier to let Sybil rant on at length about the evils of the male sex, tossing in a nod of agreement now and again by way of encouragement. When the vehement tirade finally ended, Margery was able to return to the topic that had brought her to the Queen's Head.

"I was shocked to learn about the damage to your property."

"It has wrecked all our ambition."

"Not so," said Margery. "The thing that Lawrence most admires about you is your strength of character. You have had setbacks before and risen above them."

"Those setbacks were always caused by Westfield's Men."

"Come, come—that's too harsh."

"Harsh but true," said Sybil. "This is not the first fire they have inflicted upon us. And I've lost count of the number of times a play of theirs has provoked an affray in our yard."

"You must also have lost count of the money they bring in."

"No, they've swelled our profits, I grant them that."

"And they can do so again," said Margery with a disarming smile. "When they come home in triumph from Denmark, they'll fill the Queen's Head once more."

"They'll not get the chance, Mistress Firethorn."

"But they must."

"Not while I'm landlord here," said a ghostly voice behind her. Margery turned to see Alexander Marwood standing there. "I give you my solemn word. Westfield's Men are exiled." He glanced deferentially at his wife. "Am I right, Sybil?"

"We are at one on this," she agreed.

"But you are cutting your own throats," said Margery. "Keep the company out and you bid farewell to any hope of recovery. How can you rebuild the inn without the money that only Westfield's Men will garner for you?"

Sybil was complacent. "There are other sources of money."

"A loan? Interest rates will be very high."

"I'm not talking about a loan."

"Then what—you have saved enough to pay for it all?"

"No, no," said Marwood, aghast at the very thought, "we'll not plunder our savings. What Sybil is talking about is a gift."

"A gift of money?"

"Subject to certain conditions."

"One of which," said Sybil, reserving the right to administer the fatal thrust, "is that Westfield's Men will never again perform here."

Margery was shaken. "Can this be true?"

"We've signed a contract to that effect."

"So the decision has legal force," said Marwood with a kind of morose gleefulness. "The company is banned forthwith by the terms of the contract. I rejoice in our good fortune."

"Rebuilding work begins on Monday."

"These are black tidings," said Margery, deeply upset. "I wish to see the Queen's Head rise from the ashes, of course, but not at the expense of Westfield's Men. I urge you both to think again. Tear up this contract before it commits you to a hideous mistake."

Sybil folded her arms. "It's too late for that."

"We've given our word to the gentleman," said her husband.

"What gentleman?" asked Margery, torn between anger and despair. "I see nothing gentlemanly in this. Westfield's Men are the pride of London. They've entertained the whole city for many years with comedies, tragedies, and histories. And is all this to end?"

"It already has."

"Then it's nothing short of treachery."

"It's Westfield's Men who are the traitors. They've betrayed us time and again. Their heads are now on the block."

"So do not look for sympathy from us," warned Sybil.

Margery was still dazed. "And a *gentleman* did this to us?"

"A rich merchant from York—one Master Dunmow."

"Dunmow? That name strikes a chord for some reason."

"So it should," said Marwood, "for it's engraved on our hearts. Will Dunmow was the young man burned to death in the fire that began in his bedchamber. His father, Isaac, is our benefactor."

"Does he hate the company enough to destroy them?"

"They killed his son."

"Your husband has seen the last of the Queen's Head," said Sybil, keen to reinforce the point. "Westfield's Men may be the toast of Denmark, but when they come back to London, they face destitution. They will have no home."

* * *

The *Cormorant* battled its way through the North Sea. Days were long and arduous but they were not wasted. The actors did not merely help with the extensive repairs to the ship. They rehearsed *The Princess of Denmark* every morning, and under the direction of Nicholas Bracewell, they spent hours on the fight scenes that featured in the other plays they intended to perform. There was a double purpose behind this. Not only were the lively brawls and clever swordplay made to look more convincing onstage, Nicholas was also training the actors to defend themselves better in case they were attacked by another pirate vessel.

Everyone was delighted that they would first call at Elsinore, thereby shortening the voyage and sparing them visits to other ports. There was one exception and he argued with the captain regularly. Rolfe Harling was distressed that they would not sail directly to Flushing. When he saw Nicholas talking to the captain that morning, he decided to raise the issue yet again.

"I must protest most strongly, Captain Skrine," he said.

"You have done so repeatedly, sir, but to no avail."

"Can nothing alter your mind?"

"No," said Skrine bluntly. "We sail for Denmark."

"But your orders were to call at Flushing."

"Storm and pirates intervened, Master Harling."

"And the Spanish navy has to be considered," said Nicholas reasonably. "The Dutch are at war with Spain. Because we are their allies, the Dutch granted us Flushing—or Vlissingen—as a base for our soldiers."

Harling was tetchy. "I know all this."

"What you seem to forget is that Spanish galleons—not filled with pirates this time—guard the eastern approach in order to stop our soldiers reaching land. Captain Skrine will be able to get to Flushing with greater ease if he sails south from Amsterdam with the protection of ships from the Dutch navy."

"Very true," said Skrine.

"It's too late to turn back now, Master Harling."

"This argument does not concern you."

"It concerns me very much," said Nicholas firmly. "We lost one of our actors in the skirmish with the pirates, and most of the others were injured. I'd sooner not expose them to more danger by tangling with the Spanish navy. Nor," he added with a nod in the direction of Lord Westfield, "would our patron. We'll not be able to perform a play at his wedding if more of the company are killed or wounded."

"Why are you so eager to reach Flushing?" asked the captain.

"I have business there," said Harling.

"It will have to wait."

"But it has a bearing on our visit to Elsinore."

Nicholas was interested. "Go on, sir."

"I sent letters to Denmark, telling them of our plans. Not wishing any replies to go astray at sea, I asked for them to be sent overland to Flushing. They'll be delivered to the governor and held there until we arrive."

"Then you will have to delay reading them."

"But they may contain intelligence about our visit."

"We are expected, are we not?"

"Of course," said Harling, "but we have no details. They would have been in the correspondence sent in my name. Without that, we do not know where we will stay and what is expected of us."

"That will soon become clear," said Skrine.

"Forewarned is forearmed, Captain."

"Nobody could have forewarned us about the pirates and there is no ship afloat that is completely forearmed against the North Sea. These are perilous waters, Master Harling. Be grateful that we will reach our destination in one piece."

"But you sail to the wrong port."

Skrine bristled. "*I'll* make that decision, sir."

"And I believe it to be a wise one," said Nicholas.

Rolfe Harling seethed with exasperation. Wanting to impose his authority, he was quite powerless to do so. Until that moment, he and Nicholas had always been on friendly terms, but the situation had changed. In supporting the captain, Nicholas had incurred Harling's dislike. It was he who was treated to a look of muted aggression before the other man flounced off across the deck.

"What difference will a couple of letters make?" said the captain.

"They are clearly of significance to him," concluded Nicholas.

Skrine grinned. "Could they be written by a lady, then?"

"I think not. Master Harling is more adept at finding a bride for someone else than seeking one out for himself. He has other reasons to rue the missing correspondence." Nicholas stroked his beard. "I wonder what they could be."

Sigbrit Olsen was so surprised by the news that she let out an involuntary cry of alarm. Her delicate hands came up to her face.

"They are here *already?*" she exclaimed in disbelief. "You told me not to expect them for days."

"I was wrong," said Bror Langberg, "and delighted to be so. I've sent men down to the harbor to greet them."

"How did they get here so early?"

"I'll make a point of asking them."

"And are they coming to the castle?"

"Where else, Sigbrit? You cannot invite Lord Westfield to sail all this way in order to be lodged at an inn. He will receive the honor that is due to him."

They were in her apartment, a room on the second floor that overlooked the sound. Crossing to the window, Sigbrit surveyed the harbor below and saw that a merchant ship had dropped anchor. Passengers were being rowed toward the quay in a boat. They were too far away to be anything more than a series of tiny figures but she knew that somewhere among them was her future husband.

"I am not *ready,* Uncle Bror," she said anxiously.

"I will help you."

"Where is Hansi? I need her with me."

"Your sister is on her way here, Sigbrit."

"I cannot do this without Hansi," wailed the other.

"She will arrive this evening at the latest. Now come away from that window," he went on, guiding her back into the room. "If the sight distresses you, do not look at it."

"I will not have to meet Lord Westfield, will I?"

"Not today, Sigbrit."

"But he will ask where I am."

"Leave me to deal with him. All that you must do is to calm down and compose yourself. An important event is about to take place in your life and you must revel in it."

"How can I when I have so many worries?"

"About what, child?"

"About him—about myself—about *everything*."

"Away with these silly thoughts," he said, enfolding her in his arms. "I am only doing what your parents would have done—seeking your happiness. Since you will not find it here in Denmark, you must look elsewhere. That's why I sought an English husband for you."

"I realize that, Uncle."

"And I took the utmost care when I chose one."

"You are meticulous in everything you do."

"Then no more of this foolish anxiety," he said, standing back to appraise her. "In a month's time, you will be thanking me for what I did on your behalf. Lord Westfield will make a fine husband."

"Hansi thinks that he is too old."

"Your sister is not marrying him."

"She believes I should have someone nearer my own age."

"A mature man and a young woman make an ideal match," he argued. "Look at us, for instance. Has your Aunt Johanna ever complained that I am too old?"

"No, Uncle."

"Yet we are separated by twenty years—almost as much as you and your future husband. Marriages are built on love and trust. Those are the only qualities that matter."

Sigbrit nodded then drifted back to the window. The boat had reached the quay now and the passengers were scrambling out. A coach was arriving to pick up Lord Westfield. Large carts had also been sent down from the castle to collect the actors and their baggage. It was only a question of time before she sailed away from her native land with these foreigners. Her concern was balanced by her curiosity.

"What sort of man is he, Uncle?"

"Lord Westfield? He's a handsome, vigorous, intelligent person.

He's close to the queen and has influence at court. In every way, he's a man of substance."

"But you have never actually met him."

"No," he conceded, "but I had detailed reports from Rolfe Harling, the man empowered to make the match on his behalf. Master Harling is even more scrupulous about details than I am."

"Did he tell you *why* Lord Westfield wishes to marry?"

"He has now recovered from the death of his second wife and feels ready to start a new life with someone else."

"How did she die?"

"In childbirth. Mother and baby were lost."

"How terrible! Has it made him embittered?"

"No, Sigbrit, he accepts the vicissitudes of fate without complaint. You must do the same."

"Yes," she said to herself.

"Lord Westfield has been greatly helped, of course."

"By whom?"

"His theater company," said Langberg. "They have carried him through many sad events in his private life. The fact that he lent his name to them should tell you much about the man. He is fond of all the arts and is, according to Master Harling, of mirthful disposition."

"Then he will be disappointed in me."

"Not so."

"I am not inclined to mirth, Uncle."

"You have a serious mind—he will appreciate that."

"Will he?"

"He'll admire all your virtues, Sigbrit."

She turned to face him again and conjured up a brave smile. But it did not mask the swirling fears and uncertainties that lay beneath. He kissed her tenderly on the forehead.

"Have faith in your uncle," he whispered. "All will be well."

Kronborg was at once impressive and daunting. Occupying a strategic position on a spit of land that jutted out into the sea, it guarded the straits at their narrowest point. As they stood on the quay, Westfield's Men marveled at its size, its prominence, and its cold magnificence.

Tall earth ramparts surrounded the castle, strengthening its defenses and able to withstand the heaviest cannon fire. The fortress itself consisted of a high curtain-wall, square-built on a foundation of granite fieldstone. Strong bastions had been raised at the four corners so that enemies could be shot at from a variety of angles. To the actors who viewed it from below, Kronborg looked impregnable.

"It will be a big change from the Queen's Head," said Edmund Hoode with a shiver, "but I hope that we perform indoors. It's so cold here."

"You'll feel better when you're out of this wind," said Nicholas. "They'll provide something to warm us up at the castle."

Owen Elias grinned hopefully. "Women?"

"Food and fires, Owen."

"But they have Danish beauties here as well, surely?"

"Take a vow of celibacy," advised Hoode. "After the beating you took in London, I would have thought you'd mend your ways."

"Never, Edmund. The only thing I wish to mend is this body of mine. It may be needed before long."

"It will be," said Nicholas. "Onstage in a play."

A second boat pulled into the quay and Nicholas broke off to supervise the unloading of the remainder of their baggage. Scenery, costumes, and properties were heaved onto one of the waiting carts. Everyone lent a willing hand. The coach had already set off for the castle, leaving a frothing Barnaby Gill in its wake. He stalked angrily across to Nicholas.

"This is shameful!" he protested.

"What is?"

"There was no room in the coach for me."

"Then you'll have to travel with us in the cart," said Nicholas. "It is so with the other sharers—Edmund and Owen among them."

"You know what I am talking about."

Nicholas was jabbed in the chest by a stubby finger. As well as their patron, the coach had contained Lawrence Firethorn, Rolfe Harling, and Anne Hendrik. That he had been omitted in favor of a woman was seen by Gill as a stinging insult.

"She had no right to be there," he said.

"Anne was invited."

"In place of me—it's unpardonable."

"I disagree," said Nicholas.

"She is not even part of the company."

"Anne proved her worth on the *Cormorant*. She saved lives by her prompt treatment of the wounded, and she nursed several of the actors through their injuries. You were not aware of this, Barnaby," he went on, "but it was Anne who rescued you when you were knocked unconscious. A little gratitude is in order."

"Well, it will not come from me," said Gill sourly. "I do not deny the commendable work that she did on board the ship but she has no place among us now that we have landed."

Nicholas sounded a warning note. "Anne Hendrik is here as my friend, so I'll hear no disparagement of her. Besides, she is eager to help us. We lost Harold Stoddard," he reminded Gill, "and had to bury him in a watery grave. Since he was once apprenticed to a tailor, Harold would have been both actor and tireman. While she is with us, Anne will look after our costumes instead, well-fitted for the task by her trade as a hatmaker."

"She's a woman, Nicholas—she does not *belong*."

"Nobody else has complained."

"Nobody else was ousted unfairly from that coach."

"Lord Westfield made that decision so you must take up the matter with him. Do not blame Anne. And before you claim that she does not belong with us," said Nicholas, "consider this. Anne Hendrik speaks Dutch and German, two languages that have more affinity with Danish than the one we use. She is our interpreter."

"That is not how I would describe her."

"Then correct me, if you dare."

Nicholas was issuing a direct challenge. Towering over Gill, he fixed his gaze on the actor and waited for a response. None came. After looking at the book holder's muscular frame, Gill backed away. Muttering under his breath, he went across to the first of the carts and clambered aboard. Edmund Hoode had witnessed the heated exchange from a distance. He came over.

"Is Barnaby being argumentative?"

"He knows no other way, Edmund."

"Who does he rail against this time?"

"Anne," said Nicholas. "He feels that she took his place in the coach and that offended his self-importance."

"After the way she helped us at sea," said Hoode, holding up a bandaged arm, "she deserves a coach of her own. Anne was surgeon and mother to us all on board the *Cormorant*."

"Lord Westfield recognizes that."

"Then she wrought a small miracle."

"Miracle?"

"Yes, Nick. When he stepped aboard the ship, our beloved patron could think of only one woman and that was his future wife. His princess of Denmark holds him in thrall. For Anne to capture his attention for even a moment speaks volumes in her favor. Hold on to her," he said with a confiding smile. "Anne Hendrik is a princess in her own right."

W hen may I meet the lovely Sigbrit?" said Lord Westfield impatiently.

"In due course," replied Bror Langberg.

"This afternoon–this evening?"

"Tomorrow, perhaps."

"Why the delay? I've sailed hundreds of miles to claim her as my wife yet she keeps me waiting."

"Not by design, my lord. The truth is that Sigbrit is indisposed. It is nothing serious," Langberg went on. "She has been troubled by a slight chill, that is all. She merely wishes to be at her best for you."

"I yearn for the moment when I see her."

Lord Westfield and Rolfe Harling had been conducted to the apartment used by the other man. With its high ceiling and generous proportions, it gave an impression of space and comfort. The fire that crackled in the grate illuminated the intricate tapestries that hung on the walls. After spending so long at sea, the visitors were delighted to be in such restful surroundings again. Bror Langberg had given them a cordial welcome and displayed his excellent command of English. He turned an inquiring eye on Harling.

"You came earlier than we thought."

"That was the captain's doing," explained Harling with a frown.

"We were driven off course by a storm and harried by pirates. Against my express wishes, Captain Skrine decided that Elsinore would be our first port of call."

"Oh," said Langberg, unsettled by the news. "So you did not stop at Vlissingen on the way?"

"Alas, no."

"Then you did not receive the letters I sent for you."

"Rolfe can pick them up on the way back," said Lord Westfield.

"It will be too late then, my lord."

"Why—what does the correspondence contain?"

"Details of the arrangements we made for your visit," said Langberg easily. "Your early arrival means that we have been caught unawares, but no matter for that. We are delighted that you got here."

"So are we, Bror," said Harling.

"And so, I trust, is your niece," added Lord Westfield.

Langberg beamed at him. "Sigbrit is thrilled."

"Convey my warmest regards to her, Master Langberg."

"I will, my lord."

"Where will we stay?"

"Apartments have been reserved for you and for a few of the leading actors," said the Dane hospitably, "and we will, of course, find room for the lady who arrived with you. However, Kronborg is rather full at the moment so the rest of your company will have to endure meaner accommodation."

"They are used to that," said Lord Westfield. "When they go on tour, they've been known to sleep under a hedge or in a barn. They've strong bodies and stout hearts, as Rolfe here will confirm."

"Yes," said Harling, "they acquitted themselves well when we were under attack. Three of them even manned a cannon."

Langberg chuckled. "They'll not need to do that here."

"Do you keep a large garrison at the castle?"

"Large enough, Rolfe. But you must both be tired after your long voyage," Langberg continued, crossing to open the door. "I'll have someone conduct you to your apartments."

"Thank you," said Lord Westfield.

"We will see you later, my lord."

"Do not forget to pass on my best wishes to Sigbrit."

"It will be done immediately."

Langberg shepherded him gently out of the room and exchanged farewells with him. A servant led the prospective bridegroom away. Rolfe Harling did not move. He wanted a private conversation with their host. Closing the door, Langberg swung round with a dark scowl.

"You did not reach Vlissingen? That is unfortunate."

"I did all that I could to make the captain change his mind."

"My letters were sent over a week ago."

"It pains me that I never got to read them."

"What pains me, Rolfe, is that someone else might do so."

"The governor will not open private correspondence."

"He might if it is left there indefinitely."

"Calm down, Bror," said Harling. "I'll collect it as soon as I can."

"The issues I discuss will have gone cool by then. This is very annoying–and worrying." Langberg made an effort to collect himself. "But let us turn our minds to the wedding. Lord Westfield is content?"

"He could not be happier."

"And he has no qualms about the marriage service? We are Lutherans here. Sigbrit will not forgo her religion."

"Nor will she be asked to, Bror. Lord Westfield is a tolerant man. He'll indulge his wife in this matter as in any other." Harling smiled. "He is so spellbound by her that he would agree to marry her almost anywhere, whatever her religion happened to be."

"That is music to my ear."

"What of the lady herself? Is she ready?"

There was a pause. "As ready as she'll ever be."

"You sound a trifle uncertain."

"Not at all. Sigbrit is overjoyed with the situation."

"I am sorry to hear that she is unwell."

"A temporary problem," said Langberg, flapping both hands. "Her doctor assures me that she will have recovered by tomorrow. Do not have any qualms on her account. Her young life is about to undergo some big changes. Sigbrit is fitting her mind to the future."

* * *

Seated in the window, Sigbrit Olsen was lost in thought. She knew that she should be grateful to her uncle Bror for the care he took of her, but she could still not bring herself to look with any enthusiasm on the marriage that he had arranged for her. She had lost her first husband in a hunting accident and had wept for a month afterward. Sigbrit felt that it was impossible to recapture the love and respect that she had shared with him. The notion of going to England was enticing but not if she was to be kept there in perpetuity. She did not wish to cut herself off from her friends and fellow countrymen forever. Nothing could compensate for that.

She was too preoccupied to hear the door open and shut behind her. Only when she felt a soft hand on her shoulder did she realize she had a visitor. Looking up with a start, she saw that it was her Aunt Johanna.

"Did I give you a fright?" said the older woman solicitously.

"My mind was miles away."

"I think that it should return to the present now. Lord Westfield has arrived and brought his actors with him."

Sigbrit leapt up. "You've *seen* him, Aunt Johanna?"

"I had a brief glimpse."

"What is he like?"

"He's a little shorter than I imagined he would be, and rather more solid in the body. But that's to be expected in a man of his age. He looks very personable, that I can tell you."

"How did he bear himself?"

"Very well, considering the trials they have been through."

"Trials?"

"A voyage across the North Sea is always hazardous."

"And it's one that I am doomed to make," said Sigbrit gloomily.

Johanna Langberg held her in an affectionate embrace for a few seconds and gave her a reassuring kiss. Sigbrit's aunt was a shapely woman in her thirties with a beauty that had been enhanced with the passage of years. Wife, mother, and devoted friend, she had a serenity about her that her niece had always envied. In times of stress, Sigbrit had drawn great strength from her aunt Johanna.

"Has he asked to see me?"

"I'm sure that he has," replied Johanna. "What bridegroom would not wish to see his future wife at the earliest opportunity? But your Uncle Bror had told Lord Westfield that he must wait."

"On what grounds?"

"He gave out that you were indisposed."

"That is not so far from the truth."

"Come now, Sigbrit. It's time to cast off this somber mood. A member of the English nobility has gone to immense trouble so that you may be married in the place where you were born. Anybody else in your position would be touched by the sacrifices he has made."

"I am, Aunt Johanna—touched and pleased."

"Then why this sorrowful face?"

"That is what hurts me most—I do not *know*."

"Let me tell you something," said the aunt. "I was only eighteen when I married your uncle and I had these feelings of unease as well. As soon as I became his wife, however, they disappeared as if they had never been there. They were all fantasies."

"My case is different, I think."

"Is it?"

"I was married before and I did not have the suspicion of a doubt when I went to the altar with Ingmar. I could not wait to share my life with him. Now, I feel myself holding back."

"You must conquer that impulse, Sigbrit."

"I have tried."

"Lord Westfield will expect readiness. It's his entitlement."

"I know." Sigbrit wrung her hands. "You and Uncle Bror have been so kind and patient with me, Aunt Johanna. I do not want to let you down. But the person I most want to see right now is my sister."

"That's the other news I bring you."

"Hansi is here?"

"The ship has just been sighted."

"At last," cried Sigbrit. "Hansi will make all the difference."

"That's why we sent to Copenhagen for her. Bid your fears adieu," said Johanna confidently. "Your sister is coming to help you. Hansi will know exactly what to do."

Westfield's men were disappointed. Having admired the castle from afar, they had watched it grow ever bigger and more splendid as they were driven toward it in their carts. When they entered the Dark Gate, the stone portal that fronted Kronborg Slot, they went through into a forecourt to be confronted by four smaller gates, each surrounded by elaborate stonework. They then made their way through one of the gates into the main courtyard and blinked in astonishment. Rows of tall windows surrounded them on four sides, each facade topped by gables and pinnacles, and decorated by master stonemasons. Towers increased the feeling of tremendous height. Facing them at the eastern end of the south wing was the chapel, complete with Gothic windows and a striking portal around which statues of Moses, Solomon, and King David had been set. In the center of the courtyard was a superb fountain with an intricate design.

It was a majestic fortress and they felt privileged to be invited into it. When they saw where they would be sleeping, however, they changed their minds at once. Lawrence Firethorn, Barnaby Gill, and Edmund Hoode had been given apartments but everyone else was taken down a flight of stone steps into the cellars. The smell of beer and the stink of salted fish told them that they were not the only inhabitants. Stretching under the castle, the casemates were dark, dank, and unwelcoming. With the only light coming from blazing torches, Westfield's Men were expected to sleep on straw mattresses in a smoke-filled cavern.

Owen Elias was the first to moan to Nicholas Bracewell.

"It's like a labyrinth down here, Nick," he said. "We'll get lost."

"Not if we stay together, Owen. This is not a place to wander off in," remarked Nicholas, looking down a long, black tunnel. "There'll be dungeons down here somewhere."

"We are staying in one now."

"It's the same for the soldiers. They sleep down here as well."

"But we are *guests*. We deserve more."

"I'm sure that our patron will speak up for us. Meanwhile," said Nicholas cheerfully, "we must make the most of our situation. Think of the consolations."

Elias was cynical. "What consolations?"

"We are safe on land, we are all together, and we will soon perform before royalty. Those thoughts will make me sleep soundly."

"They'll do nothing for me."

"Would you rather be back in London?"

"Yes, Nick. I would."

"Even though someone tried to kill you?"

"Those pirates tried to kill us all in the *Cormorant*."

"I'm talking about that beating you took," said Nicholas. "When you joined the ship, you could hardly walk. And you have still not fully recovered from your injuries."

"Nor will I if I have to lay my head in this place!"

"You are among friends—what more do you want?"

"A soft bed in a warm room."

His friend laughed. "We would all like that. On the other hand, we've had far worse lodgings than this when we toured. At least we are dry and out of that fierce wind. More to the point, we are a long way from London."

"That brings me no comfort at all," grumbled Elias.

"It should," said Nicholas. "You are out of danger."

The *Speedwell* held her course as she sailed across the North Sea. Among its passengers were Josias Greet and Ben Ryden. They had their orders. They were determined to earn their reward.

[CHAPTER NINE]

Their feelings of disappointment were soon allayed. Before they had even finished complaining about their accommodation in the cellars beneath the castle, Westfield's Men were taken up to a hut in the forecourt that was used by the officers. Seated at a long table, they were served a hearty meal that started with hot fish soup and warm bread. Plentiful supplies of beer were on hand and they discovered that the renown of Danish breweries was well earned. The beer was markedly stronger than anything they had tasted in England, and since it was free, they consumed it with additional relish.

Lawrence Firethorn, Barnaby Gill, and Edmund Hoode joined them for the meal and a sense of camaraderie returned. Still battered by their encounter with the pirates, they began to feel, for the first time, that they were recovering. Their injuries no longer smarted quite so much and their bruises had faded. More beer was served, toasts were drunk, and singing started. Before the actors lapsed into a stupor, Firethorn decided to tell them what he had learned.

"We come somewhat before our time, lads," he announced in a voice that compelled attention, "and we caught them short of preparation. I am assured that things will soon improve."

"They've done so already," said Elias, quaffing his beer.

"You merit better lodging than a dark cavern."

"Then surrender your room to me, Lawrence."

"Have you met the king yet?" asked James Ingram.

"King Christian is not yet in residence but he will arrive here in time for the wedding."

"When will that be, Lawrence?"

"At the end of the week."

"So soon?"

"Lord Westfield is a lusty bridegroom. He abhors delay."

"Where will we perform?" asked Hoode. "In the courtyard?"

"Too cold."

"In the hall?" said Gill.

"I perform best in the bedchamber," boasted Elias.

"But no spectators would pay to watch you," Firethorn told him over a burst of raucous laughter. "They've left the choice to us so I'll take Nick's advice. The hall is used as a meeting place for the councillors and may not be large enough for our purposes. The other place suggested was the ballroom."

"Ballroom?" echoed Gill. "They have a ballroom here?"

"The finest in Europe, I hear, and certainly the longest. The late King Frederick built it for his wife because she was so fond of dancing."

"Then that must be our playhouse. Let a dancer decide."

"The dowager queen is not enamored of comic jigs, Barnaby. She'll want no village antics here. The pavane, the galliard, and the volta are more to her taste."

"I can dance *anything*, Lawrence."

"He's like a bear on a chain," joked Elias. "Give him a prod and Barnaby will dance to order. And as with a bear, beware his embrace."

There was some good-natured baiting, and for once, Gill took it in good part. Like the others, he was relieved to be there after their testing voyage and was refreshed by the delicious meal. It was now possible to enjoy their adventure.

"Above all else," continued Firethorn, rising to his feet with a drink in his hand, "remember this. We are not only here to support our esteemed patron. We have the signal honor of representing our country and displaying the talent that she has nurtured. Let us show these Danes why English actors are the best in the world." He raised his tankard. "To England!"

"England!" they chorused with patriotic fervor.

Nicholas Bracewell had slipped out earlier. Having eaten his dinner, he wanted to make sure that Anne Hendrik had also been fed and looked after. Since none of the guards on duty seemed to speak English, he had some difficulty tracking her down in the long, cold corridors. He eventually found her in a tiny room used by one of the servants. It was bare and featureless but it gave her a privacy that he and the others did not share. They began with a warm embrace.

"Have you eaten?" he asked.

"Extremely well," said Anne. "I had my dinner served in here."

"We've been well fed and given as much beer as we can drink. That will mean tired actors with very sore heads."

"Does Lawrence mean to rehearse today?"

"No, Anne. He wants to give the company time to get over the rigors of the voyage. Most of us are lodged in the casemates. They have all protested bitterly about it but I'll wager that every man among them will sleep as soundly as a baby tonight."

"They need rest. Wounds take time to heal."

"There speaks a ship's surgeon!" They shared a laugh. "Forgive us. I'm sorry that we've brought you so far out of your way."

"I'm loving every moment of it, Nick. I'll be made welcome in Amsterdam but I'll certainly not stay in a splendid castle like this. Have you had time to explore it?"

"Not yet."

"One of the servant girls showed me around," she said. "It took my breath away. The rooms are lined with gilt leather or hung with rich tapestries. Ceilings are finely ornamented. There are wonderful paintings everywhere and the views from the windows made me gape."

"Keep away from the casemates, Anne."

"Why?"

"It's a different world down there. We sleep among beer barrels and stores of salted fish. It's cold and airless. There are no windows and a strong chance that we'll have rats. Kronborg is clearly a castle of two halves—you are in the better half."

"Then I'm taking up a bed that you deserve."

"I would only sleep in it if you were beside me." He kissed her and pulled her to him. "Do you realize? This is the first moment we have had alone since we left London."

"I hope that there are others before I leave."

"There will be, Anne. I promise." He released her. "We came here in a rattling cart," he went on with mock envy, "but you arrived in style with Lord Westfield. What happened?"

"We were met by a man named Bror Langberg. He appears to be in charge here."

"Rolfe Harling told us about him. He's one of the king's leading councillors and the uncle of the lady whom our patron is to marry."

"He and Master Harling met like old friends, though they hardly have much in common. Bror Langberg is genial and good-humored."

"Then he's the opposite of Rolfe Harling."

"They spoke together in Danish."

"Is everything in hand for the wedding?"

"Apparently."

"Good," he said. "For that's what brought us all this way."

"I'd like to see the town before I go."

"I'll make sure that you do, Anne. We do not perform here until the end of the week. Lawrence is already talking about staging a play in the town beforehand—more than one, perhaps. It's needful."

"Why?"

"We must have revenue," he said. "Lord Westfield has paid for our passage here and he will open his purse again when we sail home. Elsewhere, we must look to ourselves."

"You will be paid to perform at the wedding, surely?"

"Handsomely, I expect, but we have many expenses. If we can play in Elsinore itself a couple of times, it will stand us in good stead before we visit other towns."

"Not too many of them, Nick," she warned playfully. "I want you back home with me."

"When will you sail for Amsterdam?"

"After the wedding. The *Cormorant* leaves on Sunday."

"There are still more repairs to be made first and Captain Skrine will need to hire new men for his crew. He lost five in all when we were attacked. But for you," he added gratefully, "that number would have been even higher. The captain will be pleased to see you on board again."

"First, I offer my services to the company."

"You are one of us now."

"Lord Westfield insists that I stay for the wedding."

"Your skill with a needle may well be wanted," Nicholas said. "Our costumes are always in need of a stitch or two. And we must look our best for the performance of *The Princess of Denmark*."

"Your patron cannot wait to meet his bride in the flesh."

"We are all curious to see this lovely creature."

Anne's memory was jogged. "That's why it was so odd."

"Odd?"

"Yes, Nick—the look that the servant girl gave me."

"The one who showed you around?"

She nodded. "Having no English, she talked to me in German."

"You have a good grasp of the language."

"I did at one time but I'm woefully out of practice. However, I think that I made myself understood in the end."

"What did you say?"

"That I'd heard how beautiful the lady was."

"We both saw her portrait, Anne."

"Lord Westfield must have shown it to everyone on board. He is so proud of her. The miniature of Sigbrit Olsen reveals her to be a gorgeous young woman."

"What was the girl's reply?"

"That was the odd thing," said Anne, still puzzled. "She didn't make one. She just gave me this strange look as if she had no idea what I was talking about."

The arrival of her sister had transformed Sigbrit Olsen. Her sadness vanished, her face lit up, and her confidence came flooding back. Hansi Askgaard was only two years older but she had a poise and wisdom beyond her age. She lived in Copenhagen with her husband, a close adviser to the new king, and entertained lavishly. While her younger sister tried to avoid it, Hansi savored public attention and she dressed accordingly. None of Sigbrit's muted colors would suit her. She preferred bright apparel and wore it with sublime assurance.

"Enjoy yourself, Sigbrit," she urged. "That is all you have to do. Enjoy the whole occasion."

"I will try."

"You have something to celebrate. You will be a wife again."

"Yes," said Sigbrit, "and that appeals to me. But I worry that I am being disloyal to Ingmar in marrying again."

"Pah! The only way to get over the death of one husband is to take another. No disloyalty is involved. Ingmar will never be forgotten," said Hansi, "and he will always remain special to you. But it's time to come out of mourning and seize this wonderful opportunity."

"You make me feel so much better about it all, Hansi."

"That's why I'm here."

Hansi kissed her sister on the cheek, then noticed that one of the paintings on the wall was awry. She set it straight. They were in Sigbrit's apartment and her sister appraised it critically. There was an air of neglect about the chamber as if its occupant had grown careless and jaded. Hansi clicked her tongue.

"You've been here too long, Sigbrit. It's not healthy."

"I walk around the ramparts every morning."

"What use is that apart from exciting the guards?"

"It's good exercise."

"It's not your body that needs exercising, it's your mind. As long as you remain here, you look inward. You mope. That's why you must get away and why this proposal from Lord Westfield is a godsend."

"You thought that he was a trifle old."

"Too young a man would be wrong for you."

"That's what Uncle Bror said. He believes that I need a more mature husband, one with some experience of the world."

"I agree with him."

"If only he did not live so far away."

"England is not on the other side of the world," said Hansi briskly. "We shall certainly visit you there and so will Uncle Bror."

"He and Aunt Johanna have vowed to come next spring."

"Then we may well sail with them. You'll be mistress of your own house once more, Sigbrit, and you'll entertain us royally."

"Thank you, Hansi. My spirits are lifted already."

"They should never have been allowed to droop."

"I do not have your certainty."

"I've always known what I wanted," said Hansi with a brittle laugh, "but I look upon that as the right of every woman. At the moment, I know what I want for my sister and that is to see her happy and settled. This marriage will *redeem* you, Sigbrit."

"If my husband finds me acceptable."

"He has already accepted you."

"He has accepted what Uncle Bror has told him about me, and it's inspired him to travel all the way here. But I'm bound to wonder why Lord Westfield has not chosen an English bride."

Hansi pulled a face. "Have you *seen* Englishwomen?"

"Not really."

"Then you should talk to our ambassadors. Whenever they come back from London, they complain about the appearance and the manners of the court ladies. Queen Elizabeth is over sixty," Hansi said as if the attainment of such an age were indecent. "Her teeth are black and her face is painted white. What sort of an example is that to set?"

"Lord Westfield's other wives were English."

"Then he knows the deficiencies of the breed."

Sigbrit laughed. "You make them sound like cattle."

"From what I hear, many of them are little better."

"I refuse to believe that."

"Then believe the evidence of your own eyes," suggested Hansi. "A member of the English nobility could have almost any woman he wanted in his own country, provided that she was available. Instead of that, he has chosen my sister. He loves you, Sigbrit."

"But he has never set eyes on me."

"He loves the idea of you and that is what is important. You are young, full of charm, and you are Danish. To someone like Lord

Westfield, you are eminently *different*. That is why he'll adore you, Sigbrit, and that is why you must take him as a husband."

"Oh, Hansi!" cried her sister, tears of joy streaming down her face. "Thank heaven you came! You've made me feel so happy."

The Trumpeter's Tower was the tallest in the castle. Situated in the middle of the south wing, it soared up into the sky like a cathedral spire. Climbing up the steep stairs to the top gallery of the turret took them some time but Nicholas Bracewell and Lawrence Firethorn were rewarded with the most spectacular views. In one direction they could see the town of Elsinore, in another, the coast of Sweden, and if they turned with their backs to the courtyard, they could gaze at the Baltic Sea as it broadened out in the distance.

Firethorn's attention was fixed on the high-pitched castle roofs, glistening brightly in the late-afternoon sun as if made of gold.

"Look at that, Nick," he said in amazement. "Sheets of copper."

"They have severe winters here, Lawrence. Copper will keep out the snow and rain though it will cost far more than tiles, of course."

"Denmark must be awash with money."

"There's the reason why," said Nicholas, pointing at the three ships sailing toward the harbor. "Each vessel has to pay sound dues before she is allowed through. That's why this castle was built. It's less of a royal residence than a sumptuous tollhouse. It's also a symbol of Danish power."

"So are all those cannon on the ramparts. It would be a bold enemy who dared to attack this place. It's astounding, Nick. I thought it would be made of a dull, gray stone. It has so much color."

"The redbrick and sandstone dressings were chosen for that purpose. So were the other materials. But it's the clever decoration that interests me most. Stonemasons have been busy *everywhere*." Nicholas let his gaze travel slowly around the courtyard. "No wonder Anne likes being here so much."

"It's a far cry from her house in Bankside."

"She's very fond of Dutch architecture," said Nicholas, "and this is the image of it in many ways. Anne says that it reminds her of a square she knows in Amsterdam. However," he went on, striking a businesslike note, "I did not bring you up here simply to admire the finer aspects of the castle."

"No," said Firethorn, nudging him, "you wanted to see if I could manage the long climb after all that drink."

"This is where the trumpeters play. Their fanfares ring out across the castle for all to hear. I think we should use the tower for *The Princess of Denmark*. Martin Yeo can signal the start of the play."

"Dressed as a woman?"

"He'll need to be in costume for the performance."

"No trumpeter has ever worn a skirt up here before."

"Martin will be heard but not seen," said Nicholas. "Everyone will be sitting in the audience. And the beauty of it is that we are directly above the ballroom. When he has discharged his duty up here, Martin will be able to come down the spiral staircase into the ballroom and make his entrance as a lady-in-waiting."

"You have decided on the ballroom, then?"

"I think so. Let me show you why."

They descended the staircase. Feeling slightly giddy, Firethorn made sure that Nicholas went first so that the book holder could break his fall if he lost his footing. As it was, the actor managed to get down the steps with relative safety, although his shoulders bounced off the walls many times as he did so. They came into the ballroom and stood side by side to take its measure. It was vast. Well over sixty yards in length, it was more than a dozen yards wide and had a row of high windows running down one side of it.

"You see how much natural light is admitted?" said Nicholas with a gesture. "We'll not have to use candles or torches in here."

Firethorn studied the floor. "I love all this marble," he said. "It will be perfect for us to dance upon for we must have a galliard to end the play. What is a wedding without a lively dance at its conclusion?"

Above them was a beamed ceiling and along the wall was a continuous narrow frieze with a succession of battle scenes painted on it. Below those was a selection of finely woven tapestries and gilt-framed paintings. At one end of the ballroom was a decorated wooden screen with a gallery above it for the musicians. Nicholas led the way purposefully toward it.

"They have designed the scenery for us," he pointed out. "We'll make use of the gallery and build a low stage in front of the screen."

"I agree," said Firethorn, looking around. "This place answers all our demands. The hall would be more compact but less imposing. Besides, the ballroom has an attribute that no other room in the castle could possibly match."

"What's that, Lawrence?"

"It will carry my voice."

He opened his mouth and emitted a long, loud, rising roar of anger that filled the entire ballroom like the report of a cannon. Firethorn chortled with satisfaction but the noise caused disturbance elsewhere. A door opened and Bror Langberg swept into the ballroom with Rolfe Harling at his heels. When they saw the two men there, they went over to them.

"We wondered what that sound was," said Langberg.

Firethorn gave a bow. "I was just exercising my lungs."

"They must have heard you in the town," said Harling with frank disapproval, "if not in Copenhagen itself."

"I wanted to see how my voice sounded in here."

"Like a veritable siege gun, Master Firethorn," complimented Langberg, rubbing his hands together. "I acted when I was a student but I had none of your skills."

"Few people do," said Nicholas.

"I've yet to meet one of them," added Firethorn proudly before bringing Nicholas forward. "This, by the way, is our ever-reliable book holder, Nicholas Bracewell." He indicated the Dane. "Our host, Master Langberg."

"It's an honor to meet you, sir," said Nicholas.

"And I'm pleased to make your acquaintance. I've been hearing about your exploits aboard the ship from Rolfe. Is it true that you put paid to some pirates?"

"That was all my doing," asserted Firethorn. "Once I had been taught how to fire a cannon, I brought their mast down."

"It was frightful," recalled Harling.

"We beat the curs!"

"Then changed course and missed our visit to Flushing. That

was most inconvenient for some of us, Master Firethorn. That rash decision has created a lot of problems."

"None that cannot be overcome," said Langberg quietly.

"If you say so."

"I do, Rolfe. I do." Langberg's smile broadened. "While you are here, Master Firethorn, exercising those powerful lungs of yours, perhaps I might have a word with you?"

"Of course," said the actor.

"It concerns the town," said Langberg, taking him by the arm to lead him away. "As soon as I knew that we would be graced by your presence, I passed on the tidings. It is not only here that we long to see your company perform."

They moved down the ballroom out of earshot, leaving Nicholas to initiate a conversation with Rolfe Harling. On the *Cormorant,* the latter had been patently ill at ease. In the castle, he was much more at home, clearly used to being in the company of statesmen.

"You do not care for the playhouse, I fancy," said Nicholas.

"I never have time to visit it."

"So you know nothing of our work at the Queen's Head?"

"Only by report," said Harling.

"Good report or bad?"

"It came from your patron."

"Ah," said Nicholas, "then you heard from our dearest friend."

"He loves the company this side of idolatry and wears it around his neck like a chain of office."

"We pray that his new wife will look kindly on us as well."

"I'm sure that the lady will."

"Lord Westfield must have the highest opinion of you to entrust such an important mission to you," said Nicholas, studying him.

"I believe that I've earned that high opinion."

"I do not doubt it. Have you done this work before?"

Harling stiffened. "That question borders on impertinence."

"Then I withdraw it at once. It's simply that you seem so adroit as a matchmaker that I assumed you were well versed in the art."

"My life has been dedicated to rather more serious business than finding wives for eligible widowers," said Harling sharply. "I've written learned books and traveled around the universities of Europe. All that I have done in this instance is to assist a friend."

"For a fee?"

"You are being impertinent again, Master Bracewell."

"Will you be staying for the wedding?"

"That's what brought me here and I'll see it through to the end. Immediately afterward, however, I'll take the first ship to Flushing."

"The *Cormorant* sets sail on Sunday."

"I would never put myself into Captain Skrine's hands again."

"He's a fine seamen."

"Then why did he change course unnecessarily?" said Harling.

"He explained that."

"Not to my satisfaction."

"With respect, Master Harling, it was more important to get an entire company to Elsinore than to oblige the sole passenger who had business in Flushing."

Harling glared at him. "You may regret that remark one day."

Before Nicholas could reply, he saw Lord Westfield enter the ballroom, waddling along in his finery and waving a hand to them.

"There you are, Rolfe!" he said.

"Did you want me, my lord?"

"I thought you were going to play chess with me."

"I was," said Harling, "but, when I came to your room after dinner, I found you fast asleep. I thought it best to leave you."

"I dozed off for an hour, that is all. I am ready to do battle now." Lord Westfield looked at Nicholas. "Do not meet him over a chessboard," he cautioned, "for it is impossible to win. Rolfe plays the game as if he invented it."

"Concentration is the secret," said Harling.

Nicholas smiled. "You have an unlimited supply of that."

There was a momentary silence. It was broken by the sound of the door opening at the far end of the ballroom. For a second, a woman's face appeared and they were rooted to the spot, struck by the sheer force of her beauty. Embarrassed to have stumbled upon them, the woman withdrew at once and left her memory hanging in the air. Lord Westfield had seen those sculptured features before.

Snatching the portrait from his pocket, he compared it to the vision that had just appeared before him. He was ecstatic.

"It was *she*," he cried. "That was my lovely bride."

In defiance of all their fears, Westfield's Men slept relatively well in the casemate, the combination of fatigue and drunkenness making most of them oblivious to everything around them. The cold did not trouble them and the nocturnal banter of the soldiers in a nearby casemate did not wake them. It was their first night on dry land and they took full advantage of it. Heartened by a good breakfast on the following morning, they were further bolstered by the news that a request had come for them to perform in the town. Nicholas Bracewell was duly dispatched to call on the mayor, to show him their license and to see where they could best stage a play. Owen Elias went with him for company and—since she had expressed an interest in Elsinore—he also took Anne Hendrik. Blown along by a stiff breeze, all three of them marched out of the castle.

With over nine thousand inhabitants, Elsinore was the second-largest town in Denmark and also one of the prettiest. Neat stone-built houses with tiled roofs flanked every street and there was an abundance of shops. Elsinore had retained its simple basic pattern for centuries though it had now pushed out well beyond its original boundaries. Because foreign immigrants had settled here over the years, many languages could be heard. Yet there was no sign of any tension between the differing nationalities.

"I see no libels against strangers here," said Elias.

"That bodes well," said Anne. "The tavern we just passed was run by a Dutchman. And I've seen German and French names on signboards as well. They all seem to live happily cheek by jowl."

"If only that were true of London," Nicholas commented.

When he reached the town hall, he went inside to introduce himself and left his friends to explore the immediate vicinity. Nicholas spent a productive time with the mayor, a rotund, bearded, jovial man with a positive love of theater. He could not have been more helpful, and though his English was halting and his conversation punctuated by a series of loud guffaws, he told Nicholas all that he needed to know, including, importantly, the amount of money they intended to pay Westfield's Men. Taking him outside, the mayor showed him what he felt would be the ideal place to set up a stage.

By the time he left, Nicholas was in good spirits. He found the others in a nearby tavern called the White Hart. Its English landlord served Danish beer and Elias was sampling it while Anne tasted an imported German wine. Nicholas took a stool at their table.

"Well?" asked Elias.

"We've been invited to give two performances, Owen."

"Before the wedding?"

"Yes," said Nicholas. "It will give you a chance to get yourselves in good voice before we play *The Princess of Denmark*."

"Where will you perform, Nick?" said Anne.

"In the main square."

She was surprised. "In this weather?"

"The square is well-protected from the wind. As long as it remains dry, we will have no difficulties. The Danes are a hardy people. To survive their winters, they have to be."

"So the landlord told us," said Elias. "During his first Christmas here, he almost froze to death."

"What brought him here in the first place?"

"The same thing that brought all the foreigners here, Nick."

"The sound dues?"

"Yes," replied the Welshman. "Since they had to anchor here, all vessels needed the services of pilots, ferrymen, sailmakers, rope makers, ships' chandlers, and so on. That's how the population grew."

"As a payment was made," said Anne, taking up the story, "the name and nationality of every ship had to be recorded. When they came into the town to collect supplies, captains preferred to deal with someone who spoke their own language. According to the landlord, English sailors often come first to the White Hart."

"As it happens, our friend Captain Skrine was here yesterday, asking about carpenters and smiths he needed to work aboard the *Cormorant*."

"We must invite him to one of our performances," said Nicholas. "They asked for rustic comedies. I think he'd enjoy either of the plays we'll stage in the square."

Elias was practical. "What about money, Nick?"

"We are to have a generous grant from the town council and we can make a modest charge for our spectators."

"Gatherers?"

"The mayor has undertaken to provide those. They'll collect the entrance fee and pay it directly to me afterwards."

"This gets better and better."

"Who will supply the seating?" said Anne.

"That, too, will be taken care of," said Nicholas. "The mayor and the town worthies will sit on benches at the front with everyone else standing behind them. Those who live in houses that overlook the square, of course, can watch from their upper windows. The mayor assured me that we can count on large audiences."

"What about your patron? Will he have a seat of honor?"

"I think it unlikely that he'll even be here."

"Why not?"

"Because he's seen both comedies before and because he will not leave the castle while his bride is there. Lord Westfield caught his first glimpse of her yesterday," said Nicholas, "and he is enraptured."

It was evening before he had a formal meeting with Sigbrit Olsen and it was a moving experience for him. Having waited all day, he had drunk heavily to subdue his impatience and was decidedly light-headed when the precious moment actually came. Lord Westfield was conducted into the hall beside Bror Langberg and his wife, Johanna. Over thirty people had gathered there to be introduced to their distinguished visitor from England but he had eyes for only one person. When she emerged from the shadows in the candlelit room and gave him a gentle curtsy, he let out a gasp of wonder. Could this angel really be his?

Sigbrit was dressed in the German fashion with a loose-bodied gown of black and gold fitted to the shoulders and falling in set folds from the waist to the floor. The front was open, exposing the gold-embroidered dress beneath. A small, closed frill was attached to the high collar of the bodice of the undergarment. Sigbrit's fair hair was held in a network of gold thread, lined with silk. The apparel tended to conceal more than it showed but Lord Westfield did not mind. His future wife was standing only yards from him.

"This is my niece," said Langberg, easing her forward.

"Good evening, my lord," said Sigbrit demurely.

Lord Westfield gave a seraphic smile. "I'm enchanted."

As he bent forward to place a kiss on her gloved hand, he felt a thrill course through him. Whether from the excitement of meeting her or from having consumed too much wine, he did not know but he was so unsteady on his feet for a few moments that Langberg had to support him under the elbow. The prospective bride and groom exchanged a few, stilted sentences before Langberg intervened to draw his attention to the other people there. Lord Westfield was obliged to meet everyone of real significance in the castle and to make polite conversation with them.

Though they were in the same room for almost an hour, he could never get really close to Sigbrit, still less speak to her alone. Whenever he looked at her, she was surrounded by women, curious to know what she would wear at the wedding, and whenever he tried to do more than make a passing remark to her across the room, her uncle was always on hand to introduce him to some newcomers. Langberg made much of the fact that their guest of honor had had to endure a dangerous sea voyage to reach them. Before he knew it, Lord Westfield had acquired a small audience.

"Yes," he recounted, "we were set on by pirates in a Spanish galleon but we fought them off bravely. They pounded us at first but Englishmen yield to nobody in a sea battle. I was strongly reminded of *Gloriana Triumphant.*"

Langberg was mystified. "My lord?"

"It's the title of a play written by Edmund Hoode and it marked our victory over the Spanish Armada." There was murmur of approval from everyone listening. "Gloriana, as you will guess, is Her Majesty, Queen Elizabeth. She inspired us to put our enemy to flight."

"The Dutch would value such inspiration."

"We've sent men and money to help them, Master Langberg, but the war against the Spanish drags on."

"Wars are a terrible drain on any nation."

"Denmark has done well to keep out of them."

"It was not always so," said Langberg ruefully. "At the start of his reign, King Frederick was embroiled in a seven years' war to restore the Union. It was highly expensive and he was forced to borrow money from his wife's family in Mecklenburg."

"Did he win the war?"

"Nobody won it, my lord. After seven years of fighting—and after the deaths of thousands of brave soldiers—no territory changed hands." Langberg led his companion across to a portrait that hung on the wall. "The king learned his lesson. For the rest of his reign, he sought only peace and stability. And he devoted much of his energy to rebuilding this castle and strengthening its fortifications."

"He did a magnificent job," said Lord Westfield.

"He was a remarkable man."

They regarded the portrait. King Frederick II was a handsome man with close-cropped hair and well-trimmed beard and mustache. Wearing shiny black armor, he had a striking red-and-gold sash across his breastplate. He looked proud, imperious, and resolute, gazing down like a monarch in his absolute prime.

"Do you know what his motto was?" asked Langberg.

"No," said the other.

" 'Without God—nothing.' "

"I endorse that sentiment wholeheartedly."

"King Christian has taken up the same theme."

"What is his motto?"

" 'The fear of God makes the kingdom strong.' "

"Every country should take heed of that," said Lord Westfield. "I know little of political matters, I fear, but Rolfe is well versed in the affairs of many nations. What he's taught me about the history of Denmark has made me eager to take a Danish bride."

Langberg glanced around. "Where is Rolfe Harling, my lord? He was invited. I would have expected him to be here by now."

"So would I. He is never late. Where on earth can he be?"

* * *

George Dart was a poor sailor and the voyage had been a nightmare for him. Now that they had arrived, however, and were staying in a royal palace, he realized how privileged he was to be a member of Westfield's Men. No amount of teasing from the actors could make him regret that he had come. Since he had to take on so many additional duties, the days ahead promised to be onerous and that made him quail. Meanwhile, however, Dart could enjoy himself.

"Your turn now, Dick," said Martin Yeo.

"No," replied Richard Honeydew, the youngest and most talented of the apprentices. "Let George go first."

"Very well. George?"

Dart stepped forward. "Yes?"

"We will count up to fifty," said Yeo.

"Make it a hundred."

"Fifty."

"Where will I go?"

"That's up to you," said Honeydew, handing him a candle. "Hurry up, George. We are starting to count now."

Dart charged off. They were in the casemates, playing a game of hide-and-seek, having some harmless fun while at the same time exploring the labyrinthine passages below the castle. It had taken them a long time to find Martin Yeo's hiding place. Now that it was his turn, Dart wanted to be just as elusive. With the candle casting a flickering light, he hurried on through the interconnecting cellars, making sharp turns to throw off pursuit and looking for somewhere to conceal himself. Eventually, he found it.

When he came into one casemate, he could pick out a series of storage bays, built of brick against the wall. Three feet in height, they were long enough to hide someone much taller than George Dart. Fish, grain, and other foodstuffs occupied some of the bays but he found one that was half-empty. Whatever it contained was hidden beneath a large sheet of canvas. It was the perfect place. The sound of distant voices told him that the apprentices were already on his trail. There was no time to lose. He cocked a leg over the wall and lifted the canvas sheet. He was on the point of blowing out the candle when he saw that someone else was already hiding in the bay.

Face contorted by violent death, Rolfe Harling lay on his back, his doublet stained with blood, his mouth wide-open in a soundless cry of protest.

George Dart fainted.

[CHAPTER TEN]

The murder threw the entire castle into turmoil. Guards were alerted, guests retreated quickly to their rooms, outer gates were locked, and every inch of Kronborg was searched for interlopers. Bror Langberg took personal charge of the hunt for the killer. Outraged that the crime should cast such a shadow over the castle when a wedding ceremony was in the offing, he insisted on a speedy arrest of the culprit. The whole atmosphere of the place suddenly changed dramatically. Instead of friendliness and cordiality, Westfield's Men were met with coldness and suspicion. There was one important consolation. Langberg was hugely apologetic to their patron over the untimely death of Rolfe Harling. Since the body had been found in the casemates, he had Westfield's Men moved out of there at once and installed in a wooden hut hastily vacated by soldiers.

Everyone in the company was shocked by the murder—George Dart was still shaking uncontrollably—but few felt a sense of real bereavement. Harling had not endeared himself to the actors during the voyage. Dry and aloof, he had made no effort to befriend them and had spent most of his time on board apart from them. It was a point that Nicholas Bracewell made when he and Lawrence Firethorn discussed the matter with their patron in his spacious apartment.

"He seemed to have no interest in us, my lord," said Nicholas.

"No," agreed Lord Westfield, sobered by the sudden turn of events. "Rolfe was too high-minded to be a playgoer."

"Then why did he travel with a theater troupe?"

"He came as my adviser, Nicholas. Without him, I would never have met my new wife. Rolfe had many virtues. He could speak Danish and got to know Bror Langberg extremely well. It would have been foolish to leave him behind."

"Did he not tell me that he sometimes visited the Continent on government business?" recalled Firethorn.

"That is so. He was known in universities throughout Europe."

"What sort of work did he do?"

"Rolfe was a kind of ambassador."

"How did you come to meet him, my lord?" asked Nicholas.

"He was recommended to me by a trusted friend."

"To what end?"

"It was common knowledge that I wished to marry again," said the patron, "but I was hindered by financial restraints. My brother's death—God rest his soul—lifted the burden of debt from me and so it was possible for me to institute a search."

"I'd not have thought it necessary," said Firethorn. "Whenever you attend a play at the Queen's Head, you are always accompanied by the most charming young ladies. Your circle is very wide. Could you not select from that, my lord?"

"You, of all people, should not need to ask that, Lawrence."

"Why not?"

"Because," said Lord Westfield, lifting an eyebrow, "there is all the difference in the world between a wife and a female friend."

Firethorn grinned. "I can vouch for that!"

"One occupies a permanent place in a man's life while the other is a temporary, if agreeable, distraction. I would never have considered using Rolfe Harling to search for a passing acquaintance. He would not have known where to look. Where such ladies are concerned, Rolfe had a touching innocence."

"Yet you trusted him to find a wife," said Nicholas.

"Only because his travels took him to a number of different countries. And he was supremely discreet."

"Why do think anyone would want to kill him?"

"I have no idea, Nicholas."

"Had he fallen out with someone inside the castle?"

"Not as far as I know. Besides," said Lord Westfield, "we have no proof that the villain actually resides within Kronborg."

"I think that we do, my lord. Only someone familiar with the castle would have known the ideal place for a dead body. There are all kinds of pungent smells in the casemates. The stink of a corpse might not have been noticed for days. It was only by sheer luck," Nicholas pointed out, "that George Dart stumbled on the storage bay."

"It gave him a dreadful fright, Nick," said Firethorn.

"Yet we must all be grateful to him."

"Why?"

"For finding Master Harling so soon after the murder. I was able to inspect the corpse before it was carried away. The body was still warm and the blood had not dried. One thing is fairly certain."

"What's that?"

"His killer is still inside the castle."

"Dear God!" cried Lord Westfield, backing away with a hand to his throat. "Does that mean the rest of us are in danger as well?"

"No," said Nicholas. "Rolfe Harling was singled out for a purpose and we need to find out exactly what that purpose was. That's why I'd like to learn more about the man. You told me yesterday that he was a chess player, my lord."

"True—he was a master of the game."

"I never have the patience to play it," said Firethorn.

"Rolfe did," said Lord Westfield with admiration. "He had the patience of a saint. He never moved a piece until he had considered all of the possible consequences. The fellow had a gift."

Calm down," said Hansi Askgaard, putting a comforting arm around her sister. "There's no need to fret like this."

"But the man was *murdered*, Hansi."

"So I understand."

"Right here in the castle."

"Uncle Bror will have the killer caught and executed."

"That's not the point."

"Then what is?"

"It's an omen," said Sigbrit Olsen, eyes widening. "Rolfe Harling was the man who arranged the match. His death is a warning sign."

"You are being silly."

"It is, Hansi. There's no other way of looking at it. We are only days away from the wedding and *this* happens. It must be a portent."

"It's an unfortunate coincidence, that's all."

Like everyone else in the castle, Sigbrit had been horrified to hear of the murder and she had hurried back to her apartment and locked herself in. When word had reached Hansi, she had come at once to be with her sister but she was finding it difficult to soothe her. She eased Sigbrit down into a chair.

"Try to put it out of your mind," Hansi advised.

"How can I?"

"By thinking of something else."

"This has ruined everything."

"Only because you are letting it do so. An hour ago, you were in the middle of a happy gathering, meeting your future husband for the first time."

"I'd almost forgotten that," said Sigbrit, slightly dazed.

"But it must have been a wonderful experience for you."

"Well, yes . . . I suppose that it was."

"You might sound a bit more pleased," scolded Hansi gently. "I know that I would have been in your place. What was Lord Westfield like?"

Sigbrit shrugged. "He was . . . very pleasant."

"That tells me nothing. Everyone makes an effort to be pleasant on first acquaintance. What about his appearance? Is he handsome or ugly? Is he fair or dark? How was he attired? Tell me about his manner and his deportment. *Describe* him."

"He was somewhat older than I expected."

"But not ridiculously so."

"No, no," said Sigbrit. "Lord Westfield was spirited enough, I grant him that, though he was a little unsteady on his feet at first."

"Overwhelmed by the importance of the occasion."

"I know that I was, Hansi. I was trembling all over."

"That's only to be expected."

"He dresses well and has a distinct nobility about him."

"What of his features?"

"Tolerable."

"No more than that?"

"I did not really have chance to see," explained Sigbrit. "As soon as we'd been introduced, I was set on by all the ladies there. They were so inquisitive. For most of the evening, Lord Westfield and I were yards apart."

"That will soon change when you are married."

"I wonder."

"What do you mean?" asked Hansi, hearing the doubt in her sister's voice. "You can surely not be having second thoughts."

Sigbrit looked uncertain. Getting to her feet, she paced the room as she tried to weigh everything in the balance. Hansi watched her carefully, waiting in silence until her sister had reached a decision. Eventually, Sigbrit came to a halt.

"I think that the wedding will have to be postponed."

"But that's out of the question," said Hansi. "Everything has been arranged. King Christian will be arriving in a few days. What will he say when you tell him there's a delay?"

"He will understand. The murder has altered everything."

"It's a tragedy, I agree, and it could not have come at a worse moment. But it should not be allowed to affect the wedding, Sigbrit. After all, Master Harling was to play no part in the ceremony."

"He helped to bring Lord Westfield and me together. For that reason alone, he had to be there, Hansi. It was his right. That's why his death is so troubling. It fills me with foreboding."

"Then you must wrestle with such feelings."

"How can I?"

"You *wish* to be the new Lady Westfield, do you not?"

Sigbrit hesitated. "I think so."

"It's too late to change your mind now," said Hansi, taking her hand. "This business has upset you—it's upset us all—but it has no bearing on the wedding."

"I fear that it has. Someone is trying to stop this marriage."

"Then they must not be allowed to do so."

"What if they should strike again?"

Hansi was firm. "There is no risk whatsoever of that."

"How do you know?"

"Because I have faith in Uncle Bror," said Hansi. "He will know exactly what to do. He'll track down the killer immediately and have the villain hanged. Do as I do in a crisis, Sigbrit."

"And what's that?"

"Rely on Uncle Bror."

Bror Langberg shook him warmly by the hand and waved him to a chair before sitting on the other side of the table. Nicholas Bracewell was glad of the friendly reception. Langberg was the person in the castle who could help him most. They met in his apartment.

"Rolfe told me a lot about you," said Langberg approvingly.

"Really? We hardly ever spoke."

"He talked of you to Lord Westfield. In fact, they discussed several members of the company. Rolfe was cautious. He liked to know as much as he could about people with whom he was dealing."

"While giving away very little about himself."

"Quite so," said Langberg. "We think of reserve as an English failing but he turned it to advantage. He hid behind it so that he could study his fellow men and he was a perceptive judge. That's why he spoke so well of you, Master Bracewell."

Nicholas was skeptical. "I find it hard to believe."

"Oh, he did not do so out of affection. Rolfe could never bring himself to like you. But that's irrelevant. What he observed was your value to the company. When your ship was attacked, it was you who held the others together."

"Only because I had more experience than they."

"Considerably more experience. Your pedigree is enviable. You sailed around the world with Drake, I gather."

"That was a long time ago."

"The voyage was an inspiration to sailors everywhere."

"Were you one yourself, Master Langberg?"

"I'm Danish," said the other with a grin. "In a country like ours, made up of small islands, we are all sailors. However," he went on, becoming serious, "we are not here to talk about that."

"No," said Nicholas, "we both want the same thing and that's the early arrest of the man who stabbed Master Harling to death. I'm hoping that we may be able to help each other."

"So am I. Feel free to ask anything you wish."

"When was he last seen alive?"

"Earlier this evening," replied Langberg. "I saw him through my window, strolling around the courtyard."

"Alone?"

"Completely. He was not given to idle chatter with strangers."

"Or with anyone else," said Nicholas.

"He was a scholar. He liked his own company."

"For that reason," suggested Nicholas, "it's difficult to see why anyone should wish to kill him. He made extremely few friends but, by the same token, he made few enemies. The wonder is that he found two of them in this very castle."

"Two?"

"If my guess is correct."

"Go on, please."

"Master Harling would never have gone willingly into the case-mates. Why should he? It's cold and dark down there. I believe that he was killed elsewhere then carried down to that storage bay. It would have taken two men to get him there."

Langberg was impressed. "I never thought of that. I assumed that he had been enticed down there before being attacked. On re-flection, I admit, it's difficult to see what possible enticement could have been used."

"I'd make another guess, sir."

"Well?"

"The killer and his confederate are employed here in the castle. They not only knew where to hide the body. They were aware of the exact places in the casemates where Westfield's Men and where some of your soldiers were housed."

"That's true. Rolfe was discovered well away from either. No-body would have cause to go anywhere near the bay where the body was left. Lord Westfield was right about you, my friend," said Langberg with a smile. "He told me that you had a keen brain. You've dealt with murder before, I hear."

"Far too often."

"Well, you'll not be involved in the search for the killer this time. He and his accomplice must still be inside the castle. I'll turn the place inside out before I find them."

"What about tomorrow, Master Langberg?"

"Tomorrow?"

"We are due to perform in the town," said Nicholas.

"Then let the performance go ahead."

"You have no objection?"

"None at all," said Langberg. "I'll not let this crime interfere with your work. In fact, I'll do my best to keep the whole business within the walls of Kronborg. Entertain the town and you'll be helping us. You'll be giving the impression that everything is as it should be here."

"Lawrence Firethorn will be delighted to hear that."

"Nothing must be affected by this, Master Bracewell. If someone is trying to disrupt the wedding or hamper your troupe, they will fail. We must be defiant."

"I agree, sir."

Nicholas was reassured. He was also grateful for the readiness shown by the other to discuss the murder with him. Bror Langberg was a statesman who had the ear of the young king. Nicholas, on the other hand, was only a hired man with a foreign theater company yet his opinions were treated with respect. Langberg leaned forward.

"Why do *you* think that anyone would want Rolfe Harling dead?"

"I have no idea," said Nicholas, concealing the vague suspicions at the back of his mind. "Do you, sir?"

"Yes. I believe he was killed for his money."

"Money?"

"He must have had a substantial amount," Langberg went on, "and, being Rolfe, he would always carry it about his person. I know that your patron had rewarded him handsomely for his services and that he intended to travel extensively in Germany after the wedding, so he would need funds to do that. He would have been very much richer than the average scholar. No wonder his purse was missing when we searched the body."

"What of his room?"

"I had that locked as soon as word of the murder reached me."

"Might he not have concealed his money in there?"

"It's unlikely," said Langberg, rising to his feet, "but we can easily find out. Let's search the room this instant."

Nicholas was pleased to go with him. Desperate to learn more about Harling, he was glad of the opportunity to go through the man's effects. Striding along with his gown brushing the floor, Langberg led him along a series of corridors before turning a last corner. After a dozen paces or more, he stopped outside a room and unlocked it with a key on the ring that dangled from his belt. A single candle burned on the table. Snatching it up, Langberg used it to light all the other candles. Small and compact, the room was also clean and comfortable. They began a methodical search.

Rolfe Harling had traveled with relatively little luggage. Since he was less interested in clothing than in scholarship, he had far more books than anything else. Nicholas leafed through them and noted their titles. Langberg, meanwhile, scoured the room for hiding places but found none. Nor did he discover any cache of money. Nicholas was not looking for a purse. What he was after were documents that told him more about the murder victim, letters that might explain the reason for his visit to Germany, or revealing papers of another kind. He searched everywhere without success. What he did uncover, hidden away beneath a shirt, was a chess set with large, beautifully carved ivory pieces. They were the most expensive items in his baggage.

It was Langberg who eventually gave up the hunt.

"His purse is not here," he decided. "Did you find anything?"

"No," said Nicholas, shaking his head. "Nothing at all."

Occupying the room of a servant had a severe disadvantage and Anne Hendrik was made rudely aware of it. In their search for the killer, the castle guards did not stand on ceremony when they reached the servants' quarters. They simply barged into the rooms unannounced and looked in every nook and cranny. Even though she was a guest, Anne was told to stand in the corridor while her room was thoroughly searched and while—to her annoyance—one of the guards went through her wardrobe. Without explanation, they then moved on. It was only by speaking to one of the servants that Anne learned about the murder.

She was stunned. Like the others, she had not found Rolfe Harling in any way likable or forthcoming but she was still upset to hear of his death. Her compassion also went out to George Dart, who had had the misfortune to find the body. Knowing how sensitive and vulnerable he was, she could imagine the shock he had suffered. But her immediate sympathy was reserved for Nicholas Bracewell. If a killer was on the loose in the casemates, the book holder might be in danger. She had to reach him.

When the initial commotion had died down in the castle, therefore, she left her room and went downstairs to the courtyard. It was pitch-dark but a series of torches in iron holders threw dazzling patterns across the stone. Shivering in the cold, she walked swiftly toward the steps that led to the casemates. Before she could descend them, however, a guard came out of the shadows to block her way. Though she could not translate the curt Danish command, she understood it perfectly when it was reinforced with a drawn sword and a hostile gesture.

Forbidden to enter the casemates, Anne withdrew at once. If Nicholas and the others were still down there, they were at least being protected. She began to retrace her steps. But this time, instead of climbing the main staircase, she elected to use the back stairs that she had been shown. It was a fortunate decision. Though she had to grope her way up in the dark, she got to the top without difficulty. As she reached out for it, the door opened in front of her and a young woman in a hooded cloak came through it, holding a lighted candle. When she saw Anne, she gave her only a cursory look, clearly thinking her no more than a servant. Brushing past, she went down the steps.

Anne was bewildered. In that startling moment of recognition, she had beheld the beautiful face of Sigbrit Olsen. Eyes, nose, cheeks, chin, even the gloriously pale complexion, were identical to those in the cherished portrait carried by Lord Westfield. The only difference was that, in real life, the woman was slightly older. Evidently, she had lost none of her charms. It was perplexing. Since Lord Westfield had called his new bride a princess of Denmark, and since she was palpably from aristocratic stock, Anne was bound to wonder why such a noble lady was furtively using the back stairs reserved for the servants.

Westfield's Men set out from the castle next morning with a mixture of relief and jubilation. They were at long last able to stage a play. With their carts loaded to capacity, they rumbled through the Dark Gate and into the sunshine beyond. They had not forgotten the fate of Rolfe Harling, and they spared him the tribute of a passing sigh, but their minds then turned to what lay ahead. Having been on tour many times, they were accustomed to performing in town squares, though, usually, when it was rather warmer. But there was no carping. The actors had an opportunity to entertain a large audience and they were determined to create a memorable experience for them.

Nicholas Bracewell always supervised the erection of a stage, the hanging of curtains, and the setting of scenery for the beginning of any play. As a rule, he and Thomas Skillen had a bevy of assistant stage-keepers to help them, but George Dart was the only survivor from the team and could not cope alone. Most of the company therefore rolled up their sleeves and offered their services. The only exceptions were Lawrence Firethorn, too busy meeting the mayor, and Barnaby Gill, who spurned manual labor because it might damage his hands. When the makeshift stage had been set up, a tiring-house was constructed behind it where the actors could change into their costumes and wait for their entrances. Predictably, it was Gill who had a criticism.

"I refuse to change while a lady is present," he declared.

"Anne is our tireman," said Nicholas. "We need someone to make repairs to our costumes and she has nimble fingers."

"That's what Barnaby is afraid of," taunted Owen Elias. "There's nothing he fears more when he takes his breeches down than a lady's nimble fingers."

"Theater is the sole preserve of men!" maintained Gill.

"Then find me one to look after the costumes," said Nicholas.

"George Dart."

"He already has a dozen other tasks allotted to him."

"Oswald Megson."

"And so does he. Necessity compels us to break with tradition, Barnaby. We play *Cupid's Folly* this afternoon. In the rough-and-tumble of the village scenes, costumes always get torn and buttons always get lost. Anne will be waiting in the tiring-house to stitch and mend." Nicholas raised his voice. "Does anyone object to that?"

"No!" came the collective response.

"It's wrong," said Gill peevishly. "It's against all custom."

Elias cackled. "Seeing you half-naked in the presence of a woman is against all decency," he jested merrily, "but we'll bear it for the sake of the company. Remember who we are, Barnaby—Westfield's Men. We do not follow tradition—we create it."

When Gill tried to argue on, several voices shouted him down.

Benches were set out in front of the stage and wooden screens were placed in rectangular shape to mark out the auditorium and keep out those who did not pay. The sea breeze was as stiff as ever but the buildings around the square deflected its bite and the sun provided a stark brightness that could easily be mistaken for warmth. Absorbed in their work, the actors did not even notice the weather. *Cupid's Folly* was a staple comedy in their repertoire, and as such it needed little rehearsal. Nevertheless, Firethorn insisted on taking his company through some of the longer scenes, giving them chance to lose themselves in their parts while, at the same time, arousing the curiosity of everyone who heard the raised voices behind the screens. The murder on the previous evening was soon a distant memory.

During a break in rehearsal, Firethorn spoke to the book holder.

"I hope that we've chosen the right play for them, Nick."

"*Cupid's Folly* is ideal," said Nicholas. "It's bursting with life and laughter. But its main virtue is that it's easy for a foreign audience to understand. It has plenty of dances and comic brawls that need no words to explain them."

"It's also about a folly common to every nation."

"Yes, Lawrence. Love can make a fool of any man. The Danes know well that Cupid's arrows can sometimes go astray."

"They have an example of it right before their eyes."

"Do they?"

"Of course," said Firethorn. "They merely have to look at what is happening at the castle. Lord Westfield is yet another victim of Cupid. Whenever he talks about his bride, he becomes a babbling imbecile."

"I excuse the lady of that. She is hardly marrying for love."

"Could *any* woman be enchanted by our patron?"

"You are unkind."

"Any respectable woman, that is."

"I think that Lord Westfield has a battered charm."

"His charm lies largely in his title and—now that he has finally shaken off his creditors—in his purse. Why else would this princess of his even deign to look at him?"

"Stranger marriages have been arranged."

"Most of them founder in the bedchamber."

"We must pray that that does not happen in this case."

"Why?"

"Because it affects our survival," said Nicholas. "Our patron has no heir. With a young wife, he must surely hope to produce children so that one of them can inherit. Should he fail in that ambition, his greater age and constant resort to pleasure mean that he'll certainly die before his wife. Our future would then rest with Lady Westfield."

Firethorn pondered. "That's a worrying thought, Nick," he said at length, "and one that had not even entered my head. Our patron will not live forever. Unless his widow takes his place, we'll vanish into thin air like so much smoke from a fire."

"Barnaby would rebel against a female patron."

"He rebels against everything we do."

"But chiefly against our use of a woman in the company. If he balks at Anne acting as our tireman for a few days, what will he say if we became, in time, Lady Westfield's company?"

"I hope we never find out," said Firethorn anxiously. "Thank you for raising the matter, Nick. There's a moral here, I fancy. We need to curry favor with the new Lady Westfield."

"The best way to do that is to woo her with our art."

"*The Princess of Denmark* will achieve that end. Edmund has tailored it carefully to her particular taste and I will pluck at her heartstrings with my performance. The play is an act of seduction in itself. But I cannot say the same of this afternoon's offering," Firethorn said, looking across at the stage. "*Cupid's Folly* is fit only for rougher palates."

"I disagree. Some of its wit can be savored by anyone."

"It's not a dish dainty enough to set before a lady."

"Have no fear on that account, Lawrence. She will not be here."

"How do you know?"

"Master Langberg told me as much," Nicholas confided. "It seems that Sigbrit Olsen was so disturbed by the murder at the castle that she will not even stir from her room."

But she cannot stay there forever," pleaded Lord Westfield, wringing his hands. "I need to *see* her."

"You saw her last night, my lord."

"Yes, Master Langberg, but that's about all I did so. Sigbrit and I were kept apart in that crowd. I want some private conference."

"And so you shall," said Bror Langberg. "In time."

"Where is she now?"

"Locked in her apartment, afraid to come out until the killer has been caught. Sigbrit sees what happened as an evil portent."

"It was simple misfortune, nothing more."

"But it occurred so close to the wedding."

"I'll not let that steer us off course," said Lord Westfield, jaw thrust out with determination. "I grieve for poor Rolfe, of course, and I look for the early capture of the villain who stabbed him. But he would not want his demise to throw our wedding into jeopardy."

"That will not happen," vowed Langberg. "I give you my word."

It was late morning and they were sitting in his apartment. Lord Westfield had come with a smile of anticipatory delight, certain that he would now be allowed to spend time alone with Sigbrit. Instead, he was as before being politely rebuffed. The murder in the casemates had put her tantalizingly out of his reach. He was more exasperated than ever. Langberg tried to appease him.

"I'm glad that you came, my lord," he said, getting up from his chair. "As it happens, I have a gift for you."

"A gift?"

"Strictly speaking, it is a form of bequest."

"From whom?"

"Our mutual friend, Rolfe Harling, of course." Langberg indicated the large oak chest in the corner. Set out on it was a board with the ivory chessmen in their rightful positions. "He told me how often you and he played during the voyage here."

"Only when the sea was calm enough. Most of the time, it was so rough that it tossed the pieces from the table." Lord Westfield crossed over to the chest. "This brings back so many memories. Chess defined the man. It's a game of subtlety, intellect, and quiet ruthlessness. Rolfe had all those qualities."

"He left other things as well—and you are welcome to have any of them—but I thought that this would be the most appropriate memento of him."

"It is, Master Langberg."

"As for his many books—"

"No, no," said Lord Westfield, interrupting him. "I'm not inclined to reading. Keep those learned tomes of his or, better still, donate them to a university. Rolfe would have endorsed that."

"An excellent suggestion, my lord."

"What about his killer? Has any arrest been made?"

"Not yet," replied Langberg. "We have had to widen the search outside the castle. One of your fellows, Nicholas Bracewell, made an astute observation."

"He's the shrewdest man in the company."

"I can well believe it. He argued that Rolfe was killed elsewhere then carried down to the casemates to be hidden. It would have taken two men to get him there—the killer and his accomplice."

"So?"

"Not long before the discovery was made, two individuals were seen leaving the castle yesterday evening. We know their names."

"Who were they?"

"Two cooks recently employed here," said Langberg. "At least, that's what the steward thought they were when he engaged the two men. It now appears as if they sought work in the castle so that they could lie in wait for Rolfe Harling."

"How did they know that he was coming?"

"That's what I long to find out, my lord, and I mean to do so. We've a dungeon in the casemates with some instruments of torture that can loosen any tongues." Langberg's eyes blazed and his voice became a growl. "I'll squeeze the truth out of them, whatever it takes. They robbed me of a good friend."

"And me."

"They also threw the castle into confusion only days before a wedding is due to take place. I'll never forgive them for that. My niece should have been allowed to look forward to the event in peace and tranquillity. Instead of which," Langberg went on angrily, "Sigbrit is cowering in her room like a frightened animal."

"Where are the villains now?"

"Somewhere in the town, I suspect. A search has begun for them." Langberg forced a smile. "I deeply regret all this, my lord. Pardon my rage. If you knew how much time I have spent on the arrangements here, you would understand it."

"I share it, Master Langberg."

"Let us think of cheerier things."

His visitor grimaced. "I do not know of any."

"Then your memory is wondrous short. Westfield's Men are to perform in the town this afternoon and I intend to be there. So will you, I daresay."

"No," said the other. "*Cupid's Folly* is a diverting piece but I'm in no mood for pastoral comedy. Had I been able to take Sigbrit, it would have been a different matter. If she remains here, then so do I."

"As you wish, my lord." Langberg turned to the chess set. "Shall I have this carried to your apartment?"

"Please. It will help me to remember Rolfe. He loved the game so much that he sometimes played against himself. Imagine that."

"I can imagine it very easily."

"I never stood the slightest chance of defeating him. His mind was always several moves ahead."

"When you played together," said Langberg, picking up a white pawn to examine it, "which color did Rolfe prefer?"

"Oh, black," replied Lord Westfield. "He always chose black."

Cupid's Folly was an unqualified success. Its simplicity made it easily accessible to an audience that was largely ignorant of the English language, and its broad comedy had an instant appeal. In the central role, Barnaby Gill was superb and it was to Lawrence Firethorn's credit that he allowed his rival to reap such a harvest of applause. Pierced by Cupid's arrow, Rigormortis, a doddering old man, fell in love with every woman he saw, and yet, paradoxically, he spurned the one female who adored him. Three of the apprentices transformed themselves into pretty country wenches, pursued in turn by the love-struck Rigormortis. The fourth, John Tallis, relegated to the ranks of older women since his voice had broken, played the part of Ursula, the ugly, slothful termagant who conceived a fierce passion for the old man and, literally, chased him around the stage.

Gill's comic gifts enlivened the whole afternoon and his jigs were greeted with a riot of laughter. The rest of the company also shone. Firethorn was Lord Hayfever, a frolicsome lord of the manor, forever sneezing when in the presence of women. Owen Elias was a lecherous priest whose attempted pounces on the wenches always ended in disaster; James Ingram and Frank Quilter were honest yokels who rescued the womenfolk from all the attacks on their virtue; and Edmund Hoode, a beacon of decency throughout, was the generous farmer who invited everyone to a feast at his home. It had fallen to Hoode to speak the prologue that set the tone of the comedy.

> *Come, friends, and let us leave the city's noise*
> *To seek the quieter paths of country joys.*
> *For verdant pastures more delight the eye*
> *With cows and sheep and fallow deer hereby,*

With horse and hound, pursuing to their lair,
The cunning fox or nimble-footed hare,
With merry maids and lusty lads most jolly
Who find their foolish fun in Cupid's folly.

At the end of the play, the whole company took part in a dance around a maypole, an example of English rural tradition that the spectators found both hilarious yet endearing. Two hours of magic had taken place in the square at Elsinore. When it was over, the ovation lasted for several minutes. Everyone on the benches rose to acclaim the troupe, nobody smacking their palms together with more zest than Bror Langberg and his wife, Johanna, captivated by the brilliance of the actors and delighted with an event that took attention away from the brutal murder at the castle.

Firethorn may have led out his actors to take their bows but it was Gill who deserved most of the praise and who lapped it up with unashamed selfishness. When the cheers began to fade and they withdrew reluctantly to the tiring-house, the clown was at his most self-absorbed, still basking in the wonderful reception he had been given by the townspeople.

"Well done, Barnaby!" said Nicholas Bracewell. "I've never seen you play the part better. You were magnificent."

"I am *always* magnificent," returned Gill haughtily.

"Yes," said Firethorn. "Magnificently good or magnificently bad. That's your weakness, Barnaby. You have no middle way. You are either conquering hero or catastrophe."

"Whereas you occupy a lowly station between the two," came the immediate riposte. "You are rooted in mediocrity, Lawrence. Having no greatness yourself, you despise it in others. Well," said Gill with a lordly wave of the hand, "I can be magnanimous. Since you earned no compliments onstage this afternoon, I'll spare you some of mine for I had far more than I need."

"Then perhaps you can spare a compliment for Anne as well," suggested Nicholas, "and couple it with an apology. Your gown was torn apart in that tavern brawl in the second act. Had it not been hastily sewn together again by Anne, you would have been dressed like a scarecrow."

"My performance did not depend on a well-sewn costume."

"But it was helped by Anne's skill as a tireman."

Gill was dismissive. "I know nothing of that."

"Then you should," said Elias, irritated by Gill's disdain. "You are ready to accept gratitude from an audience but Rigormortis is seized with *rigor mortis* when you are asked to offer some yourself." There was a loud murmur of approval from the others. "Today, we witnessed a historic event. It's the first time that a woman—a delightful one, at that—has helped Westfield's Men to stage a play."

"I hope that it will be the last," said Gill.

"Shame on you!"

"Women have no rightful place in drama."

"Then why do you insist on behaving like one?" said Firethorn spikily. "Everyone knows that this company consists of actors, apprentices, hired men—and an old woman named Barnaby Gill."

Gill's snarled protest was drowned out by mocking laughter.

Though the play had been a triumph, they now had to turn to the more mundane task of dismantling their stage and putting their scenery, properties, and costumes back on the carts. Only then could they drift off to the White Hart to celebrate. During the bustle of activity, Gill was conspicuously absent and Firethorn was taken aside by the mayor and by Bror Langberg to receive thanks on behalf of his company. Everyone else worked with commitment. When the others had departed for the inn, Nicholas was left behind with Anne Hendrik. Embracing her warmly, he gave her a kiss of gratitude.

"We could not have managed without you, Anne," he said.

"You'll have to do so when I leave on Sunday."

"No, no. We'll keep you with us forever."

"Not if I cause such discontent," she said.

"Barnaby is the only one who complained."

"One or two of the others felt uncomfortable about having me there. I could sense it. On the other hand," she went on happily, "I'd not have missed a chance like this. It was an education for me. I've seen dozens of plays onstage at the Queen's Head but I had no idea that so much went on behind the scenes."

"That's where the real work is done, Anne."

"Most of it by you, Nick. The actors would not know when to make their entrances had you not drawn up that guide for them and pinned it to the wall."

"I have to know each play scene by scene," he told her, "so that master list is for my benefit as much as theirs. And you were not the only student here. Both us were educated today. You saw something of my work and I, yours."

"Oh, I do little enough with a needle these days."

"You did enough to save us this afternoon. *Cupid's Folly* was all the better for having you here. The pity of it is that we did not have our patron in the audience with Sigbrit Olsen. But, according to Master Langberg, the lady is so distressed by what happened in the casemates yesterday that she is too frightened to leave her room."

"Is that what he said?"

"Yes, Anne. I spoke with him before earlier."

"Then we have another oddity."

"What do you mean?"

"Yesterday evening," she replied, "well after the body had been found, I saw her descending the back stairs to the courtyard."

Nicholas was taken aback. "Are you *sure*?"

"Nobody could mistake a face like that, Nick."

"I know—I had a brief glimpse of it myself."

"If the lady were so alarmed by the murder, she'd have stayed behind a locked door. What was she doing on the stairs?"

"I wish I knew, Anne. It's more than odd—it's very peculiar."

"Did her uncle know about it? I wonder."

"I doubt it," said Nicholas, "but it's not our place to tell him about the incident. Elsinore castle is certainly full of mysteries and this is only the latest one. I hope we have no more to vex us." He looked around. "Our work is finished here, Anne. Would our tire-man like to join the others?"

"If you think I'll be made welcome."

"You'll be feted." They walked off in the direction of the White Hart. "They *needed* today," he said. "They needed something to take their minds off the murder of Rolfe Harling and remind them that they belong to a theater company of rare distinction. Think of our setbacks. The Queen's Head was burned down, pirates attacked us in the North Sea, we were consigned to those gloomy casemates, and the man who arranged this marriage at our patron's behest was murdered."

"Ill fortune from start to finish," she remarked.

"At least, it *has* finished, Anne. The horror is finally over."

"Are you certain?"

"I feel it in my bones," he said, slipping an arm around her, "and they are never wrong. Westfield's Men have come through a time of trial. We are safe at last."

An hour later, the *Speedwell* came in sight of her destination. Two of the passengers viewed the distant town with special interest. Josias Greet spat into the sea and gave a lopsided grin.

"That's Elsinore ahead of us, Ben."

"Yes," said Ryden, "and not before time."

"What do we do when we land?"

"Kill him as soon as possible and get away from here."

[CHAPTER ELEVEN]

Celebrations in the White Hart went on for a couple of hours. It was almost like being back in the Queen's Head except that the landlord was friendly, the beer Danish, and the unstinting praise given in more than one language as spectators from various countries crowded in to thank the actors for coming to Elsinore. Among those who had seen the play, the vast majority fawned on Barnaby Gill, the erstwhile Rigormortis, and his admirers were puzzled by the sharp contrast between his comic brilliance onstage and his melancholy when off it. Everyone in the company enjoyed his share of free drink and congratulation. Westfield's Men felt accepted, honored, and feted. As they went back to Kronborg in their carts, there was such a general sense of well-being that they broke spontaneously into song.

Their buoyancy did not last. As soon as they entered the castle through the Dark Gate, the atmosphere changed. Guards eyed them with resentment and made derisive remarks. The smiles that had greeted their arrival were long gone. They were made to feel like the outsiders they were, a despised minority who had brought trouble and discomfort to Elsinore.

"Now we know what is like to be strangers in a country," said Nicholas Bracewell. "Your husband must have felt this animosity when he came to England."

"Dutch immigrants still arouse great bitterness there," said Anne, "as we know only too well. But I do not understand why there has been such a change of mood here."

"Put yourself in their position. Everything was in order until Westfield's Men arrived. Then a murder is committed, the castle is in a state of chaos, and some of the garrison are forced out of their hut so that we can move into it."

"They surely cannot blame you for the murder, Nick."

"One of our number was the victim. That's all they see. As a result, every soldier is on duty for long hours and those who occupied our hut have been made to sleep in the casemates. We are highly unpopular with them," said Nicholas, "and we are not exempt from suspicion. Until the killer is caught, everyone in the castle is now under scrutiny."

"Even me?"

"Yes, Anne. And you have another bad mark against you."

"Do I?"

"You are our tireman," he said with a smile, "and therefore tarred with the same brush."

They reached their hut. Nicholas made sure that everything was unloaded from the carts and stowed under cover for the night. He then went off to find their patron so that he could report what had happened. Seated beside a flagon of wine, Lord Westfield was in his apartment, seething with frustration at being unable to talk to his future wife. The redness of his cheek and the occasional slurring in his speech indicated that it was not the first flagon of wine. He gave Nicholas an offhand welcome.

"Why have you come?" he asked dully.

"Lawrence thought that you might like to hear about our success in the town this afternoon, my lord."

"Well, there has been no success here, I can tell you. My day has been a story of constant failure. I pine, I mope, I fret. They will not let me near her. My princess is here in the castle and she refuses to see anyone, not even the man who has pledged to marry her. It's too much," he insisted. "She needs me, Nicholas. I could comfort her."

"You will have time enough to do that after the wedding."

"I want to see Sigbrit *now*."

"Master Langberg says that she is too distressed by the murder to venture from her chamber."

"We are all distressed," contended the other, "none more so than me. Heavens above, I was Rolfe's friend. I liked him, I engaged him, I had complete faith in him to find me a suitable wife."

"And that's exactly what he did, my lord."

"Then where is she?"

"Trying to overcome the shock of what happened."

"I should be with Sigbrit to help her. Instead of that, I am left alone and made to feel more like a prisoner here than a guest."

Nicholas waited while Lord Westfield took a long sip from his glass. He saw no point in telling him what he had learned from Anne. It would only create another wave of self-pity if his patron knew that Sigbrit Olsen had been seen out of her apartment not long after the body had been discovered. Nicholas was baffled by her behavior. Lord Westfield would be horrified. The book holder tried to cheer him up.

"Westfield's Men were supreme today," he said. "*Cupid's Folly* was received with great acclaim in the town and your name was spoken of with thanks and admiration."

"Not by Sigbrit, alas."

"You would have been proud of your company, my lord. They were peerless—and not simply because they lacked their patron." The pun went unnoticed by Lord Westfield. "We missed you."

"I was too steeped in sadness to watch a comedy, especially one that ends with a maypole dance and a wedding. It would have rankled. Tragedy alone would match my disposition."

"We play again tomorrow, my lord."

"Then do not count on my presence."

"Master Langberg was there today with his wife. They both seemed to enjoy the performance. And the mayor thought it the funniest thing he had ever seen. Barnaby was unsurpassed."

"I need more than a prancing clown to lift my spirits," said Lord Westfield. "The only thing that would make me attend tomorrow would be the joy of having my princess of Denmark on my arm."

"By tomorrow, the lady may have recovered."

"So may I." He drained his glass and hauled himself to his feet. "I am sorry to be so liverish with you, Nicholas. It's not only Sigbrit who has brought this misery on. I mourn Rolfe Harling. The truth is that I feel, to some degree, culpable for his death."

"Why?"

"Because I was responsible for bringing him here."

"You were not to know that someone was plotting to kill him. Shed any pangs of guilt you may have, my lord. This crime should not weigh on your conscience."

"Nevertheless, it does."

"I still believe the explanation for his death lies somewhere in Master Harling's private life. The truth will only be revealed when we know who killed him."

"But we already do know."

Nicholas was surprised. "That's news to me, my lord."

"According to Bror Langberg, two men were seen sneaking away from here not long before the body was found. They had worked in the castle kitchens, it seems."

"Is there any proof that they committed the murder?"

"No, but it's reasonable to assume that they were the villains. They've not been seen since. The search has been widened to include the town itself."

"Ah," said Nicholas, recalling the many soldiers he had seen patrolling Elsinore that day. "That accounts for something that came to my notice. Yet it still does not solve the crime."

"The names of the killers are at least known."

"Possibly, my lord, and I hope that is the case. But there are other reasons that could prompt two men to flee the castle. They should not be condemned outright. Perhaps they were badly treated here or paid too poorly for work they disliked doing. Perhaps they had business that called them back home."

"Bror Langberg was convinced that they were the culprits."

"Then I would like to talk to them if they are caught."

"He intends to extract confessions under torture."

"All that interests me is their motive," said Nicholas. "Why did they kill Rolfe Harling? Why was he singled out and why was such violence used against him?"

"I wish I knew, Nicholas. None of it makes sense. A more innocuous creature never walked the earth, that's for certain."

Though he endorsed the statement with a nod, Nicholas had some reservations. He did not wish to unsettle Lord Westfield by voicing them, however, so he held his tongue. His gaze fell on the chess set that stood on a small table in the corner.

"You've been playing chess, I see," he remarked.

"I've been trying to," said the other, crossing to the table. "I was so bored with my own company that I sought solace in a game. I played against myself the way that I'd seen Rolfe do often but I lack both his patience and his cunning."

"The pieces are carved from the finest ivory."

"It seems that they are bequeathed to me."

"Did Master Harling have no family?"

"None that I know of," said Lord Westfield, running a hand through his hair. "Rolfe loved his work. He was a perpetual student, lonely and contemplative." He looked up. "Do you play chess?"

"Not well, my lord," admitted Nicholas. "I learned aboard the *Golden Hind*—or the *Pelican,* as she was when we first set sail. The ship's carpenter had made a chess set out of wood. That's why I was curious when I first saw this one."

"Curious?"

"The chessmen are so large, three or four times bigger than the ones we used. Our set could be slipped into a man's pocket and so could the board. Not this one. Then there is the expense."

"It was Rolfe's only indulgence—apart from his books, of course. He certainly did not spend money on his wardrobe," Lord Westfield said with a laugh, "and the pleasures of London were unknown to him. He bought the set in Italy." He handed a white bishop to Nicholas. "As you can see, the workmanship is exquisite."

Nicholas inspected it. "So delicate yet so solid," he said, turning it over. "I can see why he treasured the set."

"He kept it by him at all times."

"Did the game mean so much to him?"

"So it would appear."

A memory surfaced. "You told me earlier, my lord, that Master Harling had been recommended to you by a trusted friend." Nicholas returned the white bishop to him. "Could his name, by any chance, be Sir Robert Cecil?"

Lord Westfield was astonished. "It could, as it happens. How on earth did you guess that?"

Then the ugly woman, Ursula, leapt out from behind a tree and chased him around the stage until he tripped and fell into the horse trough with a splash." Johanna Langberg burst into laughter again as she remembered the scene. It was some time before she was able to continue. "After that," she said, composing herself, "Rigormortis put the three wenches aside and swore that he loved only Ursula. They were duly married."

"You clearly enjoyed the play, Aunt Johanna," said Sigbrit.

"It was a comical feast."

"What of Uncle Bror?"

"He loved it as much as the rest of us, Sigbrit. My one regret is that you were not there to share our pleasure."

"My mind was too troubled."

"*Cupid's Folly* would have dispelled all your cares."

"Sigbrit was better off here," said Hansi Askgaard. "She is not inclined to company at the moment, Aunt Johanna. It's only because I'm her sister that I'm allowed in here."

"You were not allowed, Hansi," corrected Sigbrit mildly. "You were wanted and welcomed. And so are you, Aunt Johanna."

The three women were in Sigbrit's apartment. Evening shadows had lengthened and several candles had been lit. The ones that burned beside Sigbrit illumined a face that was warped by a deep frown, pursed lips, and eyes ringed by fatigue. She looked as if she had had no sleep at all the previous night. Having listened to her aunt's account of the performance, she forced herself to show an interest.

"You say that Ursula was an ugly woman?"

"Yes," replied Johanna. "She had the features of a pig."

"Yet she was really a boy in disguise."

"That was the wonder of it, Sigbrit. I knew that he was only an apprentice but, within five minutes, he had persuaded me that he was a real woman. It was so with the others. They were such pretty country wenches that I felt they simply had to be young girls. But, no—they were artful boys."

"One of them is to play *you*, Sigbrit," said Hansi.

Her sister was alarmed. "Me?"

"That's what Uncle Bror told me. A new play has been written in your honor. *The Princess of Denmark* is dedicated to you, and Lord Westfield has asked that the apprentice playing the heroine should resemble his bride as closely as possible."

"But he has never seen me."

"Your portrait will have been shown to him."

"Yes," said Johanna, "and he will have further instruction from your future husband. Now that he has met you, Lord Westfield will be able to describe you in every detail."

"This is all very well, Aunt Johanna," said Sigbrit, "but I am very uneasy at the thought that we will all be sitting at a play while a killer is still at liberty in the castle."

"But he is not."

"He's been caught?"

"He and his accomplice very soon will be."

"It was the work of two men?"

"So it transpires," said Hansi. "Fearing arrest for the murder, two of our cooks fled from the castle. Uncle Bror has sent search parties into the town. So you no longer need to hide away in here, Sigbrit. You may breathe easily again and—yes—you may now enjoy watching *The Princess of Denmark* without the merest touch of guilt. By the time that it's performed, the villains will be safely under lock and key."

"So you can devote all your attention to the wedding," said Johanna happily. Her niece's worried expression remained. "Learn to smile again, Sigbrit," she urged. "Show pleasure. That's the least a husband can expect from you."

"He'd get more than a smile if he dedicated a play to me," said Hansi with a shrill laugh. "I can think of nothing more wonderful than to see myself portrayed onstage."

Sigbrit shuddered. "The very idea unnerves me."

"Why?"

"Because it raises me up to a position I have no desire to hold. I love the theater and I admire actors immensely but I do not want one of them to pretend to be me." She bit her lip before going on. "Thus it stands. I married my first husband out of love. Ingmar and I needed no play to mark the occasion, still less the presence of the king. We were enough for each other."

"This is a different kind of marriage," counseled her aunt.

"I know. I am taking a husband out of duty rather than love."

"Duty comes first. Love will surely follow."

"Why does Lord Westfield have to make such a spectacle of the whole event? Yes, yes," Sigbrit added before they could reply, "I know how pleased I was when I first heard that his actors would be coming here with him. But not anymore, alas. I'm overwhelmed by what lies ahead. The very title of the play bothers me."

Hansi stared. "What is wrong with *The Princess of Denmark*?"

"Two things," replied her sister. "First, I am not a real princess and have no wish to be treated as one. Second, and more importantly, the title reminds me of my birthright. I was born and raised here. I do not want to live in exile in England."

"But it will not be exile, Sigbrit."

"No," said Johanna, moving across to put an arm around her. "We will visit you so often that you'll imagine you are back here in Elsinore. Besides, you will not be going alone. You'll be taking maids and servants with you to England. They'll ensure that you are able to speak your own language every day." Johanna stood back. "Your uncle has worked sedulously on your behalf, Sigbrit. He acted purely out of love for you. Conquer these silly impulses that you have." Her smile congealed. "You do not want to let us all down, do you?"

Sigbrit capitulated. "No, Aunt Johanna."

Lawrence Firethorn was already regretting his decision to stage a play that gave prominence to the one man in the company whom he disliked. It was almost impossible to put Firethorn in the shade but Barnaby Gill had managed it that afternoon and it was like an open wound. Firethorn was in continuous pain. As he sat in his room with Nicholas Bracewell and Edmund Hoode, that pain could still be heard clearly in his voice.

"Barnaby was a disgrace to the profession," he argued.

"Nobody in the audience would have thought that," said Hoode with quiet impartiality. "They hailed him, Lawrence."

"What they hailed were his mistakes. He rewrote the play."

"To great effect."

"I'm surprised to hear a playwright condone such recklessness. Had *Cupid's Folly* been your work, Edmund, you'd have squawked like a chicken at what Barnaby did. He cut out lines that were there and inserted those that were not. Schooled to sing two songs, he decided that four were in order. And jigs that should have lasted for only two minutes went on for at least three times that length."

"Only because the spectators liked them so much."

"That's no excuse."

"Give him his due—Barnaby dazzled on that stage today."

"Dazzled!" roared Firethorn. "Do you dare to admire all that face-pulling, arm-waving, and blithe disregard of the play as written? Really, Edmund! You disappoint me." He swung round to the book holder. "Teach him, Nick. You know better than anyone else how Barnaby butchered the lines. Support me here."

Nicholas was tactful. "I think it of more use to talk about the play we stage tomorrow than the one we performed today. It's true that liberties were taken with *Cupid's Folly* but the audience were not aware of it. What they saw, they liked. Why argue about it?"

"Because it goes to the very heart of an actor's code. Our duty is to serve the playwright. When he creates a wonderful role, it behooves us to perform it as set down. Do you agree, Edmund?"

"Yes," said Hoode. "Up to a point."

"Nick?"

"The mark of a great actor," Nicholas suggested, "is that he can enhance the quality of his character by bringing all his skills to bear upon it. Whereas you do it by taking the role exactly as it is written and enlarging its compass, Barnaby prefers to adopt a much freer approach."

"Freer and more destructive."

"You cannot argue with applause, Lawrence."

"I can if it's grossly misplaced."

"Then we will be here all night," complained Hoode, normally the most quiescent of people. "If you insist on picking over each line of *Cupid's Folly*, then I'll to bed forthwith."

"Stay, Edmund," said Nicholas as his friend tried to get up. "I'm sure that Lawrence sees the futility of protesting about something that it's impossible to change. One play is gone, a second remains."

"The third will be the crowning achievement," said Firethorn with beaming certitude. "When I stride the boards in *The Princess of Denmark,* I'll reduce Barnaby to complete invisibility. Thank you, Nick. Your advice is timely. The past is past. Westfield's Men must look to the future."

"The immediate future is rosy. We had the Danish equivalent of five pounds from the mayor, and we took a tidy sum at the gate. We'll match that tomorrow with *The Wizard Earl,* then there will be an honorarium here at the castle. Beyond that is an invitation to visit Copenhagen, where, Bror Langberg tells me, we may play for a week."

"Then all our expenses are covered," said Hoode.

"And we'll have tasty profits to count," said Firethorn.

"Do not rush to spend them too soon," warned Nicholas. "When we sail back to England, we may have need of any surplus to see us through the lean months ahead. Westfield's Men will be without a home. Our landlord has closed the door on us at the Queen's Head."

"He'll open it again when you work on him," said Hoode.

"Alexander Marwood may be proof against my entreaties this time, Edmund. I think that we should brace ourselves for the worst."

"It's not like you to play the pessimist, Nick."

"No," said Firethorn, "you are ever wont to sound a cheering note. But have no fears of our lice-ridden rogue of a landlord. I've shown due care for the future of the company and found a way to confound that miserable, sheep-faced, vile-breathed knave."

"What have you done?" asked Nicholas.

"I set Margery onto him."

* * *

Among her many virtues were resilience and tenacity. Repulsed at her first attempt and stunned by the news that Westfield's Men would be ousted from the Queen's Head by legal means, Margery Firethorn did not give up. She sought out the man who was behind the vindictive decision, and since Isaac Dunmow lived in York, she made intensive inquiries until she learned that someone in London was acting for him. That information eventually took her to Anthony Rooker's office in Thames Street. Wearing her best dress for the occasion, she was at her most polite.

"I am sorry to intrude on you, Master Rooker," she began, "but I come on an errand of mercy. My name is Margery Firethorn and I have the privilege of being married to the finest actor in London."

"I am pleased for you, dear lady," said Rooker, "though I fail to see why you are here. Since I am no playgoer, the details of your domestic life have no interest for me."

"I'm here to talk about Westfield's Men."

"Ah!"

"You may well say that, sir. Are you going to offer me a seat?"

Rooker was a busy man with sheaves of documents waiting on the desk in front of him for attention. At the same time, however, he had a natural courtesy that had not entirely been blunted by his life as a merchant. He felt obliged to offer his visitor a seat and to hear her out. As she sat down, Margery bestowed her sweetest smile on him.

"You have the look of a kind man, Mr. Rooker."

"There's little room for kindness in my world, I fear."

"I understand that you work for Isaac Dunmow."

"Not *for* him," he said with unforced dignity. "I am master of my own affairs and work for nobody. There was a time when Isaac and I were partners, and because of that, I have done him a favor from time to time."

"It's one of those favors that brought me here."

He was wary. "Really? How can you possibly know what passes between Isaac and me? Such things are confidential, Mistress Firethorn, and no concern of yours."

"Then perhaps you should know that I have children to feed and servants to pay. I can do neither if my husband is prevented from practicing his craft at the Queen's Head. The fate of many men is involved here, Master Rooker, and they are all very dear to me."

"It's not my function in life to provide work for actors."

"You are ready enough to deprive them of it."

"This is not my decision. Speak to Isaac Dunmow."

Margery's bosom swelled. "I wish that I could, sir, but even my voice—loud as it can be—will not reach York. You represent him here. I expect answers from you."

"Then you expect the impossible. My hands are tied."

"A moment ago, you were the master of your own affairs," she pointed out. "I know how many warehouses you own and how many men you employ, Master Rooker. Only a wealthy man could afford an office like this," she went on, taking in the whole room with a gesture. "You are nobody's representative, sir. I see independence in your eye."

Rooker sighed. "Deliver your speech, Mistress Firethorn."

"I have no speech. I simply present you with the evidence."

"Of what?"

"Spite, malice, and cruelty."

"They're not of my making."

"I know that," she said. "I take you for a fair-minded man and ask you to give an honest judgment here. Do you think that Master Dunmow is being vengeful?"

"I have no opinion in the matter."

"Clearly, you do, sir."

"What do you mean?"

"If you enforce someone's wishes," said Margery, "then you must agree with them. When I badgered him for days on end, the landlord of the Queen's Head gave me the name of the lawyer who has drawn up this contract between Alexander Marwood and Isaac Dunmow. By its terms, you are empowered to pay the builder."

"That's true," he conceded. "Isaac could hardly do that from York. He needs someone in London to see that the work is being done properly at the inn and to pay accordingly."

"Then you *are* involved in the assassination of Westfield's Men."

"I am simply doing a favor for a friend."

"Why?"

"Because I have an obligation here," said Rooker uneasily. "When he was here in the city, Will Dunmow was a guest in my home. I had a duty of care toward him. I failed in that duty. As a result, I'm bound to help an anguished parent."

"Westfield's Men were anguished by his death as well."

"They barely knew him."

"What they did know, they liked," she said. "My husband told me what a pleasant young man he was. But let's return to this favor you are doing for the father. If he handed you a dagger and asked you to stab someone to death as a favor to him, what would you do?"

"You pose an absurd question."

"Do I, Master Rooker? Think about it."

"I've no need to do so."

"In agreeing to help a friend, what you are really doing is to stab Westfield's Men to death. This is no tragic accident like the fire that killed Will Dunmow," she said forcefully. "It is premeditated murder."

"All that I am doing is to pay someone to rebuild an inn."

"With blood money."

"I've no more to say on the matter."

"Well, I have a great deal, sir."

"Then you will have to say it to someone else," he told her as he got to his feet. "Frankly, I have no interest whatsoever in whether a theater company does or does not perform at the Queen's Head. Nothing would persuade me to enter a playhouse of any kind. But," he went on with controlled anger, "I'll not be browbeaten in my own office by a complete stranger. Good day to you, Mistress Firethorn."

"Forgive me," said Margery with blistering scorn. "I mistook you for a gentleman. I see you now for what you really are."

Storming out of the office, she left the door wide open.

As a former sailor, Ben Ryden had suffered no ill effects from the voyage, but that was not the case with Josias Greet. Hampered by seasickness for days, he still felt queasy and his feet took time to adjust to being back on dry land. When he walked, he moved slowly with his legs wide apart as if trying to compensate for the roll of the ship. They took a room at the White Hart, an English haven in a Danish town. The landlord had told them about Westfield's Men. Troubled by nausea, Greet had only half-listened to the details. After a long night in bed, his stomach was still in minor rebellion. Over breakfast next morning, his companion gobbled his food with undisguised gusto but Greet had no appetite.

"I could never be a sailor, Ben," he said. "I hate the sea."

"You get used to it after a time."

"Is it always that rough?"

"Much worse, as a rule," said Ryden, munching away. "The North Sea was very placid for a change."

"Placid! The *Speedwell* was tossed hither and thither."

"No, Josias. We sailed across a millpond." Ryden paused to release a loud belch, then punched his chest with a fist. "Think on this. It was worth the effort of coming here. Chance contrives better than we ourselves. We are in Elsinore less than a day and we already know when and where to strike."

"Right here at the White Hart."

"This is where the actors will come after their performance."

"Do we watch it, Ben?"

"Why not?" asked Ryden with a snigger. "We'll let that scurvy Welshman entertain us before we kill him."

"Burn him alive. That was our command."

"We'll have to knock him senseless first."

"Yes," said Greet, "or he'll fight like the devil. I still have the scars from that brawl we had with Owen Elias and I'll make him pay for each one of them."

Ryden was pensive. "I see a way to do it," he said, snapping his fingers. "There's straw and hay in the stables at the back of the inn. If we lug the body in there, we can roast him like a pig."

"Then what?"

"We sail on the next ship to England."

"Master Dunmow wanted certain proof of his death."

"We'll give it to him, Josias."

"How?"

"We'll cut off that ugly Welsh head and take it home in a sack."

Though it had a similar rural setting, *The Wizard Earl* was a very different play from the one performed on the previous afternoon. It had the same vitality and the same farcical brilliance but the resemblance ended there. Written by Edmund Hoode, it had been inspired by a visit the company had once made to Silvermere, a country estate in Essex, owned by Sir Michael Greenleaf. A munificent host and a devotee of theater, Sir Michael was also an experimental scientist and inventor. Unbeknown to him, he had become the Earl of Greenfield, the eponymous hero of the comedy, and he was about to demonstrate his wizardry to the townspeople of Elsinore.

Since it was a far more intricate and sophisticated play than *Cupid's Folly,* it was rehearsed at length behind the wooden screens that morning. Those who crossed the square were intrigued by the sounds they heard coming from the improvised stage and they vowed to attend the performance later on. The weather was, however, less than promising. The wind had died down but a fine drizzle had replaced it, coating the actors' faces like so much dew. They were not discouraged. Westfield's Men were so elated after their earlier success in the town that only a typhoon could have dampened their ardor.

By the time of the performance itself, a large audience had flocked to the square and the screens had to be moved outward on three sides to accommodate them all. The mayor was in the front row once more with the local worthies, and Bror Langberg had brought his wife down from the castle for the second time. There was a loud buzz of expectation. It was followed by a communal sigh of gratitude as the drizzle relented and the sun made a first appearance in the leaden sky. In the tiring-house at the rear of the stage, Lawrence Firethorn was quick to claim the credit for the improvement.

"The Wizard Earl has done it again," he announced proudly. "My invention of a machine to control the weather clearly works."

"Then raise the temperature," said Barnaby Gill petulantly. "It's far too cold for us."

"My performance will produce the heat of a furnace."

"That will make a change. You were more like an iceberg when you played the part last. I almost froze to death beside you."

"There is nothing new there, Barnaby," countered the other. "You are like a standing statue in every role you take. Old age has seized your limbs. Onstage, you are a block of wood."

"Tell that to yesterday's audience. They worshipped me."

"Then they worshipped a false god. Today, *I* will rule."

Nicholas interrupted the banter and called the actors to order. It was time to begin. They took their places. At a signal from the book holder, Martin Yeo blew a fanfare on his trumpet, then Owen Elias stepped onto the stage in a black cloak to deliver the prologue, which had been penned by Edmund Hoode after their first visit to the town square. The Welshman's voice rang out like a clarion call.

> *Today, good friends, in Denmark's pretty town,*
> *A tale of mirth and magic we set down*
> *For your delight. Enchantment we'll unfurl*
> *Before your eyes as you behold our earl*
> *Of wizardry, a conjurer supreme,*
> *Whose wondrous powers will charm you like a dream.*
> *He comes from England to this foreign shore*
> *To spread amazement throughout Elsinore.*

Elias surged on, listing various streets, statues, and landmarks in the town so that, if nothing else, the Danes in the audience would at least recognize some elements in the prologue. Broad gestures and explicit facial expressions also helped to convey meaning. At the conclusion of his speech, with a trick devised by Nicholas Bracewell, he clapped his hands hard and a small explosion took place behind his feet, loud enough to startle the audience and to give the actor time to vanish from the stage. *The Wizard Earl* was under way.

The action was swift and the pace never slackened as Firethorn, resplendent in the title role, displayed a whole series of inventions, each one more ambitious than the last. A kind man with a paternal interest in people, the earl always tried to create something that would bring benefit to one and all. His brain teemed with brilliant ideas, but when he tried to put them into practice, they rarely succeeded because Luke Bungle, his clumsy apprentice, kept putting the wrong ingredients into each experiment or losing the plan of the machine that he was supposed to be building.

As a consequence, the much vaunted inventions of the Wizard Earl had the opposite effect of the ones intended. When he showed off the machine that controlled weather, he pressed a button to create bright sunshine and brought on a torrential downpour instead. Everyone onstage scampered for cover so convincingly that the audience could almost feel the rain. Pulling a lever to stop the rain, Firethorn inadvertently started a snowstorm. In trying to dispel that, he plunged his whole estate into thick fog and there was sustained hilarity as the actors groped their way blindly around and bumped into each other.

Barnaby Gill excelled as Bungle but it was Firethorn's play. He was in his element as the genial inventor, ever sanguine, ever ready to attempt something new. The summit of his achievement was a potion that made the taker fall madly in love with the person he or she first saw. Hoode explored all the comic possibilities of the situation. At one point, the earl had three nubile ladies fighting over him while Bungle, having mistakenly allowed some of the potion to be fed to the animals, aroused the passion of an amorous goat—Owen Elias with horns—and was pursued with unflagging persistence.

The sheer comic verve of *The Wizard Earl* made it irresistible, and being peppered with so much action, mime, dance, and special effects made it comprehensible to the audience. Nicholas was pleased with the way that it was received, but Anne Hendrik was not able to follow the play. She was too busy behind the scenes, sewing on buttons, mending ripped costumes, and repairing hats that had been damaged in one of the many lively stage fights. Two hours sped by in a torrent of laughter and cheering. When the play ended, it gained an even longer ovation than its predecessor.

Firethorn was satisfied. He was back where he belonged at the head of his troupe, the undisputed leading actor who had put the upstart Gill firmly back in his place. After taking the last of several bows, Firethorn led the actors offstage and took the opportunity to get in another sly dig at his sworn foe.

"Congratulations, Barnaby," he said. "A fine performance."

Gill was on his guard. "Thank you, Lawrence."

"Edmund has finally shaped a role to suit your unique talents as a bungler. You bungled superbly as Bungle."

"Stop crowing," said Hoode, stepping in to stop another quarrel before it had really started. "Both of you served my play well, as did the whole company. I reserve a special word of praise for you, Owen," he went on, turning to Elias. "Your goat was incomparable." There was concerted agreement in the tiring-house. "The chase after Bungle was one of the triumphs of the afternoon."

"It's in my blood, Edmund," said Elias. "The Welsh have always had a goatish disposition. We are naught but lechery on four hooves." Becoming aware of Anne's proximity, he bit back the lewd jest that he was about to make. "I'll graze in pastures new," he went on. "Here's one goat who seeks the company of a White Hart."

"The rest of us will join you there," said Nicholas.

"If they will let us in," observed Firethorn. "So many people wish to meet us that there's scarce room enough in the inn. The landlord does well to let us drink at his expense for we have trebled his custom at the White Hart. In deference to the popularity we've bestowed upon it, he should call it the Westfield Arms."

"Was our patron in the audience today?" asked Hoode.

"Alas, no," replied Nicholas. "He's keeping vigil at the castle. Lord Westfield says that he is not in a laughing vein at the moment. He prefers to spend time alone."

Frederick Arbiter, first Baron Westfield, pored over the table as he considered his next move. Unable to get near to his princess yet again, he had remained in his apartment and sought to while away the lonely hours with a game of chess. Rolfe Harling had played against himself on many occasions, losing himself in the contest for hours as he regarded move and countermove. Lord Westfield lacked his rigid impartiality. Wanting to let the white chessmen win, he favored them at every turn, yet the black somehow retained the upper hand. It was eerie. He had the unsettling feeling that Harling was playing against him from the grave. Eventually, his patience snapped.

"Enough of this!" he exclaimed, using an arm to sweep every piece from the board and scatter them across the room. "This is no game for me. I want to see Sigbrit."

Sitting back in his chair, he mused on the cruelty of it all. The woman he loved enough to marry was less than twenty yards from where he sat but she was as unattainable as if she were in another country. Why was she keeping away from him? Had she been so disappointed when they met that she was wallowing in regret at her acceptance of him as a husband? Could it be that Bror Langberg's excuses for her absence hid the fact that Sigbrit was ill? The thought worried him. During the hour they'd spent in the hall, she did not have the bloom that he had expected. Was she still unwell? Or was there a more sinister explanation why he was being kept apart from her? It was a time when he most needed Rolfe Harling's advice but the man was no longer available to serve him.

Lord Westfield was in despair. Taking her portrait from his pocket, he held it in the palm of his hand and scrutinized it. To his eye, Sigbrit was the personification of beauty. Even in miniature, she was a woman in a thousand, and a loving impulse made him press his lips to the portrait. When he looked at her again, however, he saw something that suddenly alarmed him and made his brain whirl. What disconcerted him was that he had absolutely no idea what it was.

Before he adjourned to the inn after the others, Nicholas Bracewell took care to see that the scenery and the stage were struck, and that everything was loaded onto the waiting carts. The mayor had provided some constables to stand guard over them so Nicholas felt able to escort Anne to the White Hart. The atmosphere in the inn was raucous but she felt at ease among so many friends. Surrounded by admirers, Lawrence Firethorn was declaiming one of the speeches from *The Wizard Earl*. When he saw the newcomers, he broke off.

"Here's the real wizard," he said. "It was Nick who contrived all those bangs and flashes you saw. He's a genius with gunpowder. And he rehearsed us in every brawl we had onstage. A round of applause, please, for the man who holds us together—and for the lady who kept us so well attired this afternoon."

Nicholas and Anne acknowledged the clapping then found a corner in which to sit. Neither enjoyed being the center of attention. They were grateful when it shifted back to Firethorn, who lapsed into the role of the earl once more and sang the comic song that had amused the audience so much. Anne was interested.

"Is this what happens at the Queen's Head after every play?"

"Sometimes," said Nicholas. "If it has gone well."

"What about the night of the fire?"

"The performance went rather too well, Anne. It ensnared Will Dunmow completely. He kept asking Lawrence and the others to recite speeches from the play so that he could applaud once more. We always seek recognition of our work but Will went beyond that."

"And yet he rarely went to a play," she recalled.

"There was little opportunity to see actors in York, and in any case, his father thought that playhouses were dens of sin and corruption. If a company came to town, he stopped his son from going to see them. That's why we caught Will's imagination, I think," said Nicholas sadly. "Our preeminence was due to the flatness of the surrounding countryside. Because he had nobody with whom to compare us, he conceived a higher opinion of Westfield's Men than he might otherwise have had."

"It's impossible to have too high an opinion of you," she said. "You are head and shoulders above any other company and one of the main reasons for that is sitting opposite me."

"Waiting for a drink. Will you join me?"

"Yes, please."

"We deserve to celebrate."

"Must the celebrations be confined to the White Hart?"

Nicholas grinned. "No, Anne. I'm sure that we can have more privacy back at the castle."

Ben Ryden and Josias Greet bided their time. During the play, they had laughed as readily as anyone and had reserved their loudest guffaws for the smitten goat. But that did not deflect them from their purpose. In killing Owen Elias, they stood to earn a large amount of money and would avenge the injuries they had sustained at the Welshman's hands. When the notion of sailing across the North Sea to commit murder had first been put to Greet, he had thought it ridiculous. Now that they were actually here, he saw the advantages.

They were anonymous faces in a foreign country. Nobody would be able to identify them. Once the deed was done, they would board a ship that was sailing for Amsterdam on the morning tide. From there, they would reach London on another vessel. It was all planned. They would be clear of Denmark before the hullabaloo caused by the crime had even died down. The likelihood of arrest was negligible. It would be a perfect murder. Greet was pleased about something else as well. His appetite had returned. He could eat and drink once again.

"How much longer will he be, Ben?" he asked.

"Give him time. He'll have to go soon."

"That's the fourth tankard of beer he's quaffed. He must have a bladder the size of small barrel. Look at him."

"I've not taken my eyes off him," said Ryden. "Drink on, Owen," he murmured, "for it's the last time you'll be able to do it."

"What about his friends?"

"They'll be too busy carousing in here, Josias."

"Supposing one of them goes out with him?"

"Then he'll wish that he didn't."

"We kill him as well?"

"No," said Ryden, "we just give him the biggest headache he's ever had in his life. This is our chance. Nobody will rob us of it."

The two men were standing near the door, drinking beer and pretending to join in the fun. Over the heads of the other actors, they could see Owen Elias, reveling in the company of his friends and oblivious to being in such danger. The more beer he consumed, the more relaxed and jovial he became. A dagger was hanging from his belt but they did not intend to let him use it. Surprise was their main weapon. It would never even cross Elias's befuddled mind that two hired killers would come hundreds of miles in search of him. Onstage, he had been a rampant goat. To the watching Greet and Ryden, he was a lamb to the slaughter.

Their wait was soon over. Feeling the need to relieve himself, Elias put his half-empty tankard on a table and lumbered off toward the door. Ben Ryden nudged his friend.

"Here he comes," he whispered. "Get ready."

[CHAPTER TWELVE]

Nicholas Bracewell picked up the two cups of wine from the counter then eased his way gently through the crowded taproom to the table in the corner. Anne Hendrik took the drink that he offered her.

"Thank you, Nick."

"We earned this," he said, lowering himself onto the stool.

"Did you have to pay?"

"Everything is free to Westfield's Men. We bring in so much business for him that the landlord would like to keep us for a month." He gave a mirthless laugh. "What a pity he does not own the Queen's Head as well!"

"Yes," she said. "To have an agreeable landlord there would be a welcome change for you. The wonder is that you've managed to stay so long in Gracechurch Street. Alexander Marwood hates the company. He's tried to evict you a dozen times before now."

Nicholas was not listening. Over her shoulder, he had just seen something through the window that made him leap to his feet. As Owen Elias walked across the yard toward the privy, a man came up behind him to deliver a vicious blow to the back of his skull with the butt of a pistol. Nicholas put his wine on the table. He did not ease his way through the press this time. He moved fast and used his elbows to clear a path to the door. When he came into the yard, he saw that Elias's attacker had dragged him into the stables where a second man was trying to ignite some hay. Unconscious, and with blood oozing from his head wound, Elias was utterly helpless. The intention was clear. They meant to burn him alive. Without bothering to call for help, Nicholas ran forward and dived at the man who was holding Elias, pulling him away and flinging him against a wall. Josias Greet was momentarily dazed by the impact. Letting out a string of expletives, he then reached for the pistol in his belt, but Nicholas was too quick for him. Jumping forward, he grappled with the man and kept banging him against the bare brick. Ben Ryden, meanwhile, had started the fire and was piling hay onto it. The crackling noise put fresh urgency into Nicholas. After exchanging punches with Greet, he brought his knee up hard into his groin and made him gasp. As the man bent forward in agony, Nicholas hit him with a powerful uppercut that sent him tumbling to the ground.

Instinctively, Nicholas swung round. He was just in time to ward off an attack from Ryden, who came hurtling at him with a dagger in his hand. Nicholas moved smartly sideways to avoid the weapon's thrust, then roughly pushed his attacker away. Rushing to the stable, he tried to stamp out the fire but Ryden came after him. Nicholas threw a handful of burning hay into his face to force him back, but it only bought him a few seconds. They circled each other warily and Nicholas wished that he had been wearing his dagger. Elsinore was obviously not as safe as he had imagined. Two men were set on murdering Elias in broad daylight and dispatching Nicholas after him. There was no room for error on the book holder's part.

Greet was slowly recovering. Still in some pain, he shook his head to clear it then took stock of the situation. Ryden slashed wildly with his dagger but to no effect. Nicholas evaded the weapon nimbly. Ryden backed him against a fence. Smoke was now coming from the stables and the two horses stalled there were protesting with frenzied neighs and loud kicks. Ryden needed to act fast. It was only a matter of time before someone came out of the inn. Feinting with his dagger, he went down on one knee to deliver a murderous thrust that would have ripped Nicholas's stomach apart. But Nicholas saw it coming and eluded it swiftly, reaching out to grab the wrist that held the weapon. The two men grappled wildly.

Greet was incensed. Climbing to his feet, he pulled the pistol from his belt and tried to aim it at Nicholas, but the two bodies kept twisting and turning so rapidly that he could not shoot.

"Stand aside, Ben," he called. "I'll finish him."

Seeing the danger, Nicholas responded at once, holding his man even tighter and using him as shield against the accomplice. Greet came forward and tried to pull Ryden away from his target. Nicholas assisted him, promptly leaving go of the man and pushing with all his might. Ryden smashed into Greet and sent him flying, and with a loud report the pistol went off accidentally and the ball hit Ryden's back. Staggering forward, he let out a cry of anguish and put both hands to the exit wound. Blood spurted everywhere. The commotion brought many curious faces to the door and windows. Greet thought only of escape. He grabbed his stricken companion and hustled him quickly out of the yard into the gathering dusk.

Nicholas was far more interested in saving his friend than in chasing the would-be killers. He snatched up a pail of water that stood beside the well and flung it over Owen Elias to douse the flames that were licking at his clothes. He then handed the pail to the first man who emerged from the inn.

"Fill it up again!" he ordered.

"Yes," said the other, gaping at the scene.

"Be quick, man!"

Taking Elias by the feet, Nicholas dragged him to safety, then checked that he was still breathing. When he saw that the Welshman was still very much alive, he went back to the stables and stamped on the burning hay. Other people hurried to help him, and under the onslaught of a dozen feet, the fire was soon contained. A second pail of water put out the last of the flames and it was then possible to calm the frightened horses. Westfield's Men formed a circle around their fallen colleague, horrified at the sight of the injury to his skull. It was left to Anne Hendrik to bathe and bind up the wound. When he began to regain consciousness, Elias let out a long groan and put a hand to the back of his head.

"What happened?" he asked.

"You were attacked by two men," said Nicholas. "They tried to burn you alive in the stables."

"I thought the Danes were a friendly people."

"They are, Owen. These villains were English."

Bror Langberg kissed her gently on the forehead and smiled at her.

"I am glad to see that you have come to your senses, Sigbrit."

"I had a long talk with Aunt Johanna," she said, turning to her sister, "and with Hansi, of course. They persuaded me that I should have no fears about this marriage."

"None at all," said Hansi.

"I am beginning to look forward to it, Uncle Bror."

"And so you should," he said. "Had you been in the square this afternoon, you would have seen what a wonderful company you are about to inherit. Westfield's Men are the toast of Elsinore. They have brought so much merriment to the town."

"Good."

"On Saturday, they will perform in the castle ballroom."

"I still have qualms about that," admitted Sigbrit.

"They will disappear the moment the play begins."

Langberg was pleased that his niece's doubts seemed to have been overcome and he was grateful to her sister for the help that she had given. He now felt able to take more cheering news to the bridegroom. After bidding farewell to the two women, he went along the corridor with a spring in his step until he came to the apartment set aside for Lord Westfield. When he was admitted, Langberg saw that the chess pieces were in an untidy pile on the table.

"Rolfe Harling would never have left them like that," he noted.

"No," said the other. "He kept them neatly in a box."

"Everything about him was neat and meticulous."

"Have his killers been caught?"

"Not yet, my lord, but they will be. They will be."

Langberg studied his guest. Lord Westfield looked more jaded and world-weary than ever. His visit had so far delivered none of the joys that he had expected. All of his natural zest had deserted him.

"I bring you good tidings," said Langberg.

"Are there such things?"

"I've not long returned from the town, my lord. The performance of *The Wizard Earl* was the finest I have ever seen upon a stage. Since I speak English, I was able to appreciate its full value, but even those who could not understand a word of the language enjoyed it hugely. Your actors floated on a sea of laughter."

"Whereas I am becalmed in the shallows," said Lord Westfield.

"Take pride in the achievement of your company."

"I always do, Master Langberg. But there are times when comedy strikes a jarring note inside my head. This is one of them."

"Then let us see if we can cure you of that discord."

"Only one person could do that and she is not here."

"She soon will be," said Langberg happily. "That's the other news I bring you. Sigbrit sends word. She apologizes for being unable to see you and wants you to know that she is feeling markedly better."

"That *does* cheer me," said the other, shedding his malaise in an instant. "Can we meet properly at last?"

"Sigbrit will dine with you tomorrow, my lord."

"Why must I wait until then?"

"That is her request."

"Then I'll willingly abide by it," agreed Lord Westfield. "It's the privilege of a bride to keep her husband waiting and I'll not cavil at that. Had she felt able to attend the play today, I'd have enjoyed it at her side. As it is, we will watch *The Princess of Denmark* together and she will see what a precious gift I offer her in the form of my theater company."

"Precious and unique."

"Indeed. They have had the honor of playing before Her Majesty, Queen Elizabeth, many times."

"They will soon perform before a king," said Langberg, moving to the door. "I wonder if you would care to come with me, my lord? There is something I wish to show you."

"Where?"

"Here in Kronborg. We will not have to leave the castle."

"Then I'll gladly accompany you."

Opening the door, Langberg took him out and ushered him along the corridor until they reached the end. When they turned at right angles into another passageway, they stopped at the first window. Langberg gestured his companion forward.

"Behold, my lord."

"All that I can see is an empty courtyard."

"Look at the window opposite."

"Which one?"

"The one near the corner," said Langberg. "Do you see her?"

Lord Westfield tingled. "Is it Sigbrit?"

"Who else?"

Pressing his nose against the glass, Lord Westfield stared across the courtyard at the young woman in the window directly opposite. She was some distance away and light was fading but he was still able to recognize her as his bride. Framed in the window, she waved to him and he lifted a hand in acknowledgment. The more he stared, the clearer he could see her. He did not need to take out the portrait this time. Her beauty identified her at once. Doubts that he had felt earlier now disappeared. His gloom and irritation were replaced by a sense of pure joy. There was another treat to come. Putting her hand to her lips, she blew him a kiss across the courtyard. He was enraptured.

"Sigbrit!" he murmured. "I love you!"

The attempted murder of Owen Elias brought the festivities at the White Hart to a sudden end. Alarmed that such a thing could happen on his premises, the landlord insisted on summoning a surgeon so that the wound could be properly examined, and he also sent for constables. A search of the immediate vicinity began but there was no sign of the two men. Evidently, they had gone to ground somewhere, aided by the fact that it was growing steadily darker.

Westfield's Men waited until the surgeon had inspected and rebandaged Elias's injury, giving the Welshman an herbal compound to ease his headache and to help him sleep. Nicholas Bracewell assisted him back to the cart and they set out for Kronborg. Once they were safely back in the castle, Lawrence Firethorn stalked off to his apartment with Nicholas and Edmund Hoode in tow.

"This is intolerable!" he protested as they entered the room. "We have unseen enemies in Denmark. First of all, Rolfe Harling is killed. Today, it was Owen's turn to be attacked."

"The two crimes are not linked," said Nicholas.

"They must be," argued Hoode.

"No, Edmund. It may look like that, I agree, but I ask you to compare the cases in detail."

"Two of our number have been attacked, Nick. That's all the detail I need. Someone has a grudge against Westfield's Men."

"Then why did they single out Master Harling?" asked Nicholas. "He came here with us but not as one of the company. He was simply a friend of our patron. If someone wanted to harm us, they'd have picked another victim."

"They did," observed Firethorn sharply. "Owen Elias."

"This has to be the work of the same villains," said Hoode.

"Then why did they wait so long to strike?" asked Nicholas. "We have been here for days. After *Cupid's Folly,* Owen drank just as heavily at the White Hart as he did today. If the same killers are involved, why did not they assail him then? No," he went on, trying to work it out in his mind, "these crimes are definitely not connected. Bror Langberg is certain that the two men who stabbed Master Harling worked as cooks. They fled for their lives. It would be madness for them to lurk in the town when they were being hunted. Would you do so in their situation?"

Hoode pondered. "Nick argues well. He is right."

"I disagree," said Firethorn testily. "The coincidence is too great to ignore. We have enemies here. In future, we must stay together and arm ourselves if we go abroad."

"There is no need of that, Lawrence," said Nicholas.

"I say that there is."

"Then I ask you to look at the way Master Harling was killed."

"He was stabbed to death."

"Why was Owen not dispatched in the same way?"

"What does it matter?"

"It matters a great deal," asserted Nicholas. "I was a witness when Owen was knocked out with the butt of a pistol. Those ruffians could easily have thrust a dagger through his heart or simply shot him dead. Instead, they wanted him to be burned alive."

"Such a hideous way to die!" gasped Hoode.

"Does it remind you of someone else?"

There was a long pause. "Will Dunmow."

"Exactly," decided Nicholas. "That's the explanation here. My guess is that the two men who lay in wait for Owen today were the selfsame villains who ambushed him in London."

Firethorn was incredulous. "That's absurd, Nick. Why would two men come all the way from England in pursuit of Owen?"

"Because they were extremely well paid."

"By whom?"

"Will Dunmow's father," said Nicholas. "He was furious at what happened to his son and I think that Owen bore the brunt of that fury. You must remember that it was he and James Ingram who put Will to bed that night. Owen gave a full account of it to Master Rooker, the friend who was charged to look after Will while he was in London."

"This is idle supposition."

"I wonder," said Hoode.

"I still see a pattern here," argued Firethorn.

"Then you must open your eyes much wider," advised Nicholas. "The men who killed Master Harling were Danish. Those who sought Owen's life were English."

"That proves nothing. There are several Englishmen living in Elsinore. It could have been any of them."

"You would not believe that if you'd talked, as I did, to the landlord of the White Hart. Two men arrived from London yesterday evening on the *Speedwell*. They lodged at the inn for one night. They also questioned the landlord closely about Westfield's Men and were delighted to hear that we'd be performing in the square today."

"They probably wished to be in the audience," said Firethorn.

"I'm sure that they were," Nicholas resumed, "and I'm equally sure that they went to the White Hart to await our arrival. These men are strangers to the town, Lawrence."

"If they lodged at the inn," said Hoode, "they'd have given their names to the landlord. Did you ask what they were called, Nick?"

"Of course."

"Then we know who they were."

"I fear not, Edmund. They were too cunning to give their real names. One of them was called Ben—I heard it called out. Neither of them gave that name to the landlord."

Firethorn scratched his beard. Nicholas was so sure of his facts that his judgment had to be respected. The actor-manager had been badly shaken by events at the White Hart. He wanted no repetition.

"Owen must never be left alone," he decreed. "Someone must protect him at all times."

"He's safe within the castle," said Nicholas. "Every gate is locked and guarded. Those villains would never be able to get anywhere near Owen. Besides, one of them was shot in the back. Instead of trying to take someone else's life, he'll be hanging on to his own."

Josias Greet was in a panic. Having carried his friend to a hiding place not far from the inn, he was absolutely exhausted. Yet he knew that he had to move on. Ben Ryden was bleeding profusely. Every word he spoke was charged with pain.

"Where are we, Josias?"

"In a ditch behind the church."

"We must get away."

"You're in no condition to walk."

"Carry me," ordered Ryden. "When it's really dark, carry me."

"Where?"

"To the harbor. We'll steal aboard tonight."

"Yes, Ben," said the other, knowing full well that Ryden might not even live that long. "I'll do as you say."

"Scurvy Welshman!"

"We should have stabbed him when we had the chance."

"He had to be burned to death. That was our commission."

"Forget about it now. All that we need worry about is you."

"My body is on fire. I feel as if there's a red-hot poker in my back." A spasm of pain made him convulse. "Damnation!"

"Be quiet!" said Greet, clapping a hand over his mouth. "You'll give us away, Ben." He peered anxiously over the top of the ditch. An extension was being built to the church and they were hiding in its muddy foundations. "We cannot stay here much longer. They'll come with torches for another search. We have to sneak away."

He looked down at his companion with a mixture of sympathy and fear. Sorry that Ryden had been injured, he saw what a burden his friend had now become. If he had any hope of escape, Greet had to go alone. Ryden's body sagged and his head fell forward. Weakened by the loss of blood, he lapsed slowly into unconsciousness, his mouth agape and his breathing labored. Greet acted on impulse. After seizing the other man's purse, he also deprived him of his dagger. Then he took another look over the top of the ditch. Lanterns appeared at the far end of the street. Another search was being conducted. By staying where he was, Greet risked discovery. In trying to take Ryden with him, he would make escape virtually impossible. There was only one thing to do and he did not hesitate.

"I'm sorry, Ben," he said, raising the dagger. "I have to do this."

Then he slit Ryden's throat with a flick of his wrist.

After his glimpse of Sigbrit Olsen across the courtyard, Lord Westfield was in high spirits. He returned to his apartment and began to write a letter to her, praising her beauty and promising that he would dedicate himself to making her happy. He was not pleased to be interrupted by Nicholas Bracewell.

"Yes?" he said abruptly, holding the door open.

"I want to speak to you about this afternoon, my lord."

"Bror Langberg has already done so. He told me everything that I need to hear about *The Wizard Earl.*"

"I am not here to discuss the performance."

"Talk to me another time. I am too busy now."

Nicholas held his ground. "Too busy to hear about an attempted murder?" he asked, using a palm to stop the door from being shut in his face. "One of your actors was almost killed, my lord."

"Oh." Lord Westfield stood back. "You had better come in."

Nicholas entered and closed the door behind him. He explained what had occurred at the White Hart and confided his suspicions about who the two men might be, stressing that he was relying on guesswork rather than evidence.

"In my experience," said the other, "your guesses have a habit of being remarkably accurate. How is Owen Elias now?"

"Fast asleep. He has a bad wound in his scalp."

"Will he be able to perform at the wedding?"

"I hope so," said Nicholas. "Owen is a strong man. He recovered well from the first attack on him. We trust that he'll do the same again. There is something I am bid to ask you, my lord," he went on. "We shall be rehearsing *The Princess of Denmark* tomorrow. Lawrence wondered if you wished to be present."

"No, Nicholas. I prefer to see it for the first time with the lady who inspired it. We will each come to it afresh."

"A wise decision."

"Is there anything that I can do for Owen?"

"I think not, my lord. We will all nurse him back to health."

"Have you reported the incident to Bror Langberg?"

"No," replied Nicholas, "nor will I. His hands are full with the preparations for the wedding and he already has one murder on his hands. Owen—by the grace of God—survived. There the matter ends until we return to London."

"What happens then?"

"We'll confront the man who hired those two ruffians. But I am interrupting you, my lord," Nicholas said apologetically. "I'll withdraw."

"Wait a while. I'm glad you came." Lord Westfield indicated the chessmen on the table. "I've something to show you."

"I've seen them already."

"Hear me out," said Lord Westfield. "Earlier today, I tried to play a game against myself and became so exasperated that I swept the pieces from the table. They went all over the floor. When my temper had cooled, I picked them again and noticed something that surprised me." He lifted up the black king. "This had come loose." Unscrewing the piece, he held a part in each hand. "What do you make of that, Nicholas?"

"It sorts well with Master Harling's secretive nature."

"There's a message inside—take it out."

A tiny scroll had been inserted into the upper half of the black king. It was so small that it could easily have been missed. Extracting it with the utmost care, Nicholas unrolled it. He held it close to read the minuscule hand.

"It does not make sense," said Lord Westfield. "Rolfe had a brilliant mind yet that letter is complete gibberish."

"It's not a letter, my lord."

"Then what the devil is it?"

Nicholas looked up at him. "A code."

Anne Hendrik was finding the little room irksome. Designed for a servant, it was no more than a cramped box into which no natural light strayed. The mattress was hard and unyielding. After the cozy bed in which she slept at home, it was almost punitive. The one thing that made it bearable was that Nicholas would share it with her for a short time. In spite of all that had happened, she knew that he would keep the assignation. It was hardly the most romantic place for a tryst but it would serve.

Since he would not be able to find the room without guidance, Anne had agreed to meet Nicholas at the top of the main staircase in the west wing. He slept with the others in a hut in the forecourt so it was impossible for them to go there. She longed to see him alone. Anne had spent most of the day at his side but always in the company of many people. It was vexing. She felt that an hour in his arms would atone for everything. When the appointed hour drew near, therefore, she took her candle and left the room, padding swiftly along the corridor toward the main staircase.

In the distance, she heard voices and stepped swiftly into an alcove, covering the flame with her hand to mask its light. Footsteps approached along the corridor and the voices became clearer.

"Thank you for all that you've done, Aunt Johanna."

"Your uncle and I love you."

"Without you, I could never have gone through with this."

"Are you still nervous?"

"Very nervous."

"It will soon pass, Sigbrit."

Anne could not understand all of the Danish words but she heard the names distinctly. Sigbrit Olsen was talking to her aunt, who was carrying a candelabrum. As they went past the alcove, they were within feet of Anne, with Sigbrit closer to her. The candles threw enough light for Anne to see both of them clearly. Johanna Langberg was a gracious woman who moved with dignity but she attracted no interest from Anne. The person who fascinated her was Sigbrit Olsen, walking along on dainty feet and talking to her aunt with deference. Anne only saw her face in profile but it was enough to give her a mild shock. She backed farther into the alcove.

Bror Langberg responded to the request immediately. He conducted Lawrence Firethorn to the ballroom and praised his performance as the Wizard Earl unceasingly. The actor lapped up every word like a cat with a bowl of cream. Having discussed the matter with the others, he said nothing of the drama that had followed the performance. It was a private matter that affected only Westfield's Men. There was no need for Langberg to be involved in any way.

"Well," said Langberg as they entered the candlelit ballroom, "here we are, Master Firethorn. We know that your voice carries in here so another demonstration will not be needed."

Firethorn grinned. "A few loud bellows, perhaps!"

"You would rouse the whole castle."

"Then they retire to bed too early." He became serious. "As I told you, Master Langberg, we wish to rehearse in here tomorrow morning and afternoon."

"The ballroom is at your disposal."

"I must ask that we are not interrupted, sir. Though we perform in public, we do the best of our work in private. It is there that we can put our mistakes right and polish our performances."

"I cannot believe that you are ever in need of polish."

"This is a new and untried play," said Firethorn, concealing that it was quite the opposite and that it had been rewritten and cleverly disguised by Edmund Hoode. "That means there is an element of danger. We never quite know how a new piece will be received."

"With thunderous applause, I promise you."

"We must first earn that applause."

"Westfield's Men have done so twice in the town square."

"They were merry romps, sir—lively comedies to amuse the lower orders. Our audience here will be of higher standing so a more poetic offering is in order."

"I would cheerfully watch *anything* you play," said Langberg.

"Then at least one spectator will admire us."

Firethorn explained what he would need on the following day and every single request he made was readily granted. Langberg was not only prepared to lend the company various stage properties that they lacked, he even suggested additional items that could help to decorate a scene.

"Anything in the castle is yours, Master Firethorn," he said.

The actor leered. "Does that offer include some of the buxom wenches I've seen here from time to time?"

"You can do better than servant girls and you most surely will."

"How?"

"By giving the kind of performance that we saw today," Langberg told him. "The ladies will be enthralled by you. I'll warn you now that you'll have more than one knock on the door of your apartment on Saturday night. And it will not be King Christian, come to bestow an honor upon you, much as you deserve it. You are a famous actor, Master Firethorn. You will thrill and enchant. They will buzz around you like moths around a flame." Langberg chuckled. "I will have to chain my wife to my side or Johanna will also succumb to your charms."

"The lady that intrigues me is the one beyond my reach."

"And who is that?"

"Why, your niece, of course—Sigbrit."

"A princess in all but name."

"Is she really as beautiful as we are led to believe?"

"Sigbrit is truly blessed," said Langberg airily. "She is an angel sent from above. Your patron is a most fortunate man, my friend. He is about to marry a heavenly vision."

* * *

Nicholas Bracewell was stunned by the news. His mind was racing.

"When was this, Anne?" he asked.

"Not five minutes ago."

"And you are certain that it was her?"

"Yes, Nick. Her aunt spoke the name—Sigbrit."

"But you only saw her for a second."

"It was enough," said Anne.

They were in her little room and Nicholas was trying to take in the import of what he had been told. If her instinct was right, then a number of things were suddenly explained.

"Do you remember what I told you about that servant, Nick?"

"Yes," he said. "She gave you a strange look."

"Now I know why. Sigbrit is not the beauty we all think."

"But you saw her on the back stairs that night."

"I saw someone who looked very much like her," said Anne, "but it was not the woman who walked past me earlier. Sigbrit Olsen is a very pretty young lady, nobody would deny that."

"Prettiness is not real beauty."

"It's only a pale version of it."

"So what is your conclusion?"

"Lord Westfield does not have a portrait of Sigbrit."

"Then who is the lady?" he asked.

"The same one that I saw on the back stairs and that you caught sight of in the ballroom. The likeness is so strong that they must be sisters."

Nicholas was shocked. The implications were far-reaching. It began to look as if they had been lured there under false pretenses, and he wondered if Rolfe Harling had been party to the deception. Something that Lord Westfield had told him popped into his mind.

"Our patron complained how little he had seen of her," said Nicholas. "When they met in the hall one evening, the place was so full that he could not get near her. Since he had been drinking all day, his eyesight was probably blurred."

"A fair point, Nick," Anne said, thinking of the face she had just seen in the corridor. "In subdued light, Sigbrit might conceivably have passed for the woman we saw in the portrait but not if Lord Westfield got really close to her."

"I suspect that she was carefully shielded from him."

"By whom—and for what reason?"

"I wish that I knew."

"Lord Westfield is in for a dreadful surprise," said Anne with sympathy. "He has fallen in love with one woman yet is about to be wed to another. Are you going to warn him, Nick?"

"Not until I have more proof. I'll make inquiries."

"I've said from the start that something odd is going on."

"Odd or ominous? I have uneasy feelings about all this. When he went to the hall that evening, Lord Westfield met everyone of importance in the castle. If Sigbrit Olsen has a sister, then the lady was certain to be there—yet she was not."

"We can guess why."

"Yes, Anne," he said, taking her in his arms. "I'm very grateful to you. Ever since we left London, you've been a source of immense help to the company. Even Barnaby Gill has admitted that now and it's an achievement for any woman to win a compliment from him. Since we've been here, you've made yourself indispensable. And in providing this latest intelligence, you've rendered the greatest service yet."

"I would like to think so."

"There's no question about it."

"Does that mean you are glad you came here this evening?"

"Very glad."

She prodded his chest. "Is that all?"

"What more do you require—a letter of gratitude?"

"I just want to be appreciated," she said, nestling against him.

Nicholas grinned. "I think that I can manage that."

Breakfast was served in the hut where the actors had spent the night and they were joined by the select few who had their own rooms in the castle. Lawrence Firethorn noticed at once that someone was missing.

"Where's Nick?" he asked.

"He went out an hour or more ago," replied James Ingram. "He said that he wanted some fresh air."

"Then I think we'll know where he'll find it."

Firethorn's sly grin set off a round of muted laughter. Everyone assumed that their book holder had sneaked off quietly to be with Anne Hendrik, and envious comments were passed around the table. Not until they had finished their meal did Nicholas finally return. When he told them that he had been to the town, everyone dismissed the explanation jocularly as an excuse. He had his own breakfast then went immediately to work. After collecting the items they needed for rehearsal, they went to the ballroom and Firethorn was delighted to see that Bror Langberg had honored his promise. All the things that the actor-manager had asked for had been provided.

Though he had come with the others, Owen Elias was not well enough to take part in the rehearsal. He sat in a chair as their sole spectator, still groggy from the potion he had taken. Before they began, Nicholas addressed the whole company.

"A curtain will be hung from the balcony," he said, "so that we have a tiring-house behind. Entrances can be made from either end of the curtain, or from a gap in the middle." He pointed upward. "Our music will come from above and the scenes in Sigbrit's bedchamber will be played up there."

"Our patron will play those best," said Firethorn, chortling.

"That's why I changed the hero's name to Frederick," said Hoode. "Sigbrit and Frederick, our patron, will be married in the chapel. Then they will have a second wedding here onstage."

"Let us think only of the play," suggested Nicholas. "We must leave Lord Westfield to his own devices. Now, although we will have a stage, my feeling is that we should step down from it during the dance at the end of the performance. This was built as a ballroom so we should take full advantage of that fact."

Barnaby Gill led the chorus of agreement. When the book holder had finished his instructions, he volunteered to read Elias's role in the play then handed over to Firethorn.

"This is no rough-hewn performance in a town square, lads," said Firethorn grandly. "We are here to honor our patron and his bride, and to entertain King Christian and his court. Nothing but the best of our art will suffice. This play, as you know, began life as

The Prince of Aragon, a stirring tragedy. New-minted by Edmund, it has transcended itself and is now a sprightly comedy to excite the mind and dazzle the eye. Let us do it justice."

The rehearsal began. In spite of his severe misgivings, Nicholas worked with his usual commitment, controlling everything behind the scenes while listening with a critical ear to all that took place on-stage. There were several mistakes and some scenes had to be done again and again, but the quality of *The Princess of Denmark* shone through nevertheless. During a break, Elias made that point to Nicholas.

"Edmund is a miracle worker. He has turned water into wine."

"That is unfair on *The Prince of Aragon,*" said Nicholas. "It was a fine play in its own right. What Edmund has done is to turn wine into a form of nectar."

"I have only one complaint," said Elias.

"And what's that?"

"You have usurped my role as Lars and are *better* than me."

Nicholas smiled. "I'll gladly surrender it on the day itself, Owen."

Elias rubbed his bandaged head. "If I've recovered by then. My eyes are still bleary and my mind wanders. I have all of the ill effects of drinking with none of its pleasures." He stood up and took Nicholas aside. "Where did you really go this morning, Nick?"

"To the town."

"Come now—you went to Anne's bedchamber."

"Because of you," said Nicholas, "I had to forgo that particular delight. The two men who attacked you gave false names to the landlord of the White Hart but they did not do so to the captain of the *Speedwell.* They would have had to show him their passports. I rowed out to the ship and told him about the attempt on your life. He was more than ready to give me their names."

"What were they?" demanded Elias, anger rising.

"Ben Ryden and Josias Greet."

"I'll kill the pair of the knaves."

"Ryden is already dead," said Nicholas. "They found his body in a ditch behind the church. He was not killed by the shot that was fired. They say that his throat had been slit."

"Then his accomplice must have murdered him."

"He did more than that, Owen. Not content with taking his life, Greet seems to have cut off his hand as well."

The *Endeavor* had sailed on the morning tide. She was a three-masted ship with plenty of canvas to catch the gusting wind and send her scudding over the waves. Seven passengers were aboard the merchant vessel. Six of them stood at the bulwark to survey the Danish coast as they headed toward the Kattegat, but the other remained below. Josias Greet was already feeling slightly seasick but his nausea was eased by his sense of relief. He had escaped alive. Ben Ryden had had to be sacrificed but he would never have survived for long. Instead of subjecting him to a slow, protracted, agonizing death, Greet had dispatched his friend quickly. In his purse, he now had all the money that they had been given and there was the promise of much more.

Greet glanced at the blood-soaked bag beside him and smiled.

After a couple more hours, Firethorn brought the rehearsal to an end, and although it had gone well, he felt the need to deliver a series of reprimands to keep the actors on their toes. Gill, inevitably, was singled out for a few barbs. More work was needed on specific scenes and Firethorn intended to concentrate on those after dinner, when he expected a visible improvement. The actors were chastened by his comments. Before they could disperse, however, their patron strutted into the ballroom in his finery.

"Is all well here, Lawrence?" he asked.

"Yes, my lord," returned Firethorn, greatly impressed by his blue and gold doublet with its matching breeches. "May I say how resplendent you look today?"

"With good cause."

"Are you dining with the future Lady Westfield?"

"I am indeed," said the other uxoriously. "While you rehearse one Princess of Denmark, I go to meet another."

As their patron strode off down the ballroom, Nicholas watched with mingled affection and trepidation. He was fond of him. With all his faults, Lord Westfield was a good-hearted man. Nicholas did not want to see him hurt but feared that pain was unavoidable if the wedding went ahead. The bridegroom was being duped. What taxed Nicholas's brain was how many people were involved in the ruse. He needed time alone to think. Since he would get no privacy over dinner, he waited until the others had left, then slipped off to the one place in the castle where he could count on solitude.

The chapel had been consecrated only fifteen years earlier and it still had an air of newness about it. Nicholas came into the balcony and what struck him at once was the rich elaboration of the whole place. Skilled craftsmen had left small masterpieces on every side. The wooden pews were superbly carved and ornamented, and the altar was even more extravagant. Gold leaf glistened. Tall, white stone pillars supported the beautiful vaulted ceiling. Light streamed in through the high windows to reveal the extraordinary range of colors that had been used and to show off the vivid black-and-white pattern in the marble floor.

Nicholas knelt down and offered up a prayer for guidance. He then returned to the event that had first jangled the company after their arrival in Kronborg. Still unsolved, the murder of Rolfe Harling continued to mystify him. One possible clue had emerged when Lord Westfield had knocked an ivory chess set to the floor in a moment of pique, but it was far from conclusive. Nicholas had come around to the view that Harling's death might in some way be related to the conspiracy that was taking place. When inebriated, Lord Westfield might have been deceived, but someone as quick-witted and observant as his friend would never be taken in. Had he been killed before he could discover the truth about Sigbrit Olsen?

That thought led him to speculate on why the deception was necessary. Was it so important for her to marry Lord Westfield that a portrait of her sister had to be dangled in front of him as bait? And what would happen when the husband realized that he was the victim of a trick? Having been joined in holy matrimony before God, he could hardly turn his wife out. Nicholas brooded. During their time at the castle, a number of inexplicable things had happened here. What he lacked was a common thread to pull them all together. His mind went back to a piece of paper hidden in Harling's chess set. What secret did it hold? Why had it been concealed inside the black king?

Nicholas was still wrestling with imponderables when he heard a door open below. He looked over the balcony. Wearing a cloak and hood, a woman tripped across the floor and stepped into one of the pews. As she knelt in prayer, Nicholas drew back in embarrassment, feeling uneasy at trespassing on someone else's devotions. Curiosity soon got the better of his discomfort. Peeping over the balcony again, he watched her for a long time, wondering who she was and what had brought her here. Why did she spend such an age on her knees? Was her mind troubled or was she involved in some kind of penance?

Her prayers eventually came to an end and she rose to her feet. As she did so, the hood fell back from her head to expose blond hair in a beautiful coiffure. Nicholas could see that she was young, delicate, and, from the quality of her embroidered cloak, clearly belonged to a wealthy family. Moving across the marble floor, there was nobility in her bearing. But only when she suddenly looked up at the balcony did he know for certain who she was. It was Sigbrit Olsen. She was not the woman in Lord Westfield's portrait but the likeness was strong enough to deceive a casual observer. Anne Hendrik had only seen her in profile and had described her as pretty. Nicholas was able to see her whole face and she was alarmed.

Pulling the hood quickly back up, she fled from the chapel.

Invited to join them for dinner, Anne Hendrik chose to eat alone in her room. It was not because she felt out of place as the only woman in a male assembly. Having been so closely associated with Westfield's Men over the years, she was completely at ease with them. Mindful of the effect her presence had on the actors, she had withdrawn out of consideration. It was not only the coarse banter that was suppressed when she was there. It was the comradeship that held Westfield's Men together, a unity of which she could never truly be a part.

Her meal was simple but palatable and she valued the time alone.

Having set out originally for Amsterdam, she now found herself in Elsinore, caught up in the drama that surrounded Kronborg. She was not dismayed. Being involved in two performances had given her the most intense pleasure and she was eager to unravel some of the mysteries that the castle held. When she had finished her dinner, she put the cup and plates outside the door on their wooden tray.

"Did you save none for me?" asked Nicholas as he approached.

Anne straightened up. "What are *you* doing here?"

"Scavenging for food."

"I thought you'd have dinner with the others."

"I will, Anne, but I felt that I had to have a word with you first. Your instinct was sound. She simply cannot be in two places at once."

"Who?"

"Sigbrit Olsen. Our patron is dining with her at this very moment yet I've just seen the lady in the chapel."

"The chapel? What were you doing there, Nick?"

Easing her back into the room, he shut the door behind them then told her about his visit to the chapel. All her suspicions were confirmed. The sister of Sigbrit Olsen was being used as an occasional substitute. Lord Westfield was unwittingly reveling in the company of a woman who would not stand at the altar with him.

"He must be warned," she said.

"He will be."

"It would be cruel to keep this from him."

"Leave everything to me, Anne," he said, kissing her on the lips. "I'm hungry. If you'll excuse me, I'll join the others now."

"But you haven't heard *my* news yet."

"Oh—and what would that be?"

"When I first moved in here, one of the servants showed me around the castle. We managed to understand each other in German."

"I remember. Go on."

"Well," continued Anne, "on the way back from the ballroom today, I bumped into her again. She was disturbed about the murder that took place here. She said that it made the castle very unpleasant to work in. We've all noticed how the atmosphere here has changed."

"It was bound to, Anne."

"I tried to cheer her up by telling her that the killers were no longer inside Kronborg. I explained that the two men had worked as cooks in the kitchens."

"And?"

"She gave me that look again, Nick, the one that made me feel as if I'd said something very stupid. It seems that her husband works in the kitchens. According to him, nobody at all has fled from there. Whoever committed that murder was certainly not employed as a cook. Someone is lying."

[CHAPTER THIRTEEN]

Nicholas Bracewell was in a quandary. Aware that the performance of *The Princess of Denmark* might not even take place, he had
to watch the actors working hard on the play that afternoon. If he
stopped the rehearsal, his explanation would be met with dismay
and disbelief. Yet, if he let them carry on, he would be allowing
them to think that all the scenes that were being expertly honed in
the ballroom would soon be set before a special audience. Having
uncovered deceit elsewhere, Nicholas felt that he was now guilty of
it himself. He was, in effect, letting his friends waste their time and
effort.

Preoccupied with his dilemma, Nicholas began to make some
uncharacteristic mistakes. Most of them went unnoticed by the others, but Lawrence Firethorn had sharper instincts. When the rehearsal was over, and everything had been dismantled, he took his
book holder aside for a quiet word.

"What ails you, Nick?" he asked.

"Nothing."

"Is dropping the book nothing? Is letting your attention wander
nothing? Is forgetting that you are Nicholas Bracewell and therefore a man who never errs—do you call that nothing?"

"I was a little distracted."

"By what?"

Nicholas hesitated. "I will tell you another time."

"Now," demanded Firethorn. "I want the truth *now*."

"You will not like what you hear."

"I did not like what I saw this afternoon."

It was an honest assessment of Nicholas's work and he was ready to acknowledge it. When the last of the scenery and properties had been carried away to be stored, he agreed to accompany Firethorn to his apartment. Once inside, the actor closed the door, then put his back to it.

"Now, then, Nick—what is going on?"

"Lord Westfield is being hoodwinked."

"By whom?"

"Judge for yourself."

Composing his thoughts, Nicholas gave him as clear an account as he could of what he believed was a deliberate deception. At first, Firethorn could only bluster in protest, but he listened with growing concern as the evidence mounted up. The conclusion was inescapable. Between them, Nicholas and Anne Hendrik had unearthed a cunning ruse that could have appalling consequences if allowed to continue unchecked. Firethorn was infuriated.

"This is a heinous crime!" he exclaimed.

"Yes, Lawrence, but what lies behind it?"

"A cruel sense of humor. Our patron has been enticed by a beautiful woman so that he can be married off to a plain one."

"Sigbrit Olsen is not plain," said Nicholas. "That's what made the trick possible. She has similar features to her sister but lacks her complexion and her brilliance."

"*Brilliance* is the word. She glitters like a star."

"There is something else. Anne did not notice this because she only saw one side of the lady's face and that was by candlelight. I had a much clearer view in the chapel."

"What did you see, Nick?"

"A livid scar that runs down the side of her chin. It could be largely hidden by powder when viewed by the flames of a candle. In the light of day, it's more difficult to disguise."

Firethorn was fuming. "Hell's teeth!" he cried, pacing the room like a caged animal. "Is this what we came all this way for—to see our patron married off to some scar-faced harpy?"

"You misjudge the lady. It may well be that she is quite unaware of the deception that is being practiced in her name."

"She *must* know. She's in this up to her neck."

"No," said Nicholas. "I'm not sure that she is. I only saw her for a fleeting moment but it was when she was completely off guard. Bear in mind that she had been praying there for almost half an hour. That gives you some indication of her character."

"She was seeking forgiveness for her sins," snarled Firethorn.

"That's not what I saw in her face, Lawrence. I saw honesty and decency and a kind of innocence. I begin to think that Sigbrit Olsen is as much a victim of this plot as our patron."

"Do not forget us—we are victims as well."

"Lord Westfield is the person who stands to lose most."

"He must be told directly, Nick. We can't let him marry this counterfeit princess. It's unthinkable."

"He will want to know who is behind this subterfuge."

"What will you tell him?"

"The truth," said Nicholas. "It has to be Bror Langberg."

You were quite wonderful," congratulated Bror Langberg, enfolding his niece in his arms. "You played the part as well as any actor."

"I hardly spoke," said Hansi Askgaard.

"You did not need to—did she, Johanna?"

"No," replied his wife fondly. "All that you had to do, Hansi, was to sit there and he was spellbound. Lord Westfield never took his eyes off you."

"I could wish a more handsome husband for my sister."

Langberg smiled. "His title and his fortune are very handsome."

"Sigbrit will not have to sleep with either of those."

"She'll be happy enough with the marriage."

"I hope so, Uncle Bror."

"Had it been otherwise, I'd not have commended it to her. Lord Westfield is a restless man. He yearns for the city pleasures. While he is in London, Sigbrit will have a fine country house to herself."

"I hate to think that she will be lonely."

"There's no danger of that," he assured her.

They had returned to Hansi's room after dinner to discuss what had happened. Each of them felt that it had been a success. Lord Westfield had been placed at one end of a long table with Hansi at the other. Langberg and his wife sat opposite each other on the vacant sides. They provided most of the conversation because their guest had been too engrossed with the woman he thought would be his future wife. Saying little and smiling often, Hansi let her natural radiance hold his attention. She had one grievance.

"The irony is that I will not be there at the wedding," she said.

Johanna pulled a face. "It might cause a few problems if you were, Hansi. With regard to princesses, there is a golden rule."

"Is there?"

"No husband needs two."

"Talking of husbands," said Langberg, "that's another person who has earned our undying thanks—your own husband, Wilhelm. I will make a point of writing to tell him what a clever wife he has."

"Wilhelm knows the importance of this match," said Hansi.

"We will all benefit as a result."

"Sigbrit will wed and I will go home to my husband. I do not envy my sister. She can have Lord Westfield with my blessing." She looked at Langberg. "Will she ever learn the truth, Uncle?"

"No," he said firmly. "She must never know about this little trap we set for her husband. Ignorance is a kindness to her. If she were not so trusting, we could never have embarked on this deception."

"What of the wedding itself?"

"What of it?"

"Will he not realize then that I am not Sigbrit?"

"There's no risk of that, Hansi," said her uncle. "I'll make sure that he has had so much to drink beforehand that he will not know whom he is marrying. Lord Westfield is the only one of our visitors who has seen you properly. The others will have no suspicions."

"You have thought of everything, Uncle Bror."

"It's not all my doing."

"I'll do my share as well," Johanna pointed out. "By the time I've finished powdering Sigbrit's face, I will have covered up the little scar that worries her so much. In her wedding dress, with her face half-hidden, she'll be the image of her elder sister."

"Everything is in our favor," said Langberg with complacence. "On Saturday, all our ambitions will be fulfilled. And the most satisfying part of it is that Lord Westfield will not have the slightest notion of what is really going on."

Lord Westfield was so thunderstruck by what he had heard that he collapsed into a chair and put his head in his hands. Though Nicholas Bracewell had broken the news as gently as he could, the impact had still been shattering. Having spent the last couple of hours in euphoria, Lord Westfield had now been plunged into utter dejection. When their patron's chest began to heave ungovernably, Lawrence Firethorn feared that he might be having some kind of seizure. He leaned solicitously over him.

"Are you ill, my lord?"

"Not in body," said the other, "only in mind."

"We felt that you had to know at once."

"I still refuse to accept it."

"The evidence is clear," said Nicholas quietly. "There can be no equivocation here. Anne and I have seen both sisters."

"A pox on it!" cried Lord Westfield, removing his hands from his face. "So have I, so have I! Today, I dined with one sister, and the other evening, I met her exact likeness in the hall. Which is which, please tell me! Am I to marry twins and spend my wedding night playing three-in-a-bed? What sorcery is this?"

"It's not sorcery, my lord. It's a deep-laid plot."

"Am I to be gulled?"

"Not anymore," said Firethorn. "You are rescued. Nick and Anne have saved you from making an irretrievable mistake."

Lord Westfield glowered. "Well, expect no thanks from me."

He lapsed into a bruised silence. All that the others could do was to stand there quietly while he wallowed in his desolation. During the meal, he had experienced an intense joy that he had never known before, an ecstasy that came from simply gazing upon his beautiful Danish princess. If she could excite such feelings in him when she was at the other end of the table, she would lift him to an even higher plane of exhilaration when she lay in his arms. It was a vision of paradise and Nicholas had abruptly snatched it away from him. He glared at the book holder.

"What's afoot here?" he asked.

"I've yet to find out, my lord," said Nicholas.

"But you must have your suspicions, man."

"I do."

"Then, for God's sake, let's hear them. If you are to deprive me of the greatest love I have ever felt, then give me something in return. I want reasons, Nicholas. I want explanations." He banged the table beside him and made the ivory chessmen jump in the air. "And most of all, I want solace."

"That's the one thing I cannot offer you, alas."

"Then what can you give?" howled the other.

"Calm down, my lord," soothed Firethorn.

"I've no wish to calm down."

"There's no point in upsetting yourself like this."

"Then what else would you have me do?" challenged the other. "Dance a jig around the room? By Jesu! Can you not see how much I've lost by this expedition? I invest time and money and every sinew of my being to prove my love and for what? I am made to feel like a country yokel at Bartholomew Fair, robbed of everything he owns and jeered at by his tormentors." He got to his feet. "I'll have this out with Bror Langberg immediately." He marched to the door. "I'll not be his dupe a moment longer."

Nicholas blocked his way. "I suggest that you stay here."

"Out of my way, man!"

"For you own sake, my lord, I must stop you."

"And I must do the same," said Firethorn, standing beside Nicholas.

Their patron spluttered. "What kind of conspiracy is this?" he yelled. "Do you dare to keep me against my will?"

"We have to, my lord."

"In the name of all that's holy—why?"

"Because we cannot let you put yourself in such jeopardy," said Nicholas. "If you challenge Master Langberg while you are choleric, there will be only one outcome."

"And what, pray, is that?"

"You'll not leave this castle alive." Lord Westfield recoiled with horror. "And you would not be his first victim, my lord. Bror Langberg already has blood on his hands."

Firethorn started. "What do you mean, Nick?"

"He contrived the murder of Rolfe Harling."

There is not long to go now, Sigbrit," said Hansi Askgaard. "In two days' time, you will be the new Lady Westfield."

"Yes," said her sister dully.

"Try to sound happier about it."

"I wish that I could, Hansi, but I feel so unworthy."

"Unworthy?" echoed the other. "That is ridiculous. No bride was ever more worthy of her husband. You will be the perfect wife for him."

"Will I?"

Sigbrit was seated at a little table in her apartment. On it was a gilt-framed mirror and she studied her face in it for a moment, running a finger along the scar on her chin. Hansi stood behind her.

"It will fade in time."

"I see it more clearly than ever," sighed Sigbrit. "When I met Lord Westfield in the hall that evening, Uncle Bror taught me to keep my head to one side so that it did not show. What will my husband say when he learns the truth?"

"He will be too much in love with you to notice."

"He is bound to notice. Yesterday, he sent me this letter," she said, picking it up from the table. "My English is not good enough for me to understand every word but I can see that it is in praise of my beauty. He will be so disappointed."

"Let me see," said Hansi, taking the letter and reading through it. "There you are," she added, putting it down again, "he is ensnared by your charms, Sigbrit. Lord Westfield sees only what he wishes to see and that is his gorgeous Danish princess. Love is blind."

Sigbrit rallied slightly. She got up from the table and walked to the window, looking down at the place that had been her home for so long and realizing that she would at last have to leave it. She was overcome by a sudden onset of nostalgia.

"I wish that I did not have to leave Denmark," she said.

"You will return. Lord Westfield has promised that. We will visit you next spring, then you and your husband can come back here in the summer. You will love England, Sigbrit. I've been there."

"What is it like?"

"London is the most exciting city in the world. It is so big and full of life. It makes Elsinore look like a village. I envy you so much," Hansi said, embracing her sister. "And I have the comfort of knowing that this marriage will not only make my sister happy, it will be good for our country as well. Denmark will gain from it."

"That's what Uncle Bror told me."

"Then pay heed to what he says. Left to yourself, you would simply mourn your first husband and spend your days in lonely isolation. In England, you will have a new life. It will be such an adventure for you, Sigbrit. And the person you have to thank for it all is Uncle Bror."

"Yes," agreed Sigbrit, smiling. "He has been my salvation."

Nicholas Bracewell needed proof. It was one thing to expose an act of duplicity and rescue Lord Westfield from marrying the wrong person, but it would be far more difficult to establish the purpose that lay behind the deception. In doing that, he believed, he would also solve the murder of Rolfe Harling. Looking back, Nicholas saw that Bror Landberg had been altogether too helpful. He had discussed the crime at length with the book holder, then taken him to Harling's room and allowed him to search it. The only reason he had done that, Nicholas now realized, was that he knew there would be nothing to find. Anything that might suggest a motive for his death had already been removed. If anywhere, it would be hidden in Langberg's apartment.

A decoy was required and Lawrence Firethorn was the ideal choice. Instructed by Nicholas, he called on Langberg and took him off to the ballroom, claiming that certain practical problems had come to light during the afternoon's rehearsal and asking for advice. As soon as the two men vanished around a corner, Nicholas came out of his hiding place behind a large, ornate oak cupboard that stood in the corridor. He entered the apartment quickly and closed the door behind him. He had no doubt where anything of value was kept.

Pulling out his dagger, he went across to the chest he had seen on his earlier visit. Reinforced with strips of iron, it had two large padlocks to keep out intruders. By deft use of the point of his dagger, Nicholas prized open one of the locks, but the other would not budge. He resorted to violence. Kicking hard with his heel several times, he loosened the clasp attached to the padlock, then inserted his weapon at the weakest point and used it as a lever. By applying steady pressure, he made the lock twist, squeak in protest, then fall to the ground as the clasp was finally forced out of the wood.

The chest was open. He stood a candle on the shelf above it so that he could see more clearly. Lifting the lid, he was confronted by a mass of papers, some bags of money, and an ornamental sword. On top of the papers was a small leather satchel that he recognized as having belonged to Rolfe Harling. He took it out. Inside was a mass of letters and documents. Nicholas went through them with painstaking thoroughness. Some were in Danish, even more in German, but the ones that interested him were in English.

When he saw the name of Bror Langberg at the bottom of the first missive, he read it eagerly, but its contents disappointed him. The letter simply expressed thanks that Harling had taken the trouble to visit Denmark to discuss a possible marriage and told him that preparations would soon be in hand at Kronborg. The writer's command of English was good but his grammar was rather strange at times. Nicholas found that surprising. Having spoken to Langberg a number of times, he knew what a mastery of the language the man possessed.

When he read the second letter, the same pattern was repeated. Beyond the grammatical errors, nothing could arouse the slightest suspicion. The truth then dawned with the force of a blow. Nicholas was not looking at one letter but at two. The trick that Langberg had used with his nieces was repeated in epistolary form. One thing was shown, quite another intended. From his pocket, Nicholas took out the tiny strip of paper that had been found in the chess set. It was the secret code. With its help, he saw that he was reading something entirely different. He also understood why the code had been concealed inside the black king. It represented James VI of Scotland, a name that recurred three times in the letter when it was translated.

Nicholas was excited. He had not only found clear proof that Langberg had been involved in the murder of Rolfe Harling, he knew exactly why such trouble had been taken to marry Lord Westfield to a Danish wife. It was disturbing. Langberg had ambitions that went far beyond arranging a match for his niece. Nicholas picked up another letter and discovered, when he deciphered it with the code, that it was even more explicit. He was at once shocked and fascinated by his discovery. So keen was he to look at another letter that he lost all track of time. He was barely halfway through it when the door opened and Bror Langberg came in.

"What's this?" cried Langberg, pulsing with anger. "I should have known that something was up when Master Firethorn asked me all those unnecessary questions."

"I've a few more pertinent ones to put to you," said Nicholas.

"I'll not bandy words with a thief."

"A thief is a higher vocation than a murderer." He held up the slip of paper. "We found the code in Master Harling's chess set. It helped me to see the monster that you are."

"Be quiet!"

"There'll be no wedding now. Lord Westfield has been told the truth. You showed him one niece so that you could marry him off to her sister. Like everything else that bears your name," said Nicholas, "the marriage is fraudulent."

"I'll hear no more of this," shouted Langberg, pushing past him to reach into the chest. He pulled out the ornamental sword. "Do you know what this is?" he asked, taking it from its jeweled sheath. "It's the highest honor that Denmark can bestow. It was given to me by the late King Frederick for outstanding services to the state."

"Did they include your plan to assassinate our queen?"

"Silence!"

"I cannot believe that Rolfe Harling would condone such a plot," said Nicholas, backing away. "Is that why you had him killed?"

Langberg bristled. "You know far too much for your own good, Master Bracewell."

"I know that he was not murdered by two cooks from your kitchens. That was another case of deception. Tell me, sir, have you ever done anything honest in your life?"

Langberg was enraged. Leaping forward, he swung the sword in a vicious arc, intending to slice off Nicholas's head. The latter ducked just in time, letting the blade pass harmlessly above him. He then pulled out his dagger and parried the wild slashes and thrusts that followed. But he could not do that indefinitely. Langberg was a powerful man with a superior weapon. He was bent on murder. Nicholas had to escape quickly. As he dodged and weaved around the room, he suddenly dived for the chest and picked up a handful of documents, flinging them hard into Langberg's face to confuse him for an instant.

Nicholas seized his chance. He opened the door and ran into the corridor, but Langberg had not come alone. Two armed guards were stationed outside the door and they grabbed Nicholas between them, pinning him against the wall. He fought back to no avail. They had too strong a grip on his arms. Still holding the sword, Langberg sauntered into the corridor with a malevolent grin. He was not going to be bested by a hired man from a theater company. He held the point of the sword against Nicholas's throat and was about to jab it hard when a woman's voice cried out.

"Uncle Bror," said Sigbrit in alarm. "What are you doing?"

Langberg was balked. His niece was walking down the corridor toward him. He could not commit murder in front of her. Letting the sword fall to his side, he turned a reassuring smile on her and mumbled an excuse. Sigbrit stared at him in horror. Out of the corner of his mouth, he gave an order to the guards.

"Lock him in the dungeon," he said. "I'll deal with him later."

After long hours in rehearsal, Westfield's Men were relaxing that evening in their hut, drawing themselves free tankards of beer from the cask and deciding that the effort of reaching Elsinore had been more than worth it. Some played cards, others waged money in games of dice, and the rest indulged in friendly badinage. None of them were prepared for what happened next. Flinging open the door, Lawrence Firethorn burst in and barked a command.

"Come with me, lads," he yelled. "Nick has been arrested."

"Why?" asked Owen Elias.

"I'll explain on the way. Hurry up—there's no time to waste. Bring whatever weapons you have."

"Weapons? Are we going to fight?"

"If need be, Owen." The actors were on their feet immediately, reaching for swords and daggers. "Follow me," said Firethorn, going out, "and stay close together. They can't kill the whole lot of us."

With the others at his heels, he marched across the forecourt and went through one of the gateways into the main courtyard. Elias ran to catch up to him.

"Whatever's happened, Lawrence?"

"We've all been mightily abused," replied Firethorn. "Lord West-field was brought here under false pretenses and the villain who did it was Bror Langberg."

"But he's been the perfect host."

"That was just a guise, Owen. He's a blackhearted rogue who had Rolfe Harling murdered. Nick went to search his room for evidence and was caught before he could get away. I saw guards taking him to the casemates."

"That's where Master Harling was found."

"Exactly."

As they surged across the courtyard, most of them had heard what Firethorn had said. They were roused to a pitch of anger. If their book holder was in danger, they would do everything in their power to rescue him. They gave an early demonstration of intent. Two guards stood beside the steps that led to the casemates. When they crossed their pikes to stop anyone passing, they were grabbed by the actors and thrown rudely aside. Westfield's Men went into the casemates in a solid body, picking their way through the cavernous interior by the light of torches they stole from their brackets. Finding anyone in the bewildering maze of tunnels was not easy but Firethorn knew how to do it. He filled his lungs then bellowed at the top of his voice:

"*Nick! Where are you?*"

"Here!" came a reply from Nicholas. "I'm over here, Lawrence."

Guided by the voice, they hurried down a passage to the left until they came to section of the casemates that widened out into a square. Across one corner, a series of iron bars had been fixed to the walls, creating a triangular dungeon. Nicholas Bracewell was in it. The two guards who had put him there were waiting with Bror Langberg. When they saw a dozen armed men coming at them, they drew back.

"Stay away!" warned Langberg. "There are hundreds of men in the garrison. I could have you all hacked to pieces."

"You'd die before us," said Firethorn, using his sword to force the man back against the bars. He looked at the prisoner. "Are you hurt, Nick?"

"No," said Nicholas, "but I soon would have been."

"Give that here," demanded Elias, snatching a key from one of the guards. He unlocked the door of the cage. "Come on out, Nick."

"Thank you, Owen."

"Our turn to save you for a change."

"Yes," said Nicholas, stepping out of the dungeon. "And you were never more welcome."

The sound of running feet made him look up. Hearing the noise from the dungeon, almost thirty armed soldiers had come to investigate. When they saw what was happening, they stood in a double line to block the exit. Langberg emitted a laugh of triumph.

"I think that you are outnumbered, Master Firethorn," he said.

"Stand back!" Firethorn ordered the soldiers. "Or I'll put this sword through his heart."

"Certain death would follow for the whole pack of you."

"At least, I would have the pleasure of taking you with us."

"You are beaten, man," said Langberg, gloating. "Have the sense to admit it. Nothing can save you now."

Even as he spoke, a long, strident fanfare rang out from the

Trumpeter's Tower, muffled by the casemates but audible enough for all of them to recognize what it signaled.

"The king!" exclaimed Langberg. "I must bid him welcome."

"Then we'll go with you," said Firethorn, slipping his dagger into Nicholas's hand so that he could hold a weapon against their prisoner as well. "Tell them to stand aside."

With a sword at his throat and a dagger at his back, Langberg waved an arm to his men and the soldiers moved reluctantly out of the way. Firethorn and Nicholas pushed him forward, holding him tightly. Followed by the soldiers, the actors took a tortuous route back to the exit, glad to get out of the casemates again. When they climbed the steps into the courtyard, they were met by a blaze of light that surrounded the visitors. Dozens of torches were aflame. In the middle of them, adorned in bright attire and striking an imperious pose, was King Christian IV with his personal bodyguard.

As he saw them all emerge from the casemates, the king was astonished. Firethorn and Nicholas felt obliged to release their prisoner. In the presence of the king, they had to show deference. Langberg beamed. He was safe. He spread his arms wide.

"Welcome to Kronborg, Your Majesty," he said with a bow. "You could not have come at more appropriate time."

"Arrest that man," snapped the king. "He's a traitor."

Members of his bodyguard promptly seized Bror Langberg and pinioned his arms behind him. When he tried to speak, he was clubbed into silence. Westfield's Men were saved.

The Princess of Denmark was performed in the ballroom on Saturday night after all, but not in celebration of any wedding. It was at the command of King Christian IV, the young monarch with a love of the arts and a respect for English actors. Lord Westfield sat beside him in the audience, grateful that he had been rescued from an unfortunate marriage and able to take an especial delight in the skills of his company. There were notable absentees from the ballroom. Bror Langberg was held in the dungeon while his wife and Hansi Askgaard, accomplices in the plot, were locked in their respective apartments. Completely innocent herself, Sigbrit Olsen was shocked to learn of their perfidy and appalled at the way that she was being used for political ends. She could not bear to attend a play that had been inspired partly by her.

Since the drama now had a different purport, Edmund Hoode changed the names of its principal characters to Harald and Sophie, removing all hint of their patron and his intended bride. In its first performance, therefore, *The Princess of Denmark* was seen for what it was, a sparkling comedy set in the castle at Elsinore, replete with fine poetry, poignant romance, comic brilliance, lively dances, and a plot that held them all firmly together with invisible strength. The spectators were captivated throughout, none more so than the king, who laughed in the wrong places at times but who was thrilled by the performance. Edmund Hoode had even included a reference to him in the concluding lines of the epilogue. Owen Elias declaimed them with great feeling.

> *Our lovers suffered pain while kept apart*
> *Then royalty did bring them heart to heart.*
> *For, mark it well, there is no better thing*
> *Than being rescued by a Christian king.*

The galliard with which the play ended spilled out onto the marble floor and the actors whirled within feet of their audience. Applause reverberated the length of the whole room. King Christian IV, the Christian king, clapped until his hands were sore.

Westfield's Men took their bows with particular pleasure. They were relieved to have the opportunity to stage a play on which they had spent so much time, and they put their hearts and souls into it. The whole company knew how close they had come to disaster and their performance was, to some extent, a visible sign of gratitude to the king who had averted it. No wedding might have taken place but the feast was nevertheless held after the play and the actors were invited to join in the celebrations. It was a fitting end.

Owen Elias's head injury still throbbed but it had not stopped him from giving a commendable performance as Peder Mikkelson, pickpocket and itinerant ballad singer, a lovable rogue who made the ladies titter at his lewd behavior. Before too much drink robbed him of coherent thought, the Welshman wanted clarification from Nicholas Bracewell, who sat beside him at the feast.

"Why exactly was Bror Langberg arrested?" he asked.

"How much do you know already, Owen?"

"Only that our patron was being hoodwinked. He was given a portrait of a woman that he was never going to marry."

"A beautiful woman at that," said Nicholas. "I've seen her."

"What of her sister? Is she ugly?"

"Not in the least but her face would never have brought Lord Westfield all the way to Denmark. I've spoken with the lady." Nicholas gave a wan smile. "The irony is that Sigbrit Olsen never wanted to get married to anyone. Her uncle talked her into it."

"But why, Nick?"

"To achieve his ends. He needed somewhere in England from which his confederates could work. They would have gone there as attendants to our patron's bride. Lord Westfield is often at court and, as a result, is very much aware of Her Majesty's movements. That information would have been crucial."

Elias was scandalized. "They meant to kill Queen Elizabeth?"

"Bror Langberg wanted her out of the way so that King James of Scotland could succeed. Her Majesty is old but in good health. If they wait for her to die, it might take years and he feared that another claimant might find favor in the meantime."

"So they assassinate a queen for the sake of a Scottish king."

"He has a Danish wife, Owen."

"Ah! So that's the rub."

"Bror Langberg is a close friend of hers," explained Nicholas. "Were she and her husband to sit on English thrones, he could look for great rewards from her."

"Was this plot first hatched in Scotland then?"

"No, King James and his wife are completely unaware of it."

"Then how did King Christian learn about it?" asked Elias. "When he arrived here, he called Master Langberg a traitor."

"He was set to betray the honor of Denmark," said Nicholas. "In raising a hand against Queen Elizabeth, he would have been attacking a true friend of this country. The king had suspicions of him for some time. Letters that were sent from here to Flushing were intercepted. They were addressed to Rolfe Harling but intelligencers seized them and broke the cipher. Now I understand why Master Harling was so eager to call in at Flushing on our way here. He did not want such dangerous correspondence to go astray. Unbeknown to him, it had already been seized."

"I never liked that dried fish of a man," said Elias. "If Rolfe Harling was part of this conspiracy, the villain deserved to die."

"He was working as a spy for Sir Robert Cecil and found that he and Master Langberg had similar ambitions. Both wanted a Danish queen in England. The difference was," Nicholas said over the babble of voices around him, "that he was prepared to let Her Majesty die a natural death. When he refused to condone assassination, he was killed outright because he was in a position to reveal Bror Langberg's plot." He paused to sip his wine. "My own suspicions were aroused when Lord Westfield told me how he had come to meet his friend. It was through the offices of Sir Robert Cecil, a man who keeps a small army of intelligencers. Master Harling was one of them."

"A filthy spy, was he?" said Elias with contempt. "Never trust a man who prefers chess to women, Nick. It's a game that perverts the mind. As for our patron," he went on, glancing toward the end of the table where Lord Westfield was laughing merrily beside the king, "he must learn to choose his friends with more care—and his wives."

"I'm sure that he knows that."

"So what happens now, Nick?"

"We've seen the last of Denmark for a while," said Nicholas, looking around at the happy faces of the actors. "The company has prospered from the three plays that we presented, and we made many admirers, but I cannot say that I am sorry to leave. Tomorrow, we board the *Cormorant* again. Anne will finally reach Amsterdam and we will head for home."

Elias cackled. "Think of those all those brokenhearted women who will welcome me back," he said, rubbing his hands together.

"Think instead of the man who has twice tried to kill you."

"Oh, I've not forgotten him, Nick."

"His name is Josias Greet and my guess is that he's probably sailing to London now. We'll catch up with him one day."

When he reached the capital, Isaac Dunmow rode straight to the inn and took a room. He then sent word to Josias Greet and counted out the money while he waited for the man to arrive. A letter from Anthony Rooker had informed him that Greet had returned and claimed to have good news for him. Dunmow had set out from York at once. Instead of dulling his urge for revenge, the passage of time had merely sharpened it. If their mission had been completed, his hired killers deserved their reward.

An hour later, Josias Greet was shown up to the room, almost panting with eagerness. He was carrying a bloodstained bag. Taking off his greasy cap, he gave an ingratiating smile.

"Good day to you, Master Dunmow," he said, displaying a row of misshapen teeth. "It's a pleasure to see you in the city again."

"Well, I get no pleasure from looking at your vile face. The sooner we settle this matter, the better." Dunmow regarded his visitor critically. "I had a letter from Master Rooker. He says that you've done my bidding."

"That's right, sir. Of course, I did not tell him what that bidding was. I obeyed your orders, sir. I simply went to his office and gave him the message that you wanted."

"Owen Elias is dead?"

"As a doornail."

"Burned?"

"To a cinder."

"How do I know?"

"Because I brought something for you," said Greet, opening the bag to take out a charred hand. "I cut this from his arm, sir."

Dunmow stared at the hand with distaste, then looked away.

"Where is Ryden?"

"Ah, that's the sad part of the tale, sir. He's dead."

Greet gave a rambling account of the murder of Owen Elias. He claimed that Ben Ryden had been killed when he fought with the

Welshman, leaving Greet to overpower and burn Elias. The details he gave of their voyage and of their brief stay in Elsinore sounded convincing enough but the rest of his story struck a false note. Dunmow scowled at him.

"You're lying, you scabby knave."

"I'd swear on the Bible that it's the truth, sir."

"Then your tongue would turn black."

"I did as you told me," insisted Greet, waving the scorched hand in front of him. "Where else could I have got this?"

"From anyone. How do I know it belonged to Elias?"

"You have my sacred word."

Dunmow sneered. "You've never told the truth in your life."

"As God's my witness, this is his hand."

"Get out of here!"

Greet slapped the hand on the table. "I want the money."

"Then you'll have to wait until Westfield's Men come back to England. If Elias is still alive, you'll not get a penny."

"Pay up, sir," growled the other. "You promised."

"What I promised was to pay you and Ben Ryden. That means you get only half of the fee—or none at all, if you failed to kill Elias for the second time."

"I want it all, Master Dunmow. I earned it."

"We'll only know that when Westfield's Men return."

"Give it to me!"

"I give nothing to liars," said Dunmow, crossing to open the door. "Now clear off before you stink the place out—and take that foul hand with you." Greet glowered at him. "Go on—get out."

Greet bowed his head obediently and put the hand into the bag. As he did so, he kept his back to the other man so that he could take a dagger from his belt. Dunmow would not be fooled. If they waited until Westfield's Men returned, then Greet's lies would be exposed and he would get nothing. If he wanted the money, he had to take it now. When he turned to face Dunmow, therefore, he brought his hand upward with full force, sinking the dagger into his stomach then twisting it sharply to give maximum pain. Isaac Dunmow goggled. He opened his mouth to cry for help but all that came out was a faint gurgle. Grinning with pleasure, Greet continued to twist the blade. Only when Dunmow fell slowly to the floor did he pull the dagger out again.

Stepping over his victim, he opened the bag that held the hand and scooped all that money on the table into it. Then he looked down at Isaac Dunmow, still writhing in pain as his lifeblood drained out of him. Greet gave him a gratuitous kick.

"You should have paid me when I asked," he said.

Leaving the inn by the back door, he walked back to his lodging through the crowded streets, knowing that he had enough money to last him for a year. He began to speculate on how he could best spend it. There was no thought of Ben Ryden now. The reward belonged entirely to Josias Greet and he would enjoy it to the full. The long walk took him to one of the more squalid areas of the city, a narrow, twisting lane with an open sewer running down the middle of it. When a dog came sniffing at him, he swung the bag to knock it away and it went yelping off down the lane.

Greet entered a tenement and climbed the stairs to his room. Opening the door, he crossed to the bed and emptied his booty over the soiled mattress. He let out a harsh laugh. Then he heard the door slam shut behind him. Someone had already been in the room.

"Hello, Josias," said Owen Elias. "Remember me?"

Greet was horror-struck. "No, sir," he gabbled. "I've never seen you before in my life."

"That's because you always crept up behind me before—both here in London and in Elsinore." Elias glanced at the mattress. "Would that be Ben Ryden's hand, by any chance?"

"There's been a mistake. You have the wrong man."

"It was you who made the mistake, Josias Greet—not once, but twice." Elias pulled out his sword. "You tried to kill me."

"Keep away from me," said Greet, moving to the window with his dagger in his hand. "I'll not warn you again." As Elias took a step toward him, Greet raised his weapon. "Stand back, I say."

He flung the dagger across the room. Elias ducked out of the way and it flew past him before embedding itself in the door. Greet did not stay. Flinging open the window, he jumped through it and dropped down until he landed in a pile of offal. Before he could move, a hand closed around his neck and forced his back against the wall. Nicholas Bracewell had been waiting to cut off any attempted escape.

"Stay awhile," he ordered. "We need to talk to you."

"What do you want with me?" jabbered Greet.

"We have several scores to settle with you. That's why we came here as soon as we landed. Master Rooker was kind enough to give us your address," said Nicholas. "You left it with him for Isaac Dunmow, we hear. We came straight to this rathole to find you."

Greet tried to break free but Nicholas was far too strong. Owen Elias came out of the house to join them. He looked at the prisoner with absolute disgust, then flexed both hands.

"Let me go," pleaded Greet. "I have money. I'll pay you."

"Oh, you'll pay," said Nicholas. "We can promise that."

"Master Dunmow hired us. He is to blame."

"You were the one who attacked me," said Elias. "You and that other villain whose throat you cut back in Elsinore."

"I did that as a favor to Ben," said Greet. "He was in agony."

"It's my turn to do a favor for a friend now," said Nicholas. "Before we hand you over to a magistrate, Owen would like a private word with you." He released Greet. "He's all yours now, Owen."

Alexander Marwood pointed across the innyard to the work that had been abandoned by the builders. The main timbers had been erected and the roof had been started, but that was all. There was still much to do before that side of the Queen's Head could ever be in use again.

"Look, Master Rooker!" he cried. "This is how they have left it."

"That's of no concern to me," said Rooker.

"But you pay their wages."

"I was enjoined to release funds to the builder once a week."

"Then why have you stopped?" said Marwood. "Give them their money and bring them back here."

"I've no power to do that."

"But you must." Marwood waved a document in his face. "I'll

seek redress in court for this. You are bound by the terms of the contract."

"The contract no longer exists," said Rooker coldly. "It was signed by Isaac Dunmow. When he was murdered, the contract died with him. And I have to say that I am very glad. Now that I know the full details of the bargain that you struck, I wish that I'd never been involved in it. You are a disgrace, sir."

Marwood was offended. "I deny that charge."

"Isaac Dunmow sent hired ruffians after Westfield's Men. One of them returned to kill him. I have no love of actors, but they are entitled to the freedom to practice their craft. According to the contract you had with him, you are nothing but a hired ruffian with murder in your heart. You set out to destroy the company as well."

"They deserved it, Master Rooker."

Rooker was scornful. "If everyone got their deserts, sir, then the Queen's Head would fall down around your miserable ears. My business with you ends here and I have never been so glad to rid myself of a client."

Pursued by Marwood's wild imprecations, he went out of the yard and vanished into Gracechurch Street. The landlord stamped his foot then took another despairing look at the deserted building site. Grinding his teeth, he scuttled off to the taproom to unpack his woes to his wife, knowing that he was more likely to get reproach than sympathy but needing to tell someone of his cruel rebuff. Expecting to find Sybil in her usual icy and unforgiving mood, he was astounded to hear her laughing gaily as she talked to Nicholas Bracewell.

"Come in, come in, Alexander," she cooed, beckoning him over to her. "Nicholas has returned from Denmark with good news."

"It's bad news that Westfield's Men have returned at all."

"My husband jests," she said, shooting him a glare that made his blood run cold. "He was saying only this morning how much he missed the company."

"As I miss the plague," said Marwood under his breath.

"Your wife has been telling me about a contract you signed," said Nicholas. "On the condition that we never played here again, Will Dunmow's father undertook to pay for the rebuilding of the inn."

"An iniquitous contract," said Sybil with disdain. "I tried hard to stop Alexander from signing it. Fortunately," she added, riding over the objection that sprang to her husband's lips, "it no longer exists. Isaac Dunmow was murdered here in London."

"I know," said Nicholas. "Owen Elias and I had the privilege of handing over the killer to the magistrates—after Owen had exchanged a few words with the fellow, that is. So, it would seem that your contract is null and void."

"Yes, Master Bracewell," said the landlord.

"Do you regret that?"

"Very much."

"Alexander!" chided his wife.

"I do, Sybil. It was like manna from heaven."

"It was dreadful mistake and we must be honest enough to admit it. I think that a personal apology is needed to Lord Westfield." She quelled Marwood's attempted protest with another glare. "How misled we have been in our judgment of him! He is a fount of true benevolence."

"What are you talking about, woman?" said Marwood.

"Allow me to explain," said Nicholas. "Our visit to Denmark was not without its perils and we were able to save our patron from being tricked into something that he would regret for the remainder of his life. In token of his regret—and on one single condition—Lord Westfield has offered to pay for the rest of the repairs here so that the Queen's Head can return to its former glory."

"This is true manna from heaven," declared Sybil, clapping her hands girlishly together. "Say something, Alexander. Accept the offer."

Marwood was cautious. "You mention a condition."

"Just one," said Nicholas.

"What is it?"

"That Westfield's Men can play here again in perpetuity."

"My husband agrees," said Sybil over Marwood's groan of pain. "Have the contract and he will sign it if I have to hold his hand while he does it. Is that not so, Alexander?"

The landlord looked into her eyes and saw such a compound of threat, malice, entreaty, demand, and, incredibly, sexual allure that he lost all power to resist. While he was still under her spell, the door of the taproom opened and Lawrence Firethorn led in the whole troupe.

"Nick, dear heart," he said. "Do we have our playhouse?"

"I still await a reply," said Nicholas.

Everyone turned to their hated landlord, knowing that he would rather drink hemlock than invite them back to the Queen's Head. Only the generosity of Lord Westfield could win him over. Marwood glanced first at his wife. The specter of allure was still there. He summoned up a crooked smile.

"Welcome home, gentlemen," he said with forced geniality. "Sybil and I have pined for your return. I have repeated the same thing day after day. The Queen's Head is nothing without Westfield's Men."

They gave him a rousing cheer.